BOY IN THE WORLD

Niall Williams lives in Kiltumper with his wife Christine and their two children. His previous novels include *Four Letters of Love* and *As it is in Heaven* which were published to acclaim and became international bestsellers.

Visit: www.AuthorTracker.co.uk for exclusive information on Niall Williams.

Praise for *Boy in the World*:

'A tender coming-of-age novel' *Daily Mail*

'With poetic prose that could have been written by angels, combined with a pace that keeps the reader turning the pages . . . A Dickens for the 21st century. A spiritually enriching story of such beauty and magic that is deserves a place not just in the 9/11 canon, but also on the Leaving Cert syllabus as well' *Irish Times*

'At times thoughtful and moving, ultimately it is the empathy the reader feels for the young boy that allows this fine novel to resonate so well' *Sunday Business Post*

'Williams's style is reflective and moving' *Metro*

'Using some really stunning descriptive prose, Willia
gently along on a wave of sounds and pictures. He
ently, a succeeds in creating vivid images that stay i
long after the book is closed' *Sunday Tribune*

'A beautifully crafted story of discovery' *Belfast Tel*

'Emotional insightfulness saturates this novel' *Sunda*

NIALL WILLIAMS

Boy in the World

HARPER

This novel is entirely a work of fiction.
The names, characters and incidents portrayed in it are
the work of the author's imagination. Any resemblance to
actual persons, living or dead, events or localities is
entirely coincidental.

Harper
An imprint of HarperCollins*Publishers*
77–85 Fulham Palace Road,
Hammersmith, London W6 8JB

www.harpercollins.co.uk

Published by HarperCollins*Publishers* 2008
1

A catalogue record for this book
is available from the British Library

ISBN: 978 0 00 721346 7

Set in Sabon by Palimpsest Book Production Limited,
Grangemouth, Stirlingshire

Printed and bound in Great Britain by
Clays Ltd, St Ives plc

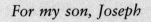

For my son, Joseph

ONE

Iamu.

   Strange sound. African sound.

   Three syllables. Iamu.

In the brief stillness of morning the boy stood and studied himself in the mirror. Beneath a lank fringe of black hair his brown eyes examined their reflection, as if for secrets. The pale brown of his skin, the prominent angle where his cheek seemed now to emerge more clearly, the darkness of his eyebrows, the squat saddle of his nose, these things he considered. The secret the boy sought was who he was to become. With the fingers of his two hands he touched the skin about his jaw to see if there was sign yet of any beard.

   Will I be bearded?

Maybe, maybe that roughening was something starting. He turned his head this way and that to look at himself sidelong.

   'I am you,' he said aloud, turning back to face the mirror, allowing himself to pose with pretend confidence. But almost at once the boy in the reflection lowered his eyes and the confidence crumbled like a mask made of flour.

   'Are you all right in there?' From just outside the bathroom

1

door a man's voice called hesitantly. And with even greater hesitation, as though the subject were one of tremendous delicacy, he enquired, 'Are they fitting?'

'Yes,' the boy said. 'Yes, they're fine.' But in fact the new shirt and jacket and trousers bought for his Confirmation that morning were still hanging off the towel rail.

'Grand, grand. I'm not rushing you,' said the man. 'There's plenty of time. But if anything needs adjusting. Oh, and I will do your tie, don't worry about that, all right?'

'Yes,' said the boy, 'fine, thanks.' He could feel the pale grey eyes outside watching the door.

'So, whenever you're ready.'

The old man moved away. He himself was already changed into a white shirt and blue suit trousers, and the tight black shoes he wore only for weddings and funerals squeaked off into the kitchen. Through the house now he had last-minute jobs of preparation, counting chairs for guests later, arranging glasses and bottles, gathering stray items of clothing that he and the boy allowed to lie around the house in the ordinary course of their living.

In the bathroom the boy was standing with his two hands pressing down on either side of the sink, looking at himself. It was not because he was vain, not because he often looked at himself in this way, or because he thought himself in any way worth looking at. Rather it was the very opposite, because to himself it seemed he had until that very morning been almost invisible. He had not really thought about what he looked like, or whom he looked like, or what changes were happening in the map of his face. Nor had he thought about what lay ahead for him. Not really. But in the week at school just finished, with the preparations at their most intense, this was the thing the Master had emphasized.

'You are not boys and girls any longer,' he had said. He had a voice more aged than himself, sounds frayed and whispery

2

from the smoking of his youth and the whiskey of his middle life. But still he could be firm. He knew a way of telling things that made the words seem important so that even those who paid no attention to spellings or History or Maths paid attention now.

'You came into this school as boys and girls, but in a week you will be gone.'

There was a broken line of grins along the back row.

'Yes. When you see me again, in a short time, in a very short time, you will think to yourselves: how old the Master has become. You will think, how very grey is his little bit of hair, how crooked and stooped he seems.' Here the Master had stooped crookedly and peered out half-blind and the class had laughed. 'He who once was so large and full of knowledge to me, so wise,' he continued, 'will be no more the Master but just an old man. Soon, very soon; in fact for some,' and here he had looked directly at the boy, 'this has begun to happen already; you will meet me and think how little that man knows, because you will quickly know so much more than me. And while you will become even smarter,' again he singled out the boy, 'I will become to you more foolish.'

The boy had thought to make some response to this, to deny it, but was too timid to speak out loud in front of the class.

The Master paused and angled himself against the seat of his stool, his two hands thrust deep in the pockets of his tweed jacket, his soft grey eyes travelling over the pupils one by one. 'But this is no reason for sadness,' he said. 'No, no. I will not be sad. And you must not be sad. This is a cause for celebration, because it means this; it means the world is getting smarter all the time. And you will be the evidence of that, you will be the ones to save the world from the mess your parents have made of it.'

He allowed this phrase to settle over them, and it was to

each of them as if these words were new clothes that they found themselves trying for the first time. Some were uncomfortable, some delighted and proud. The boy was not so sure. He looked at the large crinkled map of the world on the wall behind the Master. He had stared up at it for years in that classroom and knew his way from one country to the next with his eyes closed. But the world was a big place, and the idea of he and his classmates saving it from anything was hard to imagine. He looked along the wall at the posters they had made in preparation for the Confirmation, pictures of the Apostles with yellow crayoned flames touching their foreheads, and he was wondering if the flames burned and hurt when the Master continued.

'Here, I will remain. And I will know that I have done a very good thing when you are gone from this school. I will have done what I can to teach you what I know. And we will have shared that important time, perhaps that most important time together. But now, you have arrived at a threshold, a doorway. When you leave in a week's time, you will be leaving something important. Do you know what it is?'

Some hands were raised. Some guesses given: their school, their classroom, their desks with the names written underneath. But each guess the Master patiently dismissed.

'No, no,' he said at last, 'the thing you will be leaving behind is your childhood.'

There had fallen a silence then, as if a gap opened in the air between the Master and the pupils.

'Now the question you have to begin to ask yourselves is this: what kind of man or woman am I going to become?'

Again the Master allowed his question to hang in the air before them. Then, when he was sure it had begun to play in their minds, he added in a lighter tone, 'Because of course to some passing by outside this might seem to be only a small country schoolhouse in the middle of nowhere in the west of

Ireland. It might seem a quaint old place with a funny old schoolmaster . . .'

'Crooked and stooped,' said Martin Collins from the back row.

'Yes, crooked and stooped, in a place where nothing important could ever happen. Our roof is falling in. Our blackboard is grey from a hundred years of white chalk. From the skills of our footballers, some of our windows are cracked.' At this there was murmuring and laughter. 'But,' continued the Master, 'despite appearances, here something remarkable has happened. Here you have taken your first steps in becoming yourselves, in becoming who you are, and who you will be in the world.'

The Master had leaned back on the stool again and considered the faces gazing up at him. Some of the boys had begun to forget already the words he had just spoken and were restless for the bell when they could run out of the schoolyard for the last time. But not the boy. The boy thought about things deeply. This was his nature. Although he had once tried to join in and play games in the schoolyard he was not good at sports, and soon enough discovered both teams preferred it when he did not offer himself to be picked. Above all other things he enjoyed reading books. He was curious about everything in the world and had read through the small school library years before. He had read all the editions of the books of Charles Dickens there, of Robert Louis Stevenson, and Jules Verne. He had read the translations of great epic tales from Greece, of the stories of Ulysses and Odysseus, and the entire collection of slim books about the countries of the world. Although these were at least forty years out of date, some with their covers ripped off and pages marked and torn, from them he had tasted something of the places there were out there beyond the classroom. He was a boy who was interested in the how and why of all things, and whose understanding was far greater than others of his age. And this, rather than bringing him closer to adults or his contemporaries, had in fact created a distance between him and everyone else. In a row of lights strung out along a line he was a bulb too bright.

Knowing this, and considering how in the world of childhood he had had such difficulty, the boy had sat at his desk and for a moment let his eyes meet those of the Master. Who am I to become? In the grown-up world, who am I to be? Soundlessly he asked, and felt for the first time the burden of this question in his heart.

Now, in the bathroom before the mirror, he thought of all this again. He leaned against the sides of the sink and might have stayed longer if there hadn't been a tapping on the door.

'Nearly ready?'

'Yes,' he called back, 'just coming.'

Quickly then, he put on the new grey trousers and the white shirt that was stiff about the collar. When he squeezed closed the top button the shirt was still loose around his neck. In the mirror he looked ridiculous, he thought. He took the comb and drew a parting in his black hair and smoothed the line, but after an instant shook his head until the hair had returned to its usual untidiness and then he opened the door.

'Here you are.' A small man past sixty with a kindly face crinkled like a favoured newspaper stood with the boy's shoes freshly polished in his hand. His eyes did not move from the boy's. They were the pale grey of a thumb smudged with newsprint. Although he was still the Master, he did not look like the Master now. Out of the schoolroom and his faithful old tweed jacket and in the blue suit and white shirt, he looked almost a different person altogether. He was shaven very cleanly. There were tiny red nicks cut in his throat and one high on his cheek. The unruly tuft of his hair had been flattened down with water and was momentarily under control.

'Thanks,' said the boy.

'You're more than welcome. You look . . . well, fine. Yes, absolutely fine.'

The boy took the shoes and sat in the kitchen to put them on while the Master lifted two kites that were lying by the couch and carried them out to the back hall. 'Both of these are fine again,' he said. 'Maybe this evening, after the lot are gone, we might get a bit of breeze, take them out.'

'Yes,' the boy called after him. 'Thanks for fixing them.'

'No trouble. May evening, perfect for them.'

It was one of the things the Master and the boy liked best, to be standing below connected to the fluttering kite flying above.

When the boy stood up in the polished shoes the Master returned, holding out the tie.

'A tie? Do I have to?'

'Just for an hour. No more. Now, this is a tricky business,' the old man said, reaching up slightly to loop it around the boy's collar. 'When I first learned I choked myself for weeks after.' He raised his heavy eyebrows and made his eyes smile. 'Like this, you see, then over here, then under and through. It may not seem much, but to me, when I was growing up, it was like a secret, like something you had to be a certain age to know how to do, the knot. And of course there were fellows with some fancy ones and showing off and . . . well.'

The old man stopped. It was as if just then there was an obstacle in his way. Only it was invisible. He stood looking at the boy, losing any words he could say.

The boy moved the knot at his throat. 'What's the matter?'

'It's em, it's . . .'

The clock on the wall ticked loudly. The boy watched the man as he watched a memory.

'Are you all right?'

'I . . .' The Master had his lips pressed tightly together as though holding his feelings trapped there. Again the clock ticked, louder still, and the room seemed to tighten, as though a pressure had been put on the air. 'When you get old you get foolish, that's all,' the Master said at last and shrugged as though attempting to escape, and raised the eyebrows again, but this time in his eyes there was no smile.

'What is it? It's something . . . something's wrong,' said the boy. 'Tell me.'

And there was a moment, and then another. Briefly, everything was stopped, as if a hand reached out and paused the world in its turning. And inside that small cottage, in the kitchen stood a boy and an older man and the slow passing of a ghost, or maybe two. The Master saw them. One was his wife who had died when the boy was seven. She stood by the cooker now watching him, the pale blueberries of her eyes glinting with pride, her two hands brought up to her mouth the way she always did when she had feelings too large for words. The other ghost was the boy's mother, Marie, the Master's daughter who had died of cancer when the boy was two. She moved across the kitchen not a day older than the last time the Master had seen her, alive, her face pale, her auburn hair tied behind. She stood by her son and touched the side of his face, although the boy could not see or feel her.

'Tell me,' said the boy again. 'What is wrong?'

The Master was not looking at him but watching the ghost of the boy's mother and feeling all parts of himself singed with a sorrow he couldn't speak.

'Are you all right?' The boy was nudging the old man's shoulder.

'Yes,' said the Master, and again 'yes,' as though answering various questions from various speakers. He blinked and seemed to right himself.

'What is it?' asked the boy.

'Hold on.' The Master crossed the kitchen and went to a drawer in the dresser in which he kept a file of papers. The boy knew that in the wild jumble of things were kept documents of all kinds, in there were the instruction booklets and guarantees on everything, their two passports for the trip the Master was always hoping they would take together. In the file the old man hunted hurriedly and then found a cream-coloured envelope. He closed the file and put it back in the drawer and came to the boy, the envelope in his hand. He blew on it and brushed it against his sleeve. When he went to speak the words got caught on the knot of his tie and he pulled it a little to the right. Then he held out the envelope.

'What is it?' asked the boy, not taking it.

'Before your mother died, and you were only an infant, she wrote this letter to you. I watched her write it in the hospital. She wanted you to have it when you turned thirteen. But today she . . . today you . . .' The Master looked to the ghosts but they were gone. 'Well . . . the, em, the Confirmation is an important day. It seems right. Here.'

Suddenly the boy could not move. His heart was racing, his throat tight, had he already loosened the tie? Then why was it he could hardly breathe? Why was it the walls of the little kitchen seemed to pulse in and out?

Breath. In breath. Breathe.

He had to breathe.

Her letter. Breathe. This. In breath.

Don't. Can't.

No. No, he couldn't. He would not take the letter. He would not reach out and take it. No, he couldn't bear to, he silently decided.

The decision flashed in his mind like a wet knife in a dish-cloth. He wouldn't take the letter. He would wait. He would

9

take it some other day. Then he gasped a breath at last, and
the room seemed to stop pulsing.

No..

He looked down. And there in his hand he held the cream-
coloured envelope.

TWO

The boy had never known his mother other than that her name was Marie and that she was the shyly smiling young woman with brown hair in the photograph on the piano. He knew that she died after fighting cancer until her hair was gone and her hands so weak they could not hold on to him. He had no idea who his father was, nor, it seemed, did anyone. And in fact for almost all of the boy's life to that day he had not thought about it very much. His father and mother had been the Master and his wife when she was alive. They had adopted him as a baby and had loved him always.

But now he had the cream-coloured envelope in his hand. He was holding the envelope *she* had held, about to look at the page *she* had written.

'It's all right,' said the Master. 'You can read it now or you can keep it until later.' He glanced towards the kitchen door and then the windows to see if the ghosts might be lingering somewhere, but there was nothing. 'She is . . . well, she would have been so proud of you today. They both would have.' He smiled with his eyes and a hundred wrinkled lines were written around them. 'Whatever you'd like now,' he said softly, seeing that the boy was lost and unsure. 'Sometimes,' he put his arm

11

upon the boy's shoulder, 'sometimes the best thing to do is to do nothing for a while. Doing nothing at all is often the very wisest thing. Because, it was explained to me once, as the world is a ball and is turning and everything is in fact in motion all the time, doing nothing is not really doing nothing, it's allowing things to move at their own pace.

'Of course some people don't understand the wisdom of this,' the Master whispered, 'they think when men are doing nothing they are doing nothing.' Without the boy's realizing it, the old man had led him to the kitchen door. 'Take the envelope, go upstairs, do nothing. The church is in half an hour, plenty of time,' said the Master, 'go ahead.'

But the boy did not move. He looked down at the envelope in his hand. And suddenly, there opened a quake in his heart, a glaring gulf of sorrow – widening and widening – a dark nauseating chasm into which he himself was about to fall. He felt he was going to cry, but made only a small moan. Rushing up inside of him now rose a giant black wave of loss and sadness and a kind of anger at the world. The torrent roared in his ears. In it were carried the dead, the ghosts of the past he had thought buried. Before his eyes the room seemed to shimmer. The walls would give. The envelope was shaking in his hand as if electric. He could not bear it. He could not bear the hurt he would release if he opened the letter. He suddenly believed he would drown in grief. And so, perhaps even before he had made a decision, before his brain had considered its menu of options and chosen, and before there was time to stop him, he had stepped back inside the kitchen and thrown the cream-coloured envelope spinning into the fire.

'I don't want it,' the boy said, his face flushed, his eyes bright.

And with that he quickly opened the door and left the kitchen and climbed the stairs two by two until he was inside his bedroom and had thrown himself headfirst on to the blankets.

In the place where he lived the boy had no friends. Perhaps because of his great intelligence, he had found himself living on the edge of things for his entire childhood. In the classroom many might elbow him and ask in whispers for the answer to questions in English or History or Geography, but once in the open spaces of the yard they quickly ignored him. Perhaps too it was because his skin was not as pale as the others, because there was something indefinable about him that seemed *marked*, the way a boy might feel with a splashed birthmark on his face or a scar that reminded all of peril and injury. Whichever the reason, the boy had long ago begun to feel that some part of him was flawed, did not work the way things should. He imagined sometimes there was within him a real but invisible damage. And it was this of which he was most afraid.

To escape the feeling that he had no friend to confide in, the boy had a journal. To its white pages he told his thoughts. Some days there was little to tell, others there was not space enough in the calendar day for all that was hurrying through his mind. As he got older his thoughts grew more complex. Things were not so clear any more. He couldn't write down just one phrase to tell what had happened or what he thought about something. He wrote in fragments, half-questions. The boy did not name the journal, nor did he think of it in any way as a person. But by the time he was twelve years of age he could not have imagined living his life without it.

So, now, lying on his bed after throwing the cream-coloured envelope into the fire, he took out the most recent volume. It was green-covered and hard-backed and came from a supplier in Dublin the Master knew. It had a thin frayed golden ribbon that acted as a page marker. This the boy especially loved. He

13

loved when the book was closed to see how it marked his progress, and to open the journal by taking the frayed end and pulling so the pages splayed open at exactly the right place, like an invitation.

Now the invitation was urgent. He pulled open the page quickly and took a green pen from the book-stacked locker beside his bed. He looked briefly at the words he had written the night before.

> Cour-age
> Faith-age
> Believe-age
> I believe in what?

Now on a new page he wrote:

> I burnt the cream letter.
> Crimletter Criminaletter
> Why? Why?
> There is no I in why.
> There is no why.
> Because knot.
> Because I am knot.
> Because A cause B cause
> See cause I don't want to know.
> No know thatsall.
> Endofstory.

The boy lifted his pen and snapped the journal shut. That was it. He was done. Though to someone else the few phrases he had written might have seemed barely anything, almost the moment he had finished writing them the boy felt better. He sat on his bed and could breathe more easily now. It was over and done with. In a few moments he heard the

Master's heavy step on the stairs, then the knock on his door.

'Come in,' the boy said.

The Master's face was kind and full of concern, in his grey eyes something so forgiving and wise that the boy felt at once the comfort of him, like a flannel blanket.

'All right?' asked the Master.

'Yes. Fine. Thanks.'

'All right, just that it's maybe time for us to go. And you know what Father Paul's like. Want everything like clockwork. Be up since dawn with terror of the bishop coming.'

The boy stood up.

'Here,' the Master leaned forward and with a slight tugging put the boy's tie back in place. 'All right?'

The boy nodded. They went downstairs and passed through the sitting-room that was set for the guests later, the boy's seven great-aunts and their husbands. There were stacks of rough-looking sandwiches with their fillings half-falling out and bottles of various kinds of drink. 'Look all right?' asked the Master. 'You know what my sisters-in-law are like? Eat a turkey each, never mind turkey sandwiches.'

'Looks fine.'

'Good, good.' The Master crossed to the television where the news channel the boy liked to watch was reporting latest trends in world terrorism. He switched it off. 'Enough of that,' he said, 'come on.' They went outside and got into the small yellow car and drove towards the village.

It was a blue May day, the countryside they passed full of the beginnings of summer: hedgerows sprinkled with the small white blooms of blackthorn and the blaze of yellow gorse, meadows already green and grass thickening. Soon farmers would be out in tractors and morning, noon and early night would fill with the sound of mowers. The village was not far away and as they arrived at the top of its one long street there were cars parked everywhere and at all angles, as if abandoned. Banners of small triangular flags had been hung between the lamp-posts to signal the Confirmation Day and to welcome the bishop.

'We're a tiny bit late,' the Master said, 'but never mind,' he added, noting a look of concern on the boy's face. 'I'm the Master, they can't start without me.'

The boy did not say anything.

'You all right?' The Master patted him on his shoulder. 'Honestly you'll be fine. Absolutely fine.'

He stopped in the middle of the street and then began to reverse into the smallest of spaces between two cars, but as he did the engine coughed and died. The Master shrugged. 'Well, made it this far,' he said to the old car, and got out to hurry up the street.

Inside the church the choir was already singing. The parents of children from the Master's school exchanged looks of disapproval when he at last arrived. He smiled and was making a small wave at his seven sisters-in-law when the bell was rung on the altar and all stood. Mrs Conway on the organ pounded out the notes and made a jerking motion of her head, so that verse by verse her pink glasses edged further down her nose. The small timid figure of Father Paul came out; to hide his terror of the bishop, he wore a curve of smile freshly glued.

The bishop was a large man who loved himself completely. His fine black helmet of hair he considered magnificent, his nose straight, his teeth blanched and fearsome, his great girth symbolic. There was more of him than of most people.

The choir sang. The little church was hot with people, with the hundred candles and the pride of the parents. The first prayers passed over the boy, and soon he was standing and kneeling with others of his classmates but in a kind of dream. The whole event was unreal, as though he were watching it on the television, or had opened the door and come inside a theatre where a play was going on and everyone was involved except him. Everyone but him knew the lines. Or, they didn't even see him. He wasn't even there. There was just this new shirt and tie and new trousers and polished shoes in his place.

Over the weeks of preparation and drilling, the many visits the class had made down to the church, the boy knew what followed what. He knew like clockwork how the ceremony was to go, how first there was the Mass and then inside it as it were was the actual Confirmation when the boys and girls would step out of the church pews and go in line up to the bishop. He knew there were some in his class who were terrified of this. There were some whose mothers and fathers, for what reasons he was not sure, had told them horror stories from their own childhood. Had told them of bishops who smacked children hard across the face sending them spinning like tops. Bishops who asked impossible questions just to watch the humiliation burning the cheeks of the poor unfortunates. Bishops with waxy skin and hedgehog moustaches. Bishops with teeth that whistled. Bishops who smelled like burnt sausages. And when Father Paul had come to talk to the class about the Confirmation and its meaning he was a priest who was so unsure of himself, who seemed terrified that he might say the wrong thing, that he spoke in whispers. To the best that most of them could understand he had told them that after Confirmation they were all going to be soldiers.

The Master had told the boy no such tales. Rather when the boy had asked him one evening he had spoken of Confirmation as a rite of passage. 'It's a kind of gateway,' he said, 'between boyhood and manhood.'

'Other religions have them too.'

'They do,' agreed the Master. 'In the Jewish religion they have the Bar Mitzvah.'

'The Hindus have a ceremony too. The native Americans used to have one.'

17

'That's right. Jumping across fires, I seem to recall,' the Master said. 'The main point is it marks something. I suppose it's the beginning of becoming who you are. There's nothing at all to be afraid of.'

Now, as the actual ceremony continued, the boy was not frightened at all. But there was an unease gathering inside him. Something was wrong. For no reason at all he kept thinking about one of the prayers, the Creed, and its opening line, 'I believe in one God.' He had said it a hundred times, maybe more. But only now, at that very moment, did he ask himself if this was what he believed. Suddenly it seemed such a huge thing to him, such a declaration. Did he even believe he had a soul? Did he believe such a thing existed? Or had a separate life longer than his? That even then as he sat there in the church it was inside him? That somewhere his mother's soul floated?

Meanwhile the Offertory had come and gone, the gifts had been carried up. On the altar the bishop had slurped back the wine and grimaced a little at the inferior quality they used in the country village. All had proceeded with the strange order and precision of a familiar dream.

Only it was not a dream.

There was a sudden rustling of movement and now the boys and girls were standing and moving out along the bench to stand in the aisle. One girl with blonde curl-ironed hair, impatient at the immaturity of a boy in front of her who insisted on walking on the narrow kneeler as if it were a pirate's gangplank, shoved him in the back, and the whole line tottered forward. In the aisle they stopped and waited. Mrs Conway on the organ gathered steam. The Under-Tens Choir stood and battled against the mighty volume, singing as if they were sucking sour-pops. The parents leaned forward anxiously. Some fathers, elbowed that it was now time, stepped shyly into the aisle with video cameras, each one vying for a slightly better angle.

The line stood and waited. There was a music cue when they were to walk. They were to keep their eyes down. The bishop was to get up and come forward. It was practised a hundred times. One by one they would be confirmed and return to their rows while the video cameras rolled.

The Master had no camera. He watched the boy get out into the aisle, and tried to wink to him but the boy wasn't looking.

The Under-Tens reached the final chorus and the boys and girls heard their music cue to move. The bishop gave two little forward rolls and managed to rise. He moved forward with a kind of majesty, as if he imagined himself a king and the crowd cheering. Down one step, down another and forward towards the altar rails. Behind him, almost unseen, came the small crouched-over and smiling figure of Father Paul.

One by one the children stepped forward. The boy was thirteenth in the line. Already some were coming back down the aisle.

Were they confirmed now? Did they look any different?

Faith full. Faith filled.

Soldiers. Soul jeers.

Stoppit. Concentrate. I believe.

I believe in . . . NO!

There was no way the boy could have known beforehand, no way that he could have realized earlier and saved himself and the Master the embarrassment that was soon to follow. And perhaps it was just then, while Mrs Conway played a solo on the organ, her whole upper body swaying back and forth and her glasses slipping ever closer to the end of her nose, that the boy realized he couldn't continue. Perhaps it was only the motion of the line itself as it got smaller and smaller and he moved nearer and nearer to the bishop.

All he knew was a heat along his collar. Then a sense that his shoes were full of warm water, that he was finding it hard

19

to take the next step. Then the heat under his collar was rising and his breath was growing shorter and the panic of his drowning was ever more real.

Then suddenly the bishop was standing directly in front of him.

He was enormous.

'My son,' he said, and his fried breath travelled across to the boy. He had a pink palm raised and in its creases the boy could see glistenings of sweat. The bishop's eyes bulged. His lips he moistened with the tip of his tongue and then opened his mouth to proceed.

Know. No. I believe. St.

No.

'No, stop,' mumbled the boy.

The bishop ignored him.

'Stop!' said the boy much louder.

And then everything did. The bishop froze, his eyeballs huge, his mouth open. Above in the organ loft Mrs Conway stopped playing. There was a groan of sound out of the organ, a gasp, and then nothing. The church breathed in. Candles danced. There was a moment of absolute silence, as though a grave announcement had been made.

Through the congregation then there began the wave of response in which the Master's and the boy's names were whispered. From around the back of the bishop, Father Paul's small face appeared, his smile loosening in panic.

'I can't,' said the boy in a quiet voice. He said it only once, but his two words were repeated over and over as they were murmured back among parents and relatives, making a rustling like leaves in a sudden breeze.

'He can't.'

'He can't.'

'Shsh.'

'What?'

'He said he can't.'

The bishop was not about to have the Confirmation disturbed. The boy was foolish, or nervous and foolish, or stupid and nervous and foolish, and didn't know what he was doing or saying. These little hiccups in the ceremony could be overlooked. He could just carry on, he decided, as if nothing had happened. But he needed to do so quickly, because there was whispering in his church now. The rule of his majesty was under threat. He raised the sweat-glistening palm to the boy and placed it on his shoulder. 'Now my son,' he said.

But the boy stepped away from him.

'No!' he said.

The bishop made a little grasp as if the unconfirmed child was a slippery thing about to get away, but the boy pushed off the hand. He turned to where all were watching, his face burning brightly, his eyes like coals, and he ran down the centre of the aisle and out of the church.

THREE

He walked along the road out of the village. He walked quickly and did not look back. He did not think of the chaos that he had left behind him in the church, how the bishop had called out to him as he was hurrying down the aisle, how Father Paul had thrown his smile about in panic, how without her glasses Mrs Conway had suddenly started into the wedding march on the organ. He did not think of the Master's face he had glimpsed as he passed by, or those of his family. He did not think of the little cluster of video fathers that had blocked his way. He thought only:

Get away. Get away.

Go.

Go.

He walked quickly, he watched his polished shoes on the empty road. He was a hundred yards out of the village, then two hundred. It was then that the mild May breeze that was blowing between the hedgerows seemed to calm him a little and his mind began to wonder what had he done.

Or had he done anything? For a few moments it seemed that perhaps the whole thing had been a dream. Perhaps he was still in the bathroom at home and there was no cream-coloured envelope or journey to the church, no bishop or moment of un-Confirmation. He stopped suddenly in the road and waited to see if the clouds moved and the world turned. Watching the light grass of a meadow darkening under a sweep of cloud, he knew and spoke aloud: 'It's true. It happened.'

And he began to walk again towards home.

Why had he done it? Why had he not just stood before the bishop and let himself be confirmed? It wasn't as if he had decided beforehand, it wasn't as if he had chosen another faith or wanted to make some objection. The best way he could think to describe it was to say there was something that had begun in him. Something that had begun in him the night before when he lay in his bed thinking about the idea of the Confirmation and what it meant, and how before he had been able to sleep he had found himself questioning everything. Questioning why anything was the way it was. Hundreds of questions, thousands of them flying through his mind like bats as the darkness fell over the fields outside. To escape them he had turned over and over in the covers. He had tried to hum the tune of a song, but still the questions came. He was outside a mystery that was in fact himself.

Childhood. Why is it a hood?

Childs hood. Hood hiding what beneath?

What kind of man?

What kind will I be?

Will anyone like me better?

Pray God answers prayers.

If he can hear.

Even if he can hear can he understand?

Is he out of touch? What does he know about now?

If he is all-powerful why does he not appear more often?

Why is he invisible?

Why does he allow evil?

Why does he allow death? And disease. And horrible accidents?

24

If we are his creations why does he not make us good?
Is there only one God?
The dark furry wings of these questions had fluttered madly in the boy's mind one after the other until he had arrived not at any answers but at the most maddening questions of all:
Who am I?
And why?
Why?
Why am I alive? What am I for?
The cream-coloured envelope that morning had only added to this confusion. The boy felt that it was as if some power, some force had swept into his life in the last twenty-four hours and upset everything.

It was a poor excuse, he knew. It was not something he would easily be able to explain, and the Master must be ashamed of him now. The entire village must be talking about him. He walked more quickly. The stones of the road crunched under his feet. How was the Master going to explain it, how was he going to show himself in the village shops ever again? Sour yoghurt of shame settled in the base of the boy's throat. But he could not think of going back. No. Bolting as he did from the foot of the altar was the only thing he could have done; he was *propelled* to do it.

That was it, *propelled*.

But by what?

By who?

Confusion made him slow down and stop. He stood in the middle of the road, the dust blowing against his Confirmation clothes. Then he heard the Master's voice calling out from behind him.

'Don't start again for a minute.'

The boy turned and saw the old man puffing along to catch up. When he did he reached out a hand and leaned on the boy and briefly let his head drop low while he sought to catch his breath.

'I had to leave the car,' the Master said, his voice a whispery gasp. 'I thought I wouldn't have any trouble catching up to you.' He wheezed twice, 'But God bless you, the legs of you, you walk very fast.'

'I'm sorry,' the boy said.

'No need to be sorry.'

'But I ruined everything.'

'Well, there's many ways of looking at a thing,' the Master said, his head upright now and his breath coming more steadily. 'And if it wasn't what you wanted, then if you'd gone ahead with it you could say I was the one would have ruined everything.'

'But I don't know what I want.'

'I know that. And I know there's many there today standing up and being confirmed don't know what they want either but are too lazy or afraid or deceitful or dim-witted to say so. And some of them only want the envelopes with the money from the aunts and uncles.' At that, the Master paused and looked about. There were no cars coming or going on the country road and they were halfway from the village to home. He seemed to consider this for a few seconds and then said: 'Well, we might as well head on together, eh? I daresay the aunts will be hurrying off home and not coming back to the house now.'

'I'm sorry.'

'You'll have to stop saying that.'

'But . . .'

'No.'

The Master's tone was final. The boy said no more. They walked together homeward. Because in the village the Confirmation was still proceeding there was no traffic and they could walk down the centre of the road. In the stillness of the countryside there was peace, and for a time the problems that had bubbled in the boy's mind grew calm. They were just walking, that was all. There was only the blue and white sky of the May day, the fields, the cattle standing in them, the birds and their short quick flights making them seem like creatures of mission, or messengers darting through the air.

'The world is full of conundrums,' the Master said when they were not far from home. 'Conundrums, puzzlements,' he added, 'and to a young person with any intelligence it will seem as though these should be thought about and puzzled over and eventually solved. That's the thing. Solved. And as I well know, and have tried to tell you many times, you are not a boy of any intelligence, you are a boy of very great intelligence, and so these puzzlements have to seem even greater, more urgent to you. And even greater and more urgent the need to solve them.' The Master stopped in the road and put his finger in the air, as if pointing to an invisible blackboard just in front of him. 'And I know there are very many adults who, if I gave them the time, might look at you and say: the boy thinks too much, you must get him to stop thinking about things so deeply, get the boy outside, give him hard chores, something to tire him out. But you know this is not what I think. I think this would be like having a very fine racehorse and tying him to a plough. Do you understand?'

'But what's the use of being intelligent if it only makes things worse?'

The Master didn't answer this straight away. They walked forward the last few yards towards the house.

'It is all right to think about things,' said the Master. 'It is all right to find the world full of problems and to want to be able to solve them. Beginning with the ones right here in your life. And all right too not to have any idea how to proceed.'

They stepped through an overgrown arch of hedge where there was a small green gate. On the ground in front of them

27

was a wandering line of flagstones that wound its way in the form of a question mark up to the house.

'See,' the Master said. 'When I laid these I was not so sure how I was going, only where I wanted to get to.'

They arrived at the front door and stepped inside the house that had been set for the Confirmation party.

'Well now,' the Master said, his cheeks flushed and his soft grey eyes watering a little, 'I haven't walked from the village in years. Lemonade, I think.' He poured a glass for himself and one for the boy. They sat at the kitchen table and for a time the only sound was the ticking of the large clock on the wall.

Then the boy said he would go upstairs to his room and read for a while and the Master nodded. He wanted to be able to say something more to the boy but what it was or what exactly the words were escaped him, and so instead he smiled kindly.

In his room the boy threw himself on to the bed. He kicked off his polished shoes, pulled free the tie and opened the button at his collar. He let his eyes look along the titles of the books on the shelves. He had read all of them already, but sometimes liked to read over again his favourites even knowing how things would turn out. In fact sometimes the books were better for that. Now he took down the hardback *David Copperfield* the Master had given him two years before, which had been too difficult at first, but become in time one of the boy's treasures. Now he opened the first page and read the opening words as if meeting again an old friend.

'Whether I shall turn out to be the hero of my own life, or whether that station will be held by anybody else, these pages must show.'

Downstairs the Master sat in an old leather armchair. For a long time he considered what had happened and what it was

28

he should do now. He felt hurt for the boy at how things had turned out, and his hurt was so sharp and pressing that he thought of seeking relief in one of the whiskey bottles waiting for the guests that were not coming. It had been seven years now since he had stopped drinking, seven years since he had admitted to himself that he could not control the power of alcohol over him. Seven years since he had been found unconscious in the village street in the early morning. But now, the pain he felt for the boy needed some relief. He turned the bottle top of Powers whiskey and lifted it off. The strong bitter scent rose familiarly. He might have poured a glass for himself then, but the hand that reached for it stopped in mid-air. It wavered there. Involuntarily the Master touched his lips together and closed his eyes and, with no one but the ghost of his wife watching, he fought a silent battle against himself.

The boy was still reading *David Copperfield* with the light outside his window dimming when there was a knock again on his bedroom door and the Master appeared. Now changed back into his old tweed jacket and baggy trousers, he came in and sat on the end of the bed.

'*David Copperfield*?' he said.

'Yes,' said the boy, closing over the page. 'I've read it before.'

'I know you have.'

'But it's still good. It's better.'

'I daresay I could read it again myself. A book like that you should read every few years. In fact if there was enough time in the world you could read some books year after year and each time get something new from them.'

'That would be good,' said the boy.

'Yes.' The Master looked at all the books on the shelves and thought not for the first time that day how remarkable this boy was. 'Just checking that you are all right,' he said.

29

'I am.'

'Well,' the Master angled himself slightly to one side and reached into his jacket pocket, 'here are the cards from your aunts.' He held out a cluster of white envelopes.

'I shouldn't take them.'

'Of course you should. You crossed a threshold in your life today as much as anyone else in that church.'

'But . . .'

'No but, here.'

The boy took the cards and placed them on the bed.

'Oh, and here.'

There in the Master's hand once more was the cream-coloured envelope from that morning, only now its edges were black and one side was burnt away completely.

'Got it out as best I could,' he said. 'It is for you. I promised your mother I would deliver it. I don't see how it would have been right to let it burn. Read it. Read it when you're ready to, years from now if you like, and then by all means if you want to, go ahead and throw it in the fire, forget about it if you want to, but at least read it first.'

The Master stood up. His eyes were fixed directly on the boy. He knew there was more to say but couldn't think of how to say it. 'Well, anyway, all right?'

'All right.'

The quiet in the room after the Master left was deeper than before. There was a sharp expectancy, as if the air had been pulled tight as the skin of a drum and at any moment the sticks would begin to beat. The boy moved the Confirmation envelopes about on the bed with his fingers. He looked at the burnt cream-coloured one and lifted it and put it on the bookshelves behind his bed. He picked up *David Copperfield* to read some more, but as he read down a page he knew he had been following the words with his eyes only. He had no idea what he had just read. He tried again, but with no success.

He was tired. Evening had just folded into night outside. He opened his bedroom door and called out goodnight, and then got dressed in his pyjamas and into bed.

Some time before, the boy had stopped saying prayers before sleep. He was not sure God was listening. Besides there were many different Gods people all over the world prayed to, and anyway he didn't like praying for things for himself. So instead he lay in the bed and tried to think of *David Copperfield*.

When he woke it was dark. He felt a hand had shaken him by the shoulder, and as he sat up in his bed he looked around in fright, sure that someone had just been there. He turned on the bedside light but saw no one. Yet it had felt so real. His breath caught in his throat. His sleep had been full of dreams and for some moments he seemed to be clawing aside the cobwebs of them from the front of his mind. He swallowed the nothing in his throat. He closed his eyes and opened them again to see if he was still inside a dream.

'I'm awake,' he said out loud and heard himself, and with his left fingers touched his right shoulder where still as clearly as anything he could remember the feel of the hand shaking him.

The boy got out of bed then. He opened his window and felt the cool of the night. He listened to the night sounds; wind and trees and things growing.

He switched on the light. Then he reached down and took the burnt envelope in his hand. With a silver pen angled carefully, he delicately, slowly opened it. Pieces fell away as he did. When the pen reached the side that was burnt entirely a dark remnant detached and fluttered like a black butterfly to the ground.

Inside the envelope was a single page. But because of damage by the fire and the way the page had been folded a large arc on the right-hand side was missing.

The boy held the sheet in the light. The writing was in blue ink, the words on thin lines. They were written at a slight slant from left to right. Most lines had no endings because the paper had been burnt away. Such things the boy noticed at once, as if studying the letter itself and delaying as long as possible the thing he most wanted and was most afraid to do, read it.

When at last he began, his hand shook. He had to sit down and use his second hand to steady the page.

The first sentence read:

I am sorry that I am gone now, and cannot be there to hold you.

The boy lifted his eyes and looked away out at the dark in the window. He waited a few seconds. He looked there at the nothing that was, ink of sky with stars cloud-blotted, and he pictured the image of his mother.

He read on.

I thought that it would be important for you to know

Then the rest of that phrase was lost as the paper was burnt away.

The next phrase read:

love you but because your father did not know

Next bit missing.

After that: *what you should know about him is*

The fragments were maddening.

when he was still a student . . .

but his work because . . .

a writer and . . .

for him telling people what was happening in the worl . . .

and because he was not from here and was a . . .

because if I told him maybe . . .

not that he didn't because I didn't give him a

maybe was my mista . . .

but because I wasn't sure and because I couldn't imagine how . . .

32

from such different worlds, me from here and him . . .
and thought it was too important for him to
for the BBC in London or sometimes . . .

Then, a blackened hole, and the letter was finishing: *hope*
that you will forgive me and understand . . .
is name is Ah . . . Sh

Nothing. A black emptiness, the name unfinished, burnt
away. And in the bottom corner, his mother's signature,
Marie

The boy stared at the letter a long time.

In the many months he would have later to relive those
moments, sitting in buses and trains or walking long distances
alone with his thoughts, he would still not be able to say
exactly how what happened next had come about. As though
the decisions then were taken for him and it was not he himself
taking the steps. *Propelled.* He was once again propelled.
Within minutes he was in his jeans and a red hooded jumper.
He was putting on the trainers he always wore, taking from
his wardrobe his schoolbag and emptying out all the schoolbooks on to the floor. He was taking his journal and a pen,
the small case that held his wooden flute, and the copy of
David Copperfield inside which he placed carefully the burnt
letter. Then he was writing a quick note to the Master and
leaving it on his bed, picking up the Confirmation envelopes
and stuffing them in the bag, slipping down the stairs and
going to the drawer where he found his passport. Within
another minute he was at the back door turning the key. Then,
with a last look back, he stepped outside into the night and
was gone.

FOUR

The dark he plunged into was thick and blinding. Clouds obscured the stars. He walked with one hand held in front of him as if feeling a passageway between walls. Like this he came out into the road. There were no streetlights between here and the village and the way he had walked home earlier that day was now nothing but blackness. The boy stood absolutely still for some moments and closed his eyes. He had read that this was the quickest way to become accustomed to darkness, to keep your eyes shut tight until all the light *inside* had drained away. Then you could open them and find that the dark was in fact full of minute lights and shades and shadows, and by these you could make your way forward. He shut his eyes and waited in the road. He heard his heart racing louder, and felt a pulsing up along his neck, his breath rising and falling. He tried to calm himself but gave up almost at once, opened his eyes and found he could in fact see where the ditch on both sides of the road began, and where the road itself had a kind of bow shape slightly risen in the middle. He hurried away along it. He passed down by the sleeping farmhouse of the Ryans, their nearest neighbours, and had to shush-shush old Blackie as he lay against the front door and raised an eyebrow at him as if he were a ghost passing.

On he went. Shapes of black upon blackness were cattle in the fields standing. Some, hearing his footsteps along the road, started and turned about and a few bucked their hind legs and took off down the field as though escaping harm. Just so then did the boy disturb the stillness of the night as he travelled through it. It was yet hours before dawn, hours before the Master would go up the stairs to wake him and discover the note he had left.

I will be back soon. I could not tell you because I know you would want to stop me. But I have to do this. I have to do this on my own. Don't worry.

The boy hurried. He had to get through the village and out on to the main road where he might catch a lift in the early hours of the morning. That was his plan.

Well, maybe it wasn't exactly a plan, he thought to himself. Rather, what he had was a purpose. Yes. He had a purpose. His purpose was that he was going to find his father. That was it. That was the mystery that he had suddenly become aware of in the last twenty-four hours.

That was it.

Find him. End of story.

Find him because

Because of the letter. Because she wrote it. Because there's a piece missing, like a jigsaw.

Because I am a jigsaw.

'That's it,' said the boy to the darkness as he walked. That seemed right. He couldn't see the whole picture until the missing part was found. It was perfectly logical. And although he knew that with the minuscule pieces of information in the letter finding the missing part would be difficult, he did not think it would be impossible. He applied the same reasoning to this as to everything else in his life. Things could be figured out if you followed a procedure, if you followed one step at a time. And for a short while as he walked along the road this occupied his mind. But in the quiet and the dark, moments of the day gone by returned to him. He saw the scene of the Confirmation play back like a silent movie with the church pews, the organ music, the large figure of the bishop, and he felt suddenly uneasy about how he had behaved. Right then he stopped short on the road.

'Look,' he said to the night sky, 'If You exist, I'm sorry. If You were expecting me to be confirmed as one of Your soldiers and I turned my back on You and walked out it wasn't because I believed something else or in somebody else, all right? It wasn't personal. If You exist then . . .'

The boy looked about him on the road. In the dark he could make out nothing. Above him pinholes of stars uncovered glinted in the deep blue.

'Then . . .' He caught his lower lip in his top teeth and held it.

'Then You can prove it by helping me find my father,' he said. 'Then I'll believe in You, that'll be my confirmation.'

The boy hesitated briefly then, as if expecting an answer out of the dark, a sign to tell him it was agreed, that everything would be all right and that he could carry on and would be back home again soon. But there was no response, no sign, only the emptiness of the night and the light wind whispering in the bushes.

'Talking to yourself in the dark,' said the boy and shrugged his shoulders, 'so much for being intelligent.'

He hurried on. He passed in beneath the streetlights of the village where the small banner flags for the bishop fluttered overhead. The shops and the pubs and the church seemed ghostly now. There lingered a strange sadness in the street, a sense of aftermath. In no window was there light. The boy could walk down the centre of the village. Strangely he felt more alone than he had on the country road. He hurried out beyond the streetlights and into the dark once more. He was on the main road facing eastward where in a few hours the sun would rise. The road was broad and once he was used to it he could make out the faint trace of the yellow line that ran along its edge.

An hour passed, and then another. He was walking hastily, eyes downward on the yellow line, when he fell over the man.

'Hey!' a voice cried out. 'What the hell?'

The boy went tumbling face-forward, a jumble of dark over dark, and hit his shoulder hard against the road and the pain shot through him, and he was rolling over, crashing into the ditch. There was cold water and wet grass and a tangle of briars that dragged their thorns along the back of his jumper. There was a moment in which everything was upside-down, his feet in the air and his face in the ground. Then there was only the pain in his shoulder.

'Hey, what the blazes?' snarled the man's voice again. He was sitting on the edge of the road where he had been for some time.

The boy let out a groan and held his shoulder and then got himself up out of the cold ditch-water.

'Are you the devil or a ghost or what?' growled the man.

'I am a boy.'

In the dark the man was a low shape. The boy could not make out his features and at first thought he had no legs.

'A boy-devil or a boy-ghost or what?'

'Just a boy.'

'On the road?'

'Yes.'

There was a moment of nothing but the man's breathing and the dark full of shadows.

'Is it still the month of May?' asked the man.

'Yes.'

The man seemed to consider this for a short time and the boy stood and held his shoulder, and then the man named the village and asked him if it was a few miles west. The boy was not sure if this was a trick question or if the man himself did not know the answer. He told him the village was not very far.

'In which direction?' asked the man.

'That way.' The boy pointed.

'I can't see, come closer.'

The boy took a step nearer and at once the man reached up and grabbed him hard by the shoulder and pulled the boy down to him. The boy cried out with the sudden pain. Now, his face inches from that of the man, he could smell the sour smell of old beer and pee and smoke from the man's breath and see the pale whites of his eyes. The man pulled him close and squinted and showed a broken line of teeth. The sourness of him was foul and the boy struggled to get free, but the man quickly reached his other hand and grabbed on to him, floundering about until his bony fingers caught hold of the boy's ear.

'Well, well,' said the man, his voice thick and slurred as if he was unused to his own tongue. 'Are you real? Do you feel that?'

The boy cried out again and brought up his right fist quickly until it arrived with a kind of soft hardness in the man's face. The eye was pulp, the cheek bone. It was the first time the boy had ever hit anyone with his fist and through him ran the strange sensation of it. There was the shock of his own force as the man let go and fell backward, the disgusting jelly of the eye, the sharp pain in his own knuckles from striking bone. He pulled back and found his chest heaving, his heart rushing up into his throat and thumping wildly. The pain in his shoulder was worse. When he moved there were the teeth of a saw cutting into him.

The man lay out on the road and did not move. The boy watched him for some moments.

'Are you all right?' he asked.

There was no response.

'I am sorry I hurt you,' said the boy, then he turned, picked up his bag to hurry away down the dark road.

For twenty yards he did not stop. He hastened from the ugliness of the encounter with his heart still racing and a cool sweat pasted across his forehead. He expected a cry. He expected pursuit. But when none came, he grew fearful of the enormous silence behind him; he slowed and then stopped. He looked back and saw the shadow-shape of the man, that could have been a beast or a creature of any kind in that night dark.

The boy didn't know what to do. He knew the rule of the world of childhood was not to deal with strangers, but he had left that world now. Now there were only strangers. Was the man badly hurt? Had he knocked his head on the road when he fell back? What if he were dead?

The boy walked back towards the shadow, in his mouth a sour lump of dread. The black road, the wild briary fingers of the hedgerows, the unearthly silence that made the place seem nowhere and everywhere: these things entered him and registered in the catalogue of fear.

The man was not moving. The boy could not hear if he breathed. He stood and looked at the twisted dark of him, the legs awry, the head at a sharp tilt to the road.

'Hello? Are you all right?'

In that utter dark and emptiness it was a greeting weird and unearthly. There was no sign the man heard. The boy lowered his bag and bent down and put his hand on the damp shoulder and shook. Thin sticklike bone, the man was.

'Hello? Hello, can you hear me?'

And back from what other place he was, the man returned with a gurgle and a groan. He swallowed the nothings in his throat noisily and brought a hand up out of the dark by his side and patted gently the eye that was already puffy.

'I'm going to have a right one tomorrow,' he said, staring at the boy. 'It'll swell out to here, be all purple and yellow.' Instead of anger he showed pride, as if he enjoyed the wonder of himself and how well he bruised. A small laugh deep in his throat caught in phlegm and soon became a series of coughs that ended when he turned and spat sideways into the ditch. He watched after it for a moment, as though it was some part of him he regretted losing.

'You're all right so?' The boy half-turned to leave.

'I have a car back a bit there but I went over into the ditch. I need help to get her out. Just a push. Then I'll take you a piece of your way. What do you say?'

The boy did not say anything. What should he say? How was he to decide what was right or wrong here? The man had been drinking and probably drove his car off the road out of drunkenness. The boy should not take a lift from him. Besides how was he to know if the man would actually keep his word, if he wouldn't drive off the minute they got the car going, or worse if he wouldn't try and bring the boy back home? Or . . . There were a dozen reasons to say no. But then, as he was sobering now the man seemed more clear-headed and less frightening. The boy had terrified *him* falling over him in the dark as the man was curled in a nightmare. Perhaps he was just an ordinary man and only the night and the drink and the surprise had made him seem fierce. Besides, the boy would need to trust people he didn't know if his journey was to get him anywhere.

'You will take me some of the way?'

'Oh, I will,' said the man. 'You have my solemn word,' he closed his lips on what may have been a belch or a chuckle, 'as God is my witness.' And in the darkness the boy could see him raise a hand and pass it over and up in a sign of the cross. 'Help me up now will you? Good man.'

41

A pale hand reached up towards him. It hung there faintly silvered like a dim fish waiting to be caught.

'Friends, eh?' said the man. 'No hard feelin's. Good lad.'

The boy took a half-step forward. He was still unsure. He was still hearing a voice telling him to run away, *Go, go fast now,* but it was tangled through another telling him to be adult about this, be *not afraid, not a frayed boy.*

There was a moment that stretched, one in which the hand hung waveringly and the boy could feel only his own heart hammering and how huge and empty and dark was the night. The man's fingers twitched as he tried to reach another inch up to the boy. In whatever angle of starlight that fell then his eyes were caught and revealed as a metallic flash, as though they were glass or steel, one of them smaller than the other. There was the thin jagged line of his teeth, the ruined look of his mouth that opened crookedly like a drawer in the wrong place. The fingers twitched. The boy reached for them.

'Good lad,' he heard.

Then suddenly the hand he held held him. The fingers he took locked like a vice around him, crushing into the bones, as the man pulled himself up and was then standing tightly holding the boy's hand. His face came up like a ravaged moon over the boy. It was a face pocked and grained and with a rough covering of three days' silvered beard. Its right eye was swollen and pursed half-closed, its breath a sour gas full of the poison of resentment.

'Hit me would you?' said the man, his fingers around the boy's hand, pulling him forward with one hand only to poke him in the chest with his other. 'Hit me, why you . . .'

The man's hand became a fist in the boy's stomach, and the boy would have fallen backwards but for the hand still holding on to him. He felt the breath knocked out of him in an empty O and his eyes widened in astonishment and hurt.

'. . . you little . . .' the man was muttering, pulling the boy

42

about until he twisted his arm behind his back and pulled it roughly upward. The pain shot through the boy. 'You little, you're nothing but a little liar aren't you, eh? Running away, eh? Oh yes you are, aren't you, tell the truth.' The man pushed the boy's arm higher and the boy made a noise that was the noise of hurt in all languages.

'Tell the truth,' urged the man again, and lowered the boy's arm a fraction so that he could answer.

'I'll tell you the truth!' shouted the boy.

'Aha.'

The man relaxed his grip slightly further. And the boy then shouted out as loudly as he could: 'I am going to find my father!' He shouted it so loudly that whatever creatures moved in the dark turned and stopped and were startled then and flew or raced or burrowed away. He shouted it with a voice edged with pain and anger, a sharpened scream that slashed the night into pieces and let them fall away in the dark.

Then without thinking at all, without understanding the effect his words would have, he shouted out: 'I am going to find out if God is watching!'

It was not a spell, not an incantation or any part magic. It was a roar. And whether from surprise at the mention of God or the strangeness of the night or the still vivid visions of his nightmare, the man responded by lessening his hold slightly. 'Wha?' he began.

But already the boy had spun about and was freed of the man's grip on him. This time he did not hesitate. The boy stepped quickly back and then forward holding out both of his hands as if rushing to meet a wall. His hands arrived in the man's chest and shoved him backward.

At once the man lost his balance. It was like the road was pulled out from under him, and his feet flew up and he shouted out and fell down with a crash.

The boy did not wait to watch. He picked up his bag and

turned swiftly and began to run. He ran down the centre of the road into the dark. He ran with his brain whirring like a windmill. He ran and kept going while his lungs heaved and his throat tightened and burned. He ran through the dim starlight on the rough road that rose and fell and swung away into the east. He ran past the shapes of cattle in the fields, of sleeping statue-like horses and the looming darkness of trees and wild bushes. The boy ran as though a ghost was chasing him. He ran and did not stop, and did not look around to see if God was watching.

FIVE

Cold.

Cold dark and agh!

My shoulder.

He was five miles further along the empty road. He had slowed down and slowed further still as the panic in him calmed, and he realized he was not being followed. The pain in his shoulder was still there and he kept his bag on the other side. Inside his shoes his feet were wet and cold from ditch-water. He could have turned back and been almost home before the Master woke. He could have slipped in the back door and gone upstairs and lain under the warm blankets and mumbled that he was unwell and staying home when the Master called him. He could have been back in that comfort, his head pressed deep into his own pillow, his body curled in the body space in his bed, his books on the shelves beside him. If he hurried now he could still make it. He could take back the note he had left, and pull the curtains. And perhaps he could wake up again and it would still be the morning of his Confirmation. Time would go back and restart with the Master carrying the good plates and cups and saucers into the sitting-room and the Confirmation clothes waiting on a hanger. It would all be exactly as it had been.

No.

No, there was no going back. Everything had changed.

For a reason?

Why? What reason?

Letter in the drawer waiting.

Until that morning.

It was something the boy often wondered as he read novels. If David Copperfield's mother had not married Mr Murdstone, would David's life have been completely different? Would he never have met Steerforth or Agnes, or even Aunt Betsey and Mr Dick? And so did Charles Dickens sit down and draw up the whole plan of each character's life *before* he started writing? Did he live out each of their lives *before* they lived them? Or did they just sort of *happen*? Was it just chance that as he was writing the words he thought, 'this is what is going to happen here', and then made it turn out that way?

This and other things flew through the boy's mind as he hurried. In the hedgerows suddenly birds clamoured. For a few moments, so preoccupied was he with his own thoughts, that he wasn't aware of them. Then, at a turning in the argument in his head, he stopped and the noise startled him. There were sounds of every pitch and kind, shrills and thrills. Birds that sang five notes, four in quick succession, others only the one, over and over. No birds flew but the air was suddenly thick with song. The singing was so full-throated and varied, so widespread everywhere along the roadside that it seemed urgent, as if again some essential messages that could not be understood were there relayed.

Ahead of the boy in the east the dawn rose. He had seen early morning light in winter before, but never quite watched the full slow drama of the brightening of dark. The night was like a cloth whose hem was moving. Very slowly, at first. The thinnest fringe of a paler shade appeared low in the distance, so like the colour of night that at first you couldn't say that it was any different. Then, as the boy walked towards it, in the distance the hem withdrew slightly further. Whether the night was pulling back or the day pushing forward he couldn't say. But his eyes remained fixed on the thin streak of a colour somewhere between blue and purple against a pale-pale white.

Same colour as veins along the inside of the Master's arm.

The streaks of blue were not linear or evenly spaced nor any way you might consider drawn by a hand, but rather as if they were things with their own life, runs of colour and light released out of the darkness. The pallor of the horizon was delicate and fine and seemed to the boy strangely vulnerable, as if light were something really graceful, or shy, and its slow approach to the darkness uncertain and gentle. The first streaks of the dawn vanished as the night was pulled further away until there was a play of many colours.

Faint yellow buttermilk.

Washed grey school shirts.

Curved pink behind fingernails.

The colours were there for moments only. There, and then diluted into the bigger brightness. Birds took flight from the hedgerows and darted across the sky and climbed the air at upright angles. The dark was gone. He looked behind him to the west but already the morning had come over him, and he was swiftly in the new day.

The boy felt a sense of gladness then. He had the feeling of someone who has come through a test or difficulty. His first night was behind him. He was already that much closer to completing his journey, he told himself. And although he still felt pain in his shoulder, things would be all right, he thought.

But the brightness of the early morning brought with it something else too. In the daylight he was suddenly exposed on the road for anyone to see. Now, here were the first cars, and as they approached he had a dread they were coming to find him. When one then two and three passed by he released the breath caught like a bird in the cage of his chest and walked on. But he had the sense that he wore guilt like a yellow coat and that the drivers could tell.

'There's nothing I can do about it,' he told himself, 'I can't keep off the road by day and only travel by night. I have to chance it. Otherwise I will never get there.'

He walked on. He did not know exactly where this 'there' was. But in the hours since he had left home he had formulated this much: that the man he was looking for had some connection with the BBC, and so their offices in London would be the first place to enquire of him. He was a writer, perhaps a newsman. His name was Ah-Sh something.

What exactly would happen when the boy met the man, he didn't think about yet.

The approach of a large truck up the hill behind him caused the boy to stop and stand in to the side of the road. The truck laboured on the slope and made its way very slowly so that the driver had the boy in his sight a long time. When it arrived alongside him, the truck slowed to a stop. Its engine running, the truck's passenger door flew open, and above him the boy could see the driver leaning across to call down to him.

'Need a lift?'

The man was in a pale blue shirt with its sleeves rolled up. His stomach bowed outward, as though on his lap was an inflated ball. He had small curves of golden hair standing upward on his head and as he looked down at the boy there was a smile playing in his eyes and his entire face seemed on the point of laughing.

'Going along the way a bit? Hop up,' said the man. He smiled warmly, as if he had just told a wonderful story, or thought it marvellous how he had a free seat in his truck and the boy needed one.

But the boy hesitated. A car hooted at the stopped truck on the hill.

'Well lad, eh?'

Reason or random? Chance or plan?

He reached up, grabbed the door handle, climbed on to a metal step and slid in on to the seat.

'There you go,' chuckled the man, and held out a short pink hand to the boy. 'Ben Dack,' he said, 'your driver.' He thought this almost hilarious and the ball on his lap bounced up and down a few times as the humour found a home there.

Remembering the man on the road, the boy took the hand cautiously. But at once he found his fingers squeezed warmly and his arm pumped up and down vigorously while all the time Ben Dack smiled. 'Welcome aboard,' he said while the boy snapped the seatbelt. 'You're in for a smooth ride.'

The truck pulled out into the road into what was now a steady file of cars.

'Where you off to?' asked Ben. 'I'm taking her all the way across the country to Dublin today.'

'That's where I'm going. To Dublin.'

'Really?'

'Really.'

'Isn't that lucky then. By jingo it is. All the way to Dublin. I tell Josie, that's my wife, lovely lovely Josie, a saint to be married to me and I don't mind admitting it, don't mind at all. I tell Josie, I tell her I'm taking the truck up to Dublin again tomorrow, third time in ten days, and each time I'm always on the lookout, you know, for someone. Because there's always someone isn't there? I think so, I think so. I do. Someone who needs a lift, someone you can lend a hand to just by pulling over. Just as simple as that, eh?'

'Yes.'

'Because we're all in this world right?' Ben paused a moment as if he was reviewing this piece of information just for a second. 'Yep, we're all in this world and who knows I might be you one day and you might be me and even, even,' he raised his right hand off the steering-wheel and pointed at the boy, 'I might have been you, sort of, I mean I might have been a fellow on the road looking for a lift, you see, and well . . .' The idea became a little complicated then so he waved the hand slightly as though erasing it off the board. 'Well, the main thing is, the main point I told Josie was, kindness to one person is kindness to yourself. In a way, do you see?'

Trying to keep up with the logic of the point and finding himself somewhere further back in the reasoning than Ben, the boy could only nod.

'Exactly, it stands to reason doesn't it? Of course it does. Mathematical, sort of actually. And that way, oops.' A car came shooting down an avenue and out into the path of the truck, but Ben anticipated it and pulled on the wheel and swung them out of the way.

Although there had almost been a full collision he did not blast the horn or curse, but instead made a little whistle and chuckled. 'Poor fellow's probably slept it in, driving half-asleep. He's absolute awake now anyway.'

The boy said nothing. He was recovering from the near-crash, and trying to assemble in his mind the pieces of this new situation.

'Where was I? Lost my thought now.' Ben drummed his fingers on the sides of the steering-wheel, then lifted his right hand and clicked. 'Yes, that way what one person does for another one is not exactly charity, you see, because it's not like you're doing it for them, well you are, you are, but not *for them* if you see. That's what I'm always telling Josie, really it's for yourself, because, because, well, you see, as I say, I could be you.'

At that, arriving triumphantly at his main point, Ben chuckled delightedly. It was all so clear to him. It was like he had the secret of the world and was so pleased that he, just an ordinary fellow, had figured it out. His cheeks were reddened with pleasure and his eyebrows lifted to the angle of a squat roof. He let the brilliance of his argument shine for a moment and as he did so he placed the very tip of his tongue just between his lips.

The countryside flew past them.

'Dublin, eh?' he said after a while.

'Yes,' said the boy, and after a beat added, 'thank you for picking me up.'

'Oh not at all, not at all,' said Ben. 'I'll tell you something. I'll tell you something for nothing. The road is shorter with two. Have you ever noticed that? It is. Absolute gospel. I know this country back and forward. I know every corner of every road I'd say by now. I've been on the roads in this country for, what are you sixteen?'

'Yes,' lied the boy.

'Well all the years of your life then, and there's not one mile of them I'd rather travel on my own. A place can be lovely, but it can still be lonely. And sitting in this cab mile after mile listening to the radio or singing a little bit – no don't worry I won't start, Josie says I'd be second to a crow in a singing contest – is no comparison to having someone for company. So thank you. *Thank you* for coming onboard. Together the two of us will fly across this country in jig-time, absolute jig-time, whereas otherwise. That's the thing you see, the same journey right? The same one hundred and eighty or so miles right?'

'Right,' answered the boy, hoping he wasn't wrong.

'The exact same journey can be so different. Can be a different thing altogether, and so much so that you might think they were in different countries even. Different lifetimes, say. That's the thing. That's the thing to understand in life. I'm talking too much am I? Josie says I talk too much sometimes,

51

you just tell me if I am and Ben Dack will shut right up, shut right up for mile after mile if you just want me to listen. I can listen. You just say, all right?'

'Yes.'

'Good lad, you're a good fellow I can tell that. I'm a good judge of character. That's another thing about giving people a lift along the road, you get to take a sample as it were, a sample of life, just a dip in and there you have what comes up. And do you know what the surprising thing is?'

'I'm not sure.'

'No, well, you see that's because you're young still, and that's great, that's absolute. But the surprising thing is this, hold on,' Ben swung the wheel and took them round a roundabout and out on the Dublin road where he waved a hand at the policeman who was standing behind his car aiming the speed-gun. 'The surprising thing is, no matter what you hear said nowadays, no matter what you read about terrible things that happen every day to people and how dreadful things can be, the majority, and I mean ninety-nine and ninety-eight ninety-ninths of people are good. Absolute,' he said, 'no question. Good, kind, generous, bread-and-butter people. You know? That's the truth of what I found in this truck, that's the gospel according to Ben Dack.' He laughed at this and the ball rose and fell and he put one hand down to steady it.

For a time then it seemed that he had reached the end of all that was urgent in him to express and he was quiet. But not exactly still. It was as though the speeches he had made were then replaying in his head and as he watched the road he made a series of small noddings, eyebrow-raisings, head-anglings and even the slightest occasional humming sound in agreement with himself.

The road ran on. The day that rose was bright with blue sky and white clouds moving swiftly. The boy watched the miles go past. He still had a dull ache in his shoulder. The transfer of light and image on to the windscreen and sometimes up along it flowed as if it was the road travelling over them and not the opposite. As he bobbed gently in the seat the boy kept finding his thoughts going behind him now. He thought not of the way ahead and how he was going to proceed, but instead in his mind he visited the home he had left and imagined the scene of the Master's discovering the note. It was found by now. What was the first thing the Master would do? The boy pictured him standing, reading it. He pictured a scene of perfect stillness and the Master's eyes small in their nest of wrinkles while his mind whirred. Would he go directly to the police? Had he already called them? The boy pressed his lips together.

Are they after me?

Without intending to, he took a look in the rear-view mirror, but there was only the steady line of morning traffic behind them. Then again perhaps the Master wouldn't go to the police yet. Perhaps he wouldn't want to frighten the boy. Perhaps . . . It was no good, there were too many possibilities.

Of only one thing the boy was certain, and that was that there would be hurt. There would be worry. And so, sitting in the cab with Ben Dack nodding and agreeing with a silent conversation he was repeating to himself, the boy thought that if the Master knew that he was all right his hurt would be less. But he couldn't risk a phone call, couldn't risk a conversation with the Master persuading him to come back, and so instead he shut tight his eyes and concentrated.

As if he was clearing a table after breakfast, one by one he picked up and put away any thoughts that were in his mind. Then, when he was sure there was nothing left and his mind was clear, he imagined four words.

I
am
all
right.

He imagined writing them very carefully on a table. He made the four words of his message and with his eyes still closed, he thought on them with all the power he could manage. He thought on them, as if his thought were a beam of light immensely potent that could make the letters glow whitely and then burn through the air to the Master. *I am all right. I am all right.*

'Had a little nap, did you?' Ben Dack asked. 'Saw you nod off there, excellent. I have had people sleep one side of the country to the other. Truck of dreams, I tell Josie. What dreams and dreamers I have had aboard. Absolute. Had a girl one time told me everything that happened in dreams could happen, no, could be happening, that's right, in another world. Imagine that. That's what she said. There's another you and another me maybe doing different things there you see and, here's the strange bit, dreaming of here. Do you see? So. Makes you think doesn't it?' Ben nodded at the strangeness of this until he had satisfied himself, then announced: 'Café Dack, I think.'

'What?'

'Time for eats.'

He pulled the truck over into a grassy lay-by and shut it off. At once he raised his hands above his head, then groaned, then rolled his head left and then right, then reached down into a space beside the seat.

'Now,' he said, 'ham and cheese or cheese and ham?'

'I'm all right, thank you,' said the boy.

'No no, you have to eat at the Café Dack. That's the rules.'

'But you need them for yourself.'

'Josie knows I never travel alone if I can help it. She makes 'em for two people.'

'Every day?'

'Every day. Josie's a saint, absolute. One hundred and one per cent pure through and true saint. And what I did to be the lucky fellow to marry her I'll never know. Here, ham and cheese.' A second sandwich Ben Dack turned over. 'Cheese and ham for me.'

'Thank you.'

'And milky tea.'

Ben poured the boy a mug full and they sat there, windows open, flies buzzing and traffic softly passing.

'Dublin?' asked Ben after a while.

'Yes. Thank you very much.'

'Not that I'm enquiring. Nothing as quick a turnoff to people you pick up on the road than to give them the full interrogation. It's not fair, I believe. Not fair. Everyone has their own lives, haven't they? They have, and some things don't need to be enquired of, you can still be the best of companions. That's my philosophy.'

'I am on my way to see my father.'

'Oh? Right then, very glad I could be of assistance,' said Ben, and nodded at how pleased he was by this news and that he had a part in something good. 'Yes, very glad. Absolute.'

He finished four sandwiches and two mugs of tea and insisted that the boy eat just as much. Then he produced one of Josie's jam tarts for each of them and after he wiped his mouth with a blue and white chequered napkin she had given him he announced was going to take his forty now.

'Forty?' asked the boy.

'Winks, just to rest the eyes for the way into the city. Be fresher, you know? City's another world. Won't be long. No need to wake me, body's like a clock this stage, set the timer,' he reached up and screwed his ear twice, 'only joking. No, I'll wake in eighteen minutes.' And at that he released the catch in the car seat and it tilted back and he folded his short plump arms on his stomach. At once he was asleep.

A strange kind of quiet was in the truck but the boy himself could not sleep and sat still while time passed in the middle of the country. He had a sense of being somehow outside of the world, as if it was turning now without him. Everything in the ordinary world was going ahead, children were sitting in school, men and women were at work, and cars and buses and aeroplanes were travelling in constant motion. And he was still, so still that he and Ben and the truck might have been the only un-turning thing in the turning world.

After eighteen minutes Ben woke up. He stretched, righted his seat, smiled over at the boy and then turned on the engine.

'To Dublin so,' he said.

They pulled out to the edge of the road. From sandwich crumbs blackbirds in the long grass flew up and scattered. Ben eased the truck out into the steady traffic.

'Everyone's going somewhere, eh?' he said.

Two hours later they had arrived in the city. Ben followed the road in by the canal and slowly wound his way closer and closer to the docks by the river.

'Well, journey's end,' he said when they had arrived there. The boy hesitated. Now that he was here he wasn't sure that he could go on.

'Hello to your father, and good luck to you in everything you do,' Ben said and reached out his hand and vigorously shook the boy's.

'Thank you.'

Just then cars that were backed up behind the truck began hooting.

'Oops,' smiled Ben. And although the boy was not in any way prepared to leave him just then, or even sure that he wanted to, he opened the door and climbed down into the noise of the city.

Dublin. This is Dublin.

He looked up into the cab. He looked the way a boy can look to a man when standing on the precipice of a new experience, unsure that he can step off into it. He looked for courage, for faith in his own ability, for confirmation. But the moment was frayed with the blaring of car horns, and if he understood the boy's needs, Ben Dack had no time to meet them. He held up his small plump hand and waved, and, as though he was in on a secret they shared, he made a broad wink.

'Be well,' he said, 'until next time.' And then the truck pulled away, Ben Dack's face framed in the wing-mirror, and the boy watching and not moving from the spot.

SIX

In the Master's dream his wife was speaking. But although he could see her clearly and could see her mouth move and form the words, the Master could not make them out. She was saying something. She was speaking excitedly, telling him something urgent, but in the dream she appeared as in a film without sound, and though he moved about in the covers and turned his head on the pillow the Master could not hear her. *What is it? What is it? Tell me.* He turned again in the bedclothes, he screwed his eyes closed even tighter. In dreaming he moved his lips as though reading hers and saying the message in a kind of mumble. But still his brain could not grasp what she was saying. Then, in a final effort to move closer to her, he pushed over further in the bed, hit his head smartly against the bedpost and opened his eyes. The dream was gone, the message lost.

It was quiet. *Very quiet.* Mornings in the countryside were always hushed. There was only the noise of the wind in the trees or the birdsong. Nothing was ever coming or going outside, and so quietness was a condition he was used to. But that morning, the moment he opened his eyes, the Master could sense something was too quiet. He blinked and fixed his gaze very steadily on a place on the wall in front of him so as not to be distracted and tried to figure out just what it was. It was as though in everything that had been set out on a kitchen table something had been disturbed in the night, a cup lifted off a saucer and not returned. *No Joe, that's not it. Something, it is something.* He lay some moments with this feeling while the last remains of the dream of his wife vanished. Then carefully he angled his feet over the edge of the bed and into his slippers.

He left the bedroom in his pyjamas and went out into the small hallway and stopped and tried to figure it out again.

Something. Definitely something. But what he couldn't say. Still, it was there and he couldn't ignore it. It lay like a hair across his tongue. He came down the stairs like a man who vaguely remembers that he left the back door open or the tap running or forgot the fireguard in front of the fire. He came expecting to see the problem at once and that it would be something small and easily remedied.

In the kitchen everything was as it should be. The reminders of the non-party, film-covered bowls of brightly coloured jelly, bottles of soft drinks, boxes of biscuits, were lined up along the counter. In the glass doors of the cupboard he saw himself, his hair tufted, his eyebrows low in puzzlement. *What is it? Was it something I dreamt or just my old silliness?*

'No, there is something,' he said aloud to no one listening.

The Master stood then perfectly still in the centre of the kitchen and shut his eyes and tried to let some part of him that he believed in, and that was beyond his five senses, figure it out. As if his intuition were a fog or a soft creature without shape he stood and released it into the house. He did nothing. He did not move nor look about him for a few brief moments, then, as if fingers clicked inside him, he turned and hurried out of the kitchen. He bounded up the stairs quicker than another of his age and was at the boy's bedroom door before his breath.

He raised his right hand to knock. But already he knew.

That he suddenly knew was something he could not explain to himself. There was no visible sign, nothing real that was disturbed.

'But it was as if there was a cord, an invisible line that runs between me and the boy and when I woke in the morning I knew that it had somehow been pulled. Imagine there was stitching in your heart,' he would later tell the ghost of his wife, 'and the thread was yanked, something like that.'

The Master's heart hammered while his hand didn't. He stood before the bedroom door and felt the knowledge of what had happened arrive now in his brain and settle like black sludge. He pressed his lips together. It was no good, he knew, even as his hand rapped. He did not wait a second time but opened the door at once and felt the sight of the empty bed hit him hard like a fist into his chest. Immediately he saw the note on the pillow and had to hold on to the doorframe.

'Oh no.'

Here it was, here was the fracture he had felt in the morning as soon as he awoke. The boy was gone. He almost didn't need to read the note. He was stopped with sorrow and the dread of something ripping away from him. He was stopped with panic and fear and failure. *Where was he gone? How long gone?* And just *O God, is he all right?*

He was stopped while every detail of the scene in the bedroom – the bedclothes, books, an open drawer, those slippers – locked itself into his memory. He was stopped like a patient under surgery, as if his side or his chest was opened and a hand was reaching inside him to find the place where he was damaged.

'You stood there when you should have been hurrying,' he would tell himself later in the morning. 'Stood there like a fool with the clockwork of you stopped and your old brain fuddled.'

And indeed there was a forever when the Master seemed

to be able only to look at the empty room. Perhaps he was taking the meaning of the situation inside himself. Perhaps he was intuiting something from the way the room had been left. But if so, he didn't show sign of it. At last he made a small shake of his head, breaking free of some chains of the moment, and crossed and lifted the note.

It read:

Dear Joe,

I could not sleep. I read the letter in the cream-coloured envelope. Did you know what it said? Much of it was burned but some of it I understood.

I have to go and find the man who was my father. I do not think he knows I was born.

I must do this now. Something is telling me. I think she would want me to do this.

I have money and I will go to England and find him and tell him who I am. That is all. Then I will come back. It does not mean I love you less.

I am sorry for the upset. I will be all right and home again soon.

The Master read the note twice. As he read the words he saw the hand that wrote them, he saw the boy stooped close to the paper the way he had seen him a thousand times in the classroom. But this was not the classroom.

'You must do something, you old fool. Come on.'

He turned and hurried to the bedroom next door where he dressed himself quickly. As he did the ghost of his wife was sitting in the chair by the bed.

'I'm a fool,' he said to her.

'You're my fool, Joe,' she answered.

'I couldn't hear you this morning in the dream. Such a fool, such a fool, he's gone.'

62

'I know.'

'I'm going after him.'

'Of course you are.'

He stood one-legged and drew on his trousers. His large hands fumbled with the buttons of his shirt and then he picked up the letter and the agitation in him made it flap in his hand like a broken wing. He read each of the words again as if to confirm them, as if they too might be a dream. The worry in his chest tightened and he felt his breath squeezing from him. He could not breathe, such was the feeling of loss that bound him.

'Why are you not alive now to help me?' he asked the ghost of his wife. But she only smiled back at him kindly.

'It has to be my fault. I have to be the one to blame, giving him the letter yesterday. What was I thinking? Nothing but an old fool,' he said. If his wife had been living the Master would have gone to hold her then. He would have found comfort and strength in her arms and been able to gather himself before hurrying after the boy. Deeply now, he missed her and faced the difficulty of moving from where he was, so weighted with sorrow were his feet. The blame he felt was bitter like a drink of thorns. Then he said, 'You think I should call the police. I know you think that. But I don't want them hunting him down. He hasn't done anything wrong, he hasn't run away, not really. He's just gone to find someone.' He argued this out loud to himself and his wife to clarify the situation and make it seem less ominous. To lighten the weight of his blame he said in a most reasonable tone: 'He will be fine. I won't call the police. I'll go after the boy myself. I'll find him and then I'll help him.'

Quickly the Master slid his feet over the broken-down backs of his shoes, tapped his chest pockets for wallet and glasses, made a cape of his tweed jacket as he put it on and hurried out of the bedroom. At the door he paused for a second to look back to where the ghost of his wife was now gone.

63

He came downstairs and raced through the house, gathering last-minute things as he went, keys, pencil, paper, maps. As he passed through the sitting-room he stopped as though a hand caught him. There on the table were bottles of whiskey, brandy, six bottles of stout. Morning light glinted on the glass. The Master brought a hand up to his mouth as if holding back his longing to taste. He swallowed hard on nothing. He thought of having just one drink, just one to help him steady himself. *The nerves are flying all over the place. I'm as jittery . . . I need to get a hold of . . .*

No. No, you old fool. Not now.

But just one. Just.

He stood by the table and unscrewed the top of the brandy. Like a part of himself he had kept bottled, the smell escaped. He lifted a tumbler. He took the bottle by the neck and poured, a small tremor in his hand as the drink filled. Involuntarily he touched the tip of his tongue to his top lip. He blinked his eyes. The house was empty. All was perfectly still. No one would know. Worry and guilt and fear had gathered in his throat. He needed the drink to wash them away. The boy was gone.

It was my fault. I never should have brought him the letter. I never should have. He threw the thing in the fire, but I knew better. I'm bloody useless. That's what I am.

The Master carried the brandy to his lips. He closed his eyes on the memories of himself that returned, the brown corners of a hundred pubs where company had flowed around him, then deserted him, his staggering homeward. But it wouldn't be like that this time. This time he just needed one.

Just one before I go after him.

His lower lip kissed against the glass and the brandy flowed into his mouth. In that first instant it was as welcome to him as a returned friend. The sitting-room was still. Sunlight slanted in the window, timber of table and chairs outlined with urgent

64

illumination. Moments of time were wasting. But the Master stood in the room, shadows clutching the glass, like a pupil staring at an examination he had to take though he knew his result would be a fail. The first mouthful of the brandy was sweet and strong, the second sweeter. Across the floor light and shadow fought, as the big blown clouds in the sky moved eastward.

O God.

He held the bottle tilted to pour again. But as he did, by chance, his eye snagged on the title of a book that had not been tidied away but lay on the floor beside the couch. It was *The Boy's Guide to Kite Flying*. And whether it mattered that it was this book or might as easily have been another, whether there was something about kites themselves, their thin frail connection from sky to earth, or the boy's love of them, the Master could not say. But he stopped where he was.

O God, stop. Stop.

What are you doing? You've got to hurry, you've got to get the car and get it started.

Come on.

He put down the bottle, went out of the front door and closed it behind him, but he did not lock it. He hurried off on foot in the wake of the boy, breathlessly tramping down the road, his face bright red, and his jacket blowing out in flaps like wings. At every step he was imagining the boy before him.

When he arrived in the village the old car was waiting.

'Don't let me down now,' he said and tried the ignition, and then tapped the dashboard twice with thanks as the engine coughed and then fired perfectly. Rarely did the Master drive further than three or four miles from the house. The car was half his own age and was the only one he had ever owned. Before him it had belonged to a grease-faced puff-lipped mechanic called Mahoney who had bought it from scrap merchants and after significant efforts managed to give the engine the kiss of life. Only the speedometer had failed to return to itself and remained always at forty. The bucket seats in the front were wine vinyl, each of them holed in places. About the floor and elsewhere was a litter beyond category: screws, nails, scissors, thread, vice-grips, erasers, schoolbooks, a knob for the radio, handle for the passenger door, milk cartons, cough drops, newspapers or parts thereof, packets of garden seeds, and an unread copy of the Department of Education's Guidelines on Discipline. Vaguely the inside of the car smelled like its owner. It smelled of life and experience and chaos.

The Master grasped the thin black steering-wheel and drove along the country roads with his face pressed forward and his eyes scanning right and left for any sign that might reveal the boy had passed that way. He went out through the village and to the junction of the main road. There he pulled the car over on the grass and got out. From the high cabs of the lorries passing he looked like a man searching for his key. He peered down at the grass, took a few steps back and over with his head bent low. Then he stopped and scratched the tuft of his hair. It was hopeless, there was nothing. Everything was as if normal, as if the world showed no sign of loss or sorrow or joy or happiness, but turned out one day after the next, each one just the same.

'What were you expecting,' the Master chided himself, 'a sign?' *You are such an old poop. A boy slips out of the world, but still the world goes on. Things do not stop although one person's heart breaks. Who even hears it?*

He tried to imagine the boy in that place. He tried to reach that part of himself that had known something was wrong when he opened his eyes in the morning, that part of himself that was not easily explained, the stitching that he would tell the ghost of Mary had been pulled loose from his heart.

But nothing.

No. It was useless.

You're a fool, and worse, an old fool. Stitching! If you told someone else that, they would be having lads coming to have you locked up.

A line of cars whooshed past, drivers' looks quizzing the old man then forgetting about him.

Where are you? Where are you now? With a silent inner voice the Master asked. He stood on the rough grass of the ditch and in his frustration and longing and desperation he closed tight his fists and urged an answer.

Come on. Come on.

He tried to let himself be only an imagination, to be a spirit that could go back and forwards in time, and from one place to another, seeing and knowing each as clearly as here and now. He tried not to be there, not to be a man in a tweed jacket and old trousers standing by the side of the road looking lost as the traffic passed. He tried to let himself be not a body but a soul, a spirit that could transport him elsewhere or connect to the soul of the boy. If you can believe such a thing.

Where are you?

To the travellers on that road he must have appeared somewhat bizarre; an old man in baggy clothes standing by the ditch with his eyes scrunched up, his fists clenched tight and shaking slightly, and his lips mouthing words. It wouldn't be long before a car pulled over and somebody would walk back to see if he was having a heart-attack or a stroke or something.

Come on, come on!

The Master was fixed to the spot and asked the air for an answer. He let himself believe one was on the way, if only he could blot out everything else and receive it. He brought his fists up against his forehead and looked ever more a man losing his mind. In the blue of the morning, sunlight came from behind white cloud and shone upon him. Small wind moved in the trees at his back and there was leaf-sound like the last waves of a tide collapsing on the shore. There were no birds singing. There were no cars passing. There was no sound at all. There was in the darkness of his mind, where with closed eyes the Master was searching, a sudden image of the boy's face.

And something else.

Something that was too slight for sound, too fine and thin for substance at all, nothing more than a ripple in the air. He could not say it was a message. He could not say he heard words, could not assert to anyone of science that he could offer proof. But just then, he *knew* that the boy had been there. He knew in no form of knowledge that is acceptable to examination, but belonged instead to a domain of spirit and belief. For, as the Master opened his eyes on that grassy corner of the road, he read the invisible four words:

I am all right.

SEVEN

Sister Bridget was late. A small nun, twenty-three years of age, with a furrowed brow and kind deep-set brown eyes, she was flustered by the time. There was no reason why it should already be two o'clock. She had not intended to delay at the convent, but Sister Agnes and Sister Cecelia were so insistent, they wouldn't think of her simply saying hello and goodbye. It was a full year after all, a full year since she had lived there among them before she headed off to what she had thought would be Africa but had turned out to be Birmingham. Because she had taken ill even before her course of injections had finished, and because in the end Mother Clare had decided that perhaps her talents lay best in working in the Sisters' office and not in the missions in Africa. It was not how things were supposed to turn out. But the good Lord has his plans for each of us, Sister Agnes had written to console her at the time, and we hardly ever get to know them. Or at least not for a very long time. And she kept saying the same thing today when Sister Bridget stopped in to see them and show that she was well again and to tell them that she missed all in the community.

'Indeed He does, the good Lord has His plans,' Sister Agnes

repeated for the fourth or fifth time, her old green eyes content in the wisdom of this and the certainty that over numerous cups of tea and shortbread biscuits you couldn't say it often enough.

But what if you disagree with His plans? thought Sister Bridget. *What if you have your heart set on something completely different? What if the thing that you want doesn't seem to be in His plans, what do you do then?* She wondered these things but she didn't speak them. The two elderly nuns in front of her were pleased to see her looking so well. For some moments they seemed happy just to sip their tea and gaze over at her. And when she glanced at her watch and tried to say that she had to be going she did so in the gentlest way, for the idea of her leaving so soon seemed to hurt their feelings. It was as though now that she was back there they realized just how much they had missed the liveliness of her presence, and about the two nuns there was a frail shell of loneliness. So, yes, another cup of tea would be all right. And another of the biscuits, and yes, Sister Mary really did have the recipe just right now after all her attempts.

And maybe Sister Bridget could have left soon then but Sister Agnes brought up the subject that was most on her mind.

'We were all praying for your father, Bridget,' she said after a while.

'I know, thank you, Sister.'

'He passed peacefully in the end.'

'Yes.'

A cloud passed across the face of Sister Bridget and left her eyes dull. 'I was sorry that I wasn't there,' she said.

'You were on your way. You mustn't blame yourself.' Sister Agnes leaned forward with concern for the young nun.

'No, no,' agreed Sister Cecelia, her voice thin and throaty, cords in her neck moving with the words, 'you were on your way, and you were praying for him, and Our Lord took him when he was ready to go.'

'That's right, Bridget.'

'I wish I could have seen him one last time, just to talk to him.'

'Of course.' Sister Agnes nodded. 'Of course you do. But you can still talk to him.'

Bridget took the words as they were intended, as a kindness and a comfort, and did not reply that she could not be sure her father could hear her, or that she could ever again hear him. She sat and drank more tea with the two old nuns and thought of the graveyard in the middle of the country where her father was buried now beside her mother and her only brother. She thought of the moment she had left it, of going out through the black iron gate the last time and looking back at the headstones, at that strange silent population of the dead, and how terrible it had felt to walk away. The loneliness was a fierce hurt. Even though she had not seen her father in six months, now that he was gone the world seemed so empty and so huge.

'But you look so well,' Sister Cecelia was saying, 'you really do.'

'And so do you, Sister,' Bridget smiled.

'Oh now, not too bad for a pair of old ghosts, I suppose, isn't that right, Sister Agnes?'

'Indeed it is. Ghosts who like tea and shortbread biscuits.'

'Oh now, Oh now.' Sister Cecelia laughed and brought long thin fingers to her mouth to hold her teeth.

The afternoon sunlight flooded in the big windows. Down the long avenue chestnut trees in first leaf were catching the small quick May breezes that came and went, and still the three nuns sat there in the front room of the old convent. Sister Bridget delayed when she knew she shouldn't have. She stayed when she knew it must be getting late, because there was comfort and consolation there. It was still and peaceful sitting with the elderly nuns in the early afternoon. And Bridget knew that once she left she was on her way back to England, to her work; once she got up and left the convent the rest of her life was waiting for her, and it was a life without the presence in it of her father. From now on she would be on her own. And although she was an adult of twenty-three, and hadn't seen her father that much since she had entered the convent from school, still she was going to miss him. It was hard to explain to anyone who hadn't suffered that loss. It was like some part of a familiar painting, a painting that hung on your wall and that you saw day in day out and to which you didn't pay that much attention, now was erased. It was just not there, and suddenly you felt its absence terribly.

So the time had run on, and Sister Bridget had kept postponing standing up and saying goodbye. She had glanced at her watch from time to time, had watched the light changing in the trees, but not found it in herself to stand up.

At last, after their umpteenth cup of tea, Sister Agnes had sensed this hesitation in the young nun and brought the meeting to a close.

'Well, we have delayed you long enough,' she said. 'You have been so kind to visit us.'

'Perhaps you will stay for supper?' Sister Cecelia had suggested.

'No, Sister Bridget has a boat to catch, haven't you, Sister?'

Bridget knew the moment was upon her, and rose and thanked the nuns and Sister Agnes walked her down the corridor to the door.

'You will be fine, Bridget,' the old nun told her as she took the small wheeled suitcase from where she had left it by the door. 'Really, you will. You are very special, I have always thought so, you know that.' They paused on the threshold. 'You have a light in you,' said Sister Agnes, and she touched the younger nun on the forehead. 'God bless you.' Her eyes smiled with kindness and wisdom, and then – perhaps because

Bridget might not have taken the first step away – Sister Agnes stepped back inside the doorway so that it appeared Bridget was already on her way, and softly she closed the door. Click.

And almost at once, as if she was just then returned to the real world of time and schedules, Bridget had realized that she was late. *Very late, in fact.* She hurried down the avenue wheeling the case behind her, pebbles in the driveway catching in the wheels and making a dragging noise then freeing again as she went. At the end of the avenue she passed through the gates of the convent and out into the din of people and traffic and the whirl of ordinary life.

Hurry up, Bridget, hurry up. Oh for goodness sake.

She waited at the bus stop with a mother and two little girls that kept stepping down off the path on to the road and had to be screamed at and jerked back every two minutes. No sooner were they back by the mother's side then one of them grinned and stepped out again. Bridget tried a prayer, *Patience O Lord.* But she was useless at prayers and wanted to just reach out and grab the child and give her a good shaking. *I'll personally throw you in front of the bus when it comes if you step out again, all right, dear?*

Patience O Lord.

When the 77 bus came it was full and the driver only pulled over because two tourists wanted to get out at the wrong stop, thinking they were by the sea.

It moved off like an elephant along the road. Bridget checked her watch. *Late, I'm going to miss it. I am. Come on, come on.* She urged the traffic in front of them to part like a sea, but nothing changed. She was useless at miracles too. One of the girls with blonde ringlets and a blue dress pressed the snap on the nun's case so it popped open. Bridget closed it. The girl opened it again. This time when she closed it she kept her hand over it as a guard and stared hard at the demon. The girl smiled back at her, then stuck out her tongue.

Dear God, please get me out of here.

The bus turned left around a corner and there suddenly was the sea. At the next stop half the passengers got off. As Bridget climbed backwards down the steps, getting her case caught on the handrail, the two girls tried to follow and were almost off the bus before their mother realized and came after them, yanking each one back by an arm with yells of protest. As the bus drove off their two faces were pressed against the back window, and when they passed Bridget they each stuck out their tongues at her. And, quickly, sure that no one could see, she stuck out hers back at them.

Bridget had returned from England for her father's funeral by aeroplane, but some severe turbulence in the air and a sense that a plane *made of metal* could not and should not really fly, had convinced her that never again would she choose that mode of transport. There was something about being up in the air, she had told Sister Agnes, which didn't agree with her. She would not fly again until she was on her way to heaven she had joked. And so now, she arrived at the ferry port at Dun Laoghaire in Dublin, and bought a one-way ticket to Holyhead in Wales from where she would travel by bus back to Birmingham. It would take a little longer, but she had time. Besides, she was not convinced that the work she did at the office, arranging the practical business of the movement of missionary nuns to and from various parts of Africa, was all that vital. It was hard for her to believe that this was what God had intended for her when she felt she had a vocation to join the nuns. A desk in a small office in Birmingham. She shook her head slightly to dislodge any such doubts and stood before the glass panel and paid for her ticket.

For foot-passengers on the ferry there was a metal gangway that rose upward with thin rubber bumps across it. As Sister Bridget ascended she suddenly heard a clunk and felt the case twist about on its handle. A wheel had broken off. As she turned she was in time to see it roll down the slope and vanish. *Thank you, O Lord.* There was nothing Bridget could do but turn and drag the case awkwardly the rest of the way.

Once on board she moved inside the large seating area of the ferry, intending to find a place where she could stow the case and come and go as she pleased during the voyage. But because she was so late, almost the last foot-passenger of that sailing – there was only one more person coming after her – all of the seats were already taken. There were knapsacks, handbags, suitcases, plastic carrier bags of all descriptions stacked on and about every seat. There were people too of every description, from happy teasing tourists already drinking beer to women with worn-out looks, as if their faces had been used up, and only one expression was left. Some children sat with their eyes fixed on Game Boys, thumbs working. Others licked at mango-flavoured icepops from the shop and stared into space where privately they watched their dreams.

Bridget made one pass through the lounge with her twisting, tottering suitcase, and then another back the other way. The ferry was packed.

Out on deck there was hardly any breeze until the vessel pulled from the port and a warm wind blew. Flags flapped sharply. Sister Bridget stood and watched the city of Dublin retreat. Sunlight fell on the water and silver-tipped the small waves. And although it was beautiful Bridget was filled with the same sense of regret and loss that she had felt leaving the graveyard. She held on to the silver railing with both hands.

Don't cry, if you start now you may never stop.

But there were tears coming into her eyes. Her knuckles turned pale as she held on and she was thinking of the image of her father's face and the last time that she saw him and how suddenly alone she was when she heard a voice beside her.

'Excuse me, is this yours?'

Sister Bridget turned. What she saw in front of her was a boy of about fourteen years of age, she thought, thin and anxious, with black hair and brownish skin. His clothes looked travelled in, on one shoulder was a darkened stain. But it was his eyes that startled Bridget the most.

In them was a remarkable light.

In his right hand he held out the wheel from her suitcase.

How extraordinary.

EIGHT

'Yes, I think it is,' the woman said, and the boy handed over the wheel. 'Hold on, I'll just check.' She turned the suitcase over on the deck and bent to make the match. The woman was small, smaller than he was, and the boy could not tell her age. He waited beside her while she fussed with the wheel. 'Yes, it is, it definitely is,' she said, 'and it should just pop . . . back . . . in . . . here.' The wheel slipped and seemed to refuse its fitting. 'I'm useless at these things,' she said, and the boy told her he would try.

He knelt down and studied the wheel and fitting. He studied the groove and the casing and how the flange of the fitting had to slide in along it. Then he did just that. When it was in place he hit it twice with the heel of his hand to make sure it had popped in correctly.

'A miracle,' said the woman, 'thank you so much. You're very kind.'

The boy did not say anything, but made a shy smile.

'I'm Sister Bridget.'

She had not looked like a nun. She was not dressed in a habit or veil, but in a navy-blue skirt and a cream-coloured blouse with a grey cardigan. Her eyes were kind, thought the boy, but there was loneliness in them too. There was in her demeanour something unsure, as if to her too the world was a puzzle, and she was looking for answers that fitted her questions.

'What's your name?'

The boy did not like his own name, and for as long as he could remember had avoided saying it, abbreviating it to its first letter.

'J,' he said.

'Jay. Well where are you going? Well of course, England,' Sister Bridget said, 'but I mean do you live there or are you taking an early holiday? School is still on isn't it?'

These were the situations the boy was not prepared for. He was not prepared for the lies he would have to tell. At the same time he knew that he could not tell the truth, at least not the whole truth. The secret to all fictions, he had read once, was to base them in part on what was real. And to keep the story true to itself, that is, to keep the details real, and not to seem like you were telling a lie.

'Are you alone, then, Jay?' The nun was waiting for his answer. Her eyes were on his face. She may have been trying to read these thoughts or simply wondering why he was taking his time over such an ordinary question.

'I'm going to see my father,' he said at last.

'Oh I see, where does he live?'

Where? Where? Quickly. Say. Guess. Say London. Say some street.

His face was reddening. He could feel heat rising up through him, his ears must be crimson already. He couldn't look at her.

'I think I have to be going,' he said quickly, and turned.

'Oh I see. Well, it was nice to meet you and thank you very much for the wheel,' the nun called after him.

He could not look back. He hurried down along the deck

and then through the crowded lounge and out on to the starboard side of the ferry where there were fewer passengers and the view was only of the open sea. There the breeze was more brisk and the boy felt his face cool.

Idiot. Such an idiot.

Lives in Number 3. Steerforth Street. Chelsea.

He made fists of his hands and shook his head slightly. He watched the grey sea and peered over the edge to see where it washed and foamed white against the ship. In mid-air alongside were six gulls dark against the blue-white sky. They hovered without effort and kept easy pace with the ship whose engines made a constant thrum. Occasionally one of them twirled off in an arc and descended sharply into the water, crashing into it and beaking a fish. The caws and screams of the gulls rose over the engines and briefly other birds came out of the sky as if falling and sat in the sea and the ferry passed them by. But soon enough, they were again hovering alongside in the mid-distant air as though they were an escort or followed with some purpose.

After he had recovered himself, the boy felt some peace in the voyage. It was easeful and pleasant standing still on the moving ship, feeling progress was being made without his having, for a few hours anyway, to be on his guard.

It was only two hours since he had been in the middle of Dublin city. Two hours since he had stepped out of the lorry of Ben Dack and moved with the flow of people down one street and up the next. Across a traffic light and down and up again. Two hours since he had drifted in the vast sea of faces, trying to appear neither lost nor lonely, floating this way and that until at last he had found himself in the lavatory of the ticket office of Irish Ferries where he had opened his Confirmation cards, taken out the money and counted five hundred and forty-five euros. A one-way ticket as a foot-passenger cost thirty-seven euros. The man in the booth had not even questioned him.

Now, in the open air on deck, with the great engines of the ferry pulsing and the water running back in a white wake, the boy felt things were possible again. And with this ease he sat on a bench and opened his bag and drew out his journal. So much had happened he couldn't possibly make note of it all. But he needed to write the way other people needed to watch television or listen to music; it relaxed his mind. So, drawing open the page with the ribbon marker, he looked up at six seagulls flying a broken M overhead and then wrote:

> Seagulls-sign.
> M-shape.
> Are there signs?
> Is everything in code, M-code? J-code?
> Everything a puzzle?
> Me2. A knot in a tie.
> Overandbackandoverandback
> Andunder.
> Father Ahsh. Father Shshshshsh.
> Father Quiet. Who are you?

As he wrote there came over him a sudden wave of weariness. He had not slept the night before, or in Ben Dack's lorry, and as if sleep was a tide that could be pushed back only for a short time before it washed back over you, it came in now. His head nodded without his intending, and he closed the journal and propped himself back on the slatted bench with his bag beside him. He would just close his eyes for a few minutes.

justa

Your brain is in control of your body. He had read an entire *National Geographic* on this once; if your brain told your body to wake at seven-thirty in the morning, say, then your body could do just that. If you had broken your arm but had to run out of a burning building to save your life, then your brain would postpone the pain until later. Things like that had always fascinated him, and now as he closed his eyes the boy tried to imagine setting a clock inside his head, telling his body when to wake. Like Ben Dack. Eighteen minutes would do nicely. In his imagination he was turning a little winder, when suddenly the Master himself was there beside him.

'Well, how are you? Are you all right?'

'Yes, yes, I'm fine.'

'This is some boat, eh? I've never been on one this big before.'

'Me neither.'

The Master laughed. 'Of course not you neither. Sure you were never even in Dublin more than twice. Never anywhere much, except in books you were reading.'

'It's different than books.'

'What is?'

'This.'

'I suppose.'

'It is. In books everyone seems to know where they're going and one bit fits with the next bit, but this is not like that.'

'No?'

'No. It's like . . .'

'Tell me.'

'Well, it's like . . . I don't know if anything is right or not. I don't know if I should go this way or that way, if I should even have done this, or what exactly I am hoping for. And I knew that you would be upset and so in one way I shouldn't, I definitely shouldn't have gone. But then I had the letter, and . . .'

'That's all right. We're all right. See. The thing is . . .' The Master paused and brought his right hand up to stroke his chin a few times and to turn on the boy a gaze clear and steady. 'The thing is this. You cannot leave me. You cannot.

No more than I can leave my own head or my own heart. You're part of me, do you see? And it's important for you to know that any time and any place, no matter, I will be here for you. I'm like an old coin that is stuck to a sticky old sweet in the corner of your trouser-pocket. You put your hand in and you think I'm gone, and then, no, there I am, still there, bedded in. That's the nature of this. That's the nature of things when there's love, do you see?' He smiled, his entire face wrinkling and his soft grey eyes so deep that the boy felt himself as if drawn across the space between them and then falling in slow motion into them. He was falling not the way people fall in dreams, falling not with fright but with ease and comfort and contentment upon grey flannel-covered pillows. He was falling and there was music. There was a quick flutter of notes but they were not exactly sweet or in harmony. They were of no tune the boy knew or recognized. There were three or four more, then one note loud and shrill, so piercing that the boy grimaced and squeezed tight his eyes and he heard shouts, cries. One, then another, and then two more. There were shouts, someone was shouting. Shouting something. *But what?* And then again a few notes and the noise of the ferry engines and –

The boy opened his eyes to the blue sky.

'Give it back!'

'I won't. It's my turn!'

He sat upright to see identical twins in red soccer shirts fighting over his flute. Once they saw him wake, the twins, skin-tight haircuts and hard little faces that looked like things boiled, took off with the flute at top speed.

'Stop! Come back!'

They were gone in an instant, tearing off with wild whoops into the lounge and across it to the far deck where, when the boy arrived in pursuit, Sister Bridget was standing holding the flute in her hand.

82

'Ah, well now,' she said, with a smile, 'I think this must be yours.'

The boy took it. 'Thank you.'

'You're welcome. We seem to be matched somehow. Both losing things and finding them for each other.'

'I didn't lose it exactly, they took it from my bag while I was, well, while I was just resting.'

'I see.' Sister Bridget nodded, and had the look of someone who has in fact just then seen something to which she been blind before. 'I see,' she said again. 'Not easy to rest when you're on your own.'

'I am on my way to see my father,' the boy blurted suddenly.

'Yes, I remember. Good, that will be nice for him.'

'Yes.'

The boy knew the lie was on his face again and was sure that the nun could see it. He wanted to get away from her again because something about her brought out the nearness of the truth, but she had rescued his flute and he couldn't just walk away. Besides, now she knew he was on his own.

'Would you like to come and have some tea Jay?'

Yes. Can't. There will be questions.

'I, em, I don't really drink tea. Besides, I'd get seasick.'

'Something with bubbles then? That'd help.' The nun's face was a composition of caring and sympathy, the tone of her voice utterly without suspicion or motive, and yet there was in her eye a calm knowing.

'I'm all right, thank you,' he said. 'I'm not really seasick now. Thank you for my flute.'

'You are welcome.' The boy turned to go, but quickly Sister Bridget added, 'If you need any more rest there's a bench down here where I have my case.' He turned back to her. 'You could get some rest and I could keep an eye on your bag for you. Make sure those terrible twins don't come back.' She smiled and raised her eyebrows into her offer. 'It's just over here,' she said.

Moments later, the boy was sitting in the seat, his head angled against the side of the ship feeling its reverberations and falling into a fitful sleep while the nun stood by the railing and watched over him. He slept on and off for two hours, sleeping and then waking for an instant, raising his head and falling back again as the sleep came after him and pulled him back into the bits and pieces of unfinished dreams. He dreamt of his bedroom in the cottage. He dreamt of lying in bed reading a book at night after he was supposed to have turned out the light. It was a book about a boy and in its pages he lost himself the way he loved to do, his knees bent up beneath the blankets and the two pillows doubled for extra cushion. In the window there was the blue of night and a butterfly that flew in and found the light and battered against the shade and caused him to pause in his reading and look at it. He remembered the Master telling him once that some believed butterflies carried the spirits of the dead, and he put aside the book and tried to free this one. It battered its wings so. Attempting to lift off the shade, he burned his fingers on its metal frame and shook his right hand in the air as if for a moment strumming an invisible guitar. He turned the lamp upside-down to shake it free but still the butterfly flew in and around the bulb, and the more he tried to free it the less success he had. Until at last he reached right inside and with his thumb and forefinger he caught the tiny thing by one wing and plucked it out of the light. Holding it so he climbed across the tossed covers of his bed to the window and he held the butterfly outside in the night air and was about to release it when, suddenly, it made a frantic fluttering and broke away from its held wing. It beat hopelessly in the air for a second, then twirled helicoptering down into the dark below. In the boy's hand he held its wing.

He cried out and was twisting about in the seat, his eyes screwed tight, when the hand shook him awake.

'It's all right, it's a dream, you're all right.'

Sister Bridget's face floated in front of him like a planet arriving in the vision of an astronaut. For a moment he was unsure if it was real. 'You're on the ferry. Sister Bridget, remember? We're nearly there now, you can see the shoreline and the mountains, come look.'

The boy stood groggily and felt at once that his sleep had not refreshed him. He crossed over to the railing where many passengers were now looking out at the coast of Wales, as if they hadn't really expected to arrive, as if maps were not entirely trustworthy and you had to see for yourself. Well, there it was, an edge of land on the horizon, not particularly different from the one they had left behind, but still it gave the boy a shiver of apprehension at the back of his neck.

'You were talking in your dream,' Sister Bridget said.

'Was I?'

'Yes. What were you dreaming about?'

'Oh, nothing.'

'You can't remember?'

'Nothing important.' The boy kept his eyes on the coast.

'It seemed like it was.'

'No. Just something . . . A butterfly.'

The ferry drew nearer and passengers went to get ready to disembark. A weary-looking woman hurried along the deck calling after the twins to come back right now. 'Right now!' The twins stopped and when she drew nearer they ran off yelling once again. There was a general movement of preparation and anticipation as the life of the ship roused. While men and women came and went, putting on coats for the cooling of the evening, shouldering bags, readying pop-up handles on wheeled cases, the nun and the boy waited. The light was fading in the sky to the west now. Ahead of them night was already gathering.

'Well,' Sister Bridget said at last, when with short shudders the ferry docked and the loudspeakers announced their arrival. 'Here we are.'

'Yes.' The boy did not move. He couldn't. He had one hand on the railing and he was holding on to it for no reason that he knew. The nun watched discreetly. There were a hundred passengers left to disembark, then fifty, then hardly even ten, and still they waited.

'So?' Bridget said to him, and placed her hand on his shoulder. 'You're all right?'

'Yes, yes I'm fine,' said the boy and nodded as if he had just finished reading difficult instructions and understood them vaguely now.

'To London so, is it? On the bus?' she asked.

'Yes.'

'Ah, the same here,' Sister Bridget lied. 'We'll be together another while so. I think it's this way.' She pointed and led the way pulling her case and listening to see if he was following. They came off the ferry on to the crowded dock and Sister Bridget looked around and spotted the signs for the bus terminus and she headed off again and then slowed slightly so the boy was alongside her.

'Dreams of butterflies are quite special, you know,' she said. 'Some people believe they carry the spirits of the dead.'

The boy stopped short and he looked at her.

'Come on, the best seats will be gone,' Sister Bridget said. She frowned ever so slightly and shook her head at the puzzle of things just then emerging.

NINE

Perhaps it is only my imagination, the Master thought. He was still standing on the grassy bank moments after translating a ripple in the air to be the boy telling him *I am all right*. Just that. There was nothing more. But those four words he had received as clearly as he heard the birds singing just then in the chestnut trees. In response he had tried to send a message back, but whether he could not find the frequency, or the agitation of worries inside his chest did not allow him the stillness of mind needed, he could not broadcast anything. And in the end he had gone back to the car questioning that there had been any message at all. *Did I imagine it?* He got into the car in low spirits and pulled on to the road heading eastward once more. He had not gone a mile when the old car began to pitch and pull in a jolting movement, the engine coughing and the Master pressing forward and back in the seat as though trying to rock it forward. It was useless. No matter how firmly he held his foot down on the accelerator no power came in response. *Come on, come on. Not now, not now.* He slipped down a gear to see if that would improve things, but it didn't. He was slowing down all the time and in the narrow road behind him cars and lorries were queuing with drivers craning or angling in their seats to see what was the delay.

'You're a stubborn old thing, you know that?' he said, trying one last desperate measure. 'You're stubborn and useless and you should be scrap.'

No response. Cars began hooting.

'Ah come on now, come on,' the Master whispered to the dashboard, 'I'm sorry. You're not so bad, not so bad at all. You're a lovely old thing, you are, now just give me another little bit . . . come on. Here we go.'

The old car pitched forward dramatically, and for half an instant there may have been hope. But even as the Master's head was pressed back with the sudden increase in power the engine cut out altogether. The car died on a small decline and rolled until it could be turned in to the side of the road.

The Master got out of the car and looked at the sky and shook his head. 'You know I'm in a hurry,' he said, as he turned to lift the car's bonnet. 'You know what I'm doing and why I have to get after him. You know if there's one time you need *not* to break down it's this time right now.'

Steam hissed out of the radiator. The Master nodded like a man getting grim news already suspected. Beneath the bonnet the engine of the car showed all the signs of its very long life. It had over the years been many times repaired, but by methods not in its manual. The cap of the radiator was not the one designed for it but one belonging to an oil can that had been beaten out flat and then bent to a close fit tied about with nylon stocking. There were pieces of electrical tape around the battery, wire that looked suspiciously like a coat hanger connecting something with something else; one piece of hosing seemed to have been made out of the inner tube of a bicycle wheel.

'Now what have you done to yourself?' he asked, and poked in with his finger and burnt it and pulled it back.

He let down the bonnet with a clack, looked up and down the road for the nearest sign of life and began walking. The traffic passed steadily, the cars too closely together and the drivers too intent on haste to consider stopping for a wild-looking man tramping along in the grass verge. The Master did not expect a lift. He tried instead to concentrate on the boy and where he might be. He looked at the road as he passed along it, imagining the boy having been there. If it were another time and this another place there might have been obvious signs and he might have been able to read them, to track the boy all the way. But now there were none such. People had come and gone and were traceless, as if they had never been. There were no personal marks left, sometimes perhaps some thoughtless nuisance rubbish, but nothing that told anything. Yet, in the basic Science classes the Master had taught in school, he had explained to the pupils how in fact increasingly there *were* signs left behind, in crime scenes for example, where invisible evidence could be forensically gathered. There were probably a thousand tiny evidences of each of us in every place we stood or spoke or sneezed, but these for the most part were beyond our reading.

But what if?

What if they weren't? A hundred years ago no one believed we left fingerprints, thirty years ago no one believed a tissue in a bin could be traced back to its owner. There were no doubt in fact thousands of unseen unseeable traces of us left in the air afterwards, only we hadn't yet found ways of reading them. The future always proves the ideas held in the past too simple, too limited. *So, let's say, a spirit, let's say a spirit or a soul can leave a trace on the wind. Let's say we can reach each other in ways that no one believes right now, but that it's possible. Let's say in a hundred years we'll reach each other without mobile phones, that they will come to seem like bits of giant clunky old-fashioned gadgetry, that we will be able*

89

instead to feel our thoughts to each other. Let's say. And let's say we had this capacity all the time, that it has been there waiting for somebody to discover it. Overhead the sky was a clear pale blue with white clouds moving. In the fields just alongside the road cattle were grazing in placid contentment. Some turned momentarily to watch the stranger pass, then resumed. Birds, black and white, and smaller robins flew. If the air was filled with messages there was no sign of them. If the countryside was printed with evidence of souls' comings and goings, all were blind to it. There was nothing but the ordinary day and ordinary fields and hedges and the light changing.

Come on, something, show me something.

But nothing happened. Or if it did the Master was missing a dictionary to translate it. He looked to the pale sun and thought *he is gone to the east* and walked that way. At last he came to a small pub built it seemed in the side room of a family house. 'Healy's' was the name on a wooden sign hanging from a chain on the front wall. 'God bless,' he said as he entered the dark interior. It was a few moments before he could make out the burly figure of Healy himself behind the counter leaning forward in conversation with another shadow hunkered about a pint glass.

'Day to you,' Healy said, straightening up to view the stranger with suspicion. Although it was broad daylight outside the inside of the pub was dim and murky. Brown glass windows let in no light, and Healy preferred to spare the electricity. He had a puffy face with L-shaped sideburns that came to the edge of his mouth, a nose so flat it added almost no depth to his profile. His eyes were small and made smaller still by the fullness of his cheeks and his habit of frowning at everyone and everything. It had been Healy's father's bar, and the son did not care for customers but preferred to drink the business slowly away himself. He was more than halfway there. The only other customer as the Master walked in was a dirty-coated figure with a bald head and thin strands of long grey hair falling from just above his ears. He looked over his shoulder and cradled his pint of stout as if it might be taken from him.

'Get you something?' Healy frowned and placed both hands on the counter. His manner with customers was aggressive.

'Just some water please.'

'Water?'

'Yes, a couple of large bottles would be great. The car is down the road a bit.'

'Water?' Healy played deaf, his frown came up from his lips as well as down from his brow. His eyes almost vanished. The customer along the counter shuffled a little.

'For the car,' the Master repeated, and stepped forward.

'Broken down, eh?' Healy seemed to receive the message in delay. 'We were only talking about old cars, how unreliable they are. Funny that you should come in just then.'

The Master smiled thinly. It wasn't so funny.

'Very strange.' Healy scowled and with his right forefinger stroked his left sideburn. Things were curious, he thought, with the air of a man who feels he is never let in on the joke. 'This man here had some trouble with his car last night.'

'Is that right?' said the Master, considering the conversation the price for getting the water.

The dirty-coated man half-turned towards him. His face looked like it had been rubbed in something greasy. His eyes were red-rimmed.

'Tell him, Clarke,' said Healy.

'Broke down on me back the road there after I left here. Late it was, too.'

'I see.' The Master showed a slight polite interest. 'I'll hope to be all right once I get the water,' he added pointedly, looking at the barman to try and get him to move.

'You could be a long time on the road in the night, you know,' Clarke was continuing.

'Yes. I'm sure.'

'And there'd be fellows out would rob you and think nothing of it. Fellow I met last night tried to rob me, just a boy he was.'

'What did you say?' Swiftly the Master closed the distance between them and now could smell the day's drinking on him.

'What?'

'Did you say a boy?'

'A boy he was, ugly young fellow running along the road and he stepped right in on top of me, tried to rob me, gave me that,' he said, and turned fully to show with mixed pride and dismay his swollen purplish eye.

'What did he look like, this boy?'

'Ugly.' The man smiled sourly.

'What exactly?' The Master closed his fist but kept it by his side.

'What does it matter? It was dark, I told you. It was the middle of the night.'

'*What did he look like?* Tell me. It matters.'

'A boy.'

'Yes.'

'About that high.'

'Yes.'

'Kind of dark-looking.'

'Wearing what?'

'Wearing? Wearing whatever, I was being robbed I told you. He wanted to take whatever I had and put it in that bag of his.'

'Bag, brown?'

'What? I can't remember that.' The man Clarke half-turned back to the last dregs of his drink, and at once the Master grabbed him by the edge of his coat and pulled him towards him.

92

'Remember!'

There was a half-second when Healy reached below the bar counter for something, but the man spoke. 'I could remember more maybe if I had another drink, but I haven't the price of it.'

'Here,' the Master tumbled coins out on to the counter and Healy came for them. The pint was pulled. But just as Clarke was about to lift it the Master reached out and with a firm grasp held his arm. 'Tell first, you can drink after,' he said. 'The boy, what did he say? Where did he say he was going?'

'He came from the west. He was going east. In a hurry too he was.'

'Did you harm him?'

'He tried to rob me, I told you.'

The Master tightened his hold. 'Did you harm him?'

'I did not. He ran off. He was mad. He said he was going for his father, he said he was going for God.'

'What?'

'Something like that. To God. He could go to hell, I told him.'

'Which way did he go? Which?'

'East I said.'

'East.'

The Master let go of the fellow's arm. For a fraction of a second he had a sense of the boy hurrying across the night and meeting this man in the dark. He had a sense of the fright and loneliness the boy must have felt, and he hurt with longing to be able to see the boy now and know that he was all right. Before, in moments of deep feeling, he would have taken a drink to steady himself. He would have been fearful of the tide of emotions washing up from the caves inside him and feeling the air sucked away. He would have slipped out of the house and driven down the road to Breen's and taken a couple of whiskeys there. He would have felt the whiskey flame up and although the tide would not be turned back he would feel he could walk out on the water. Those old habits were in him still. The taste of the brandy earlier returned in memory. Had it helped him? Should he have another? Briefly in Healy's his eyes passed along the rows of bottles on the shelves. *One more for the road might steady me. One would be no harm.* And then he could be on his way. The boy was maybe not far away at all. Maybe he was just walking down the road ahead of him. He would find him in no time. Instinctively he touched the tip of his tongue to his lips.

'Something I can get you?' Healy asked.

And whether it was some sneering quality in his voice, some aspect of giving victory to Healy, or he was pulled back from taking a drink by some other force inside himself, the Master blinked and recovered. He came forward and took the two bottles of water and without another word hurried out.

The daylight was dazzling as he strode into it. *Fool, fool, fool.* He gave out to himself, a word with each step. *Fool, old fool, old foolish fool. You were going to. You were. And what about the boy? Start drinking in there and you would be there until they threw you out the door when every penny you had was spent. Fool! Bah!*

He came back to the car flustered and hot. He was still disturbed by the image he had in his mind of the boy encountering Clarke in the night. That this had happened while he was sleeping in his bed made it all the more perturbing. He had to hurry now. He couldn't think of the boy without feeling that he was in danger. He popped up the bonnet and fed the radiator both bottles, he adjusted fittings while muttering kind words to the engine, and then sat inside and tried the ignition. The engine coughed to life.

'Well well well, that's it now,' he said, and shut the door. 'We're not done yet.'

He drove away quickly. He sped into the great wide plains

of Tipperary and across north Munster and into the green valleys of Laois. The car had no radio. He removed the two wedges of cardboard that kept the front windows in place and sped by with the breeze blowing his hair about. Upon the windshield flies and midges spattered and sometimes he engaged the wipers and smears spread back and over until he gave up. At the long curved approach to the town of Monasterevin he came up behind a tractor and trailer that was moving slowly. The young farmer was sitting bouncing in the cab with a pair of grey ear-mufflers on. The mirrors of the tractor had long ago been broken off by some narrow laneway or overhanging branches. So, as the Master waited in the car behind, the farmer had no idea that he was there.

Come on, come on.

He was in a hurry. He couldn't delay like this, not now, not after the business in Healy's bar. He angled out for a better view of the road. There was a bend, lush overgrown bushes masking some part of it. He waited. Nothing came in the opposite direction. Still the tractor did not turn off or pull in. Another half-mile passed like this, the Master waiting, the bends continuing, progress virtually a crawl. Then, when he felt there was the best chance of getting safely past, he pulled out ever so slightly.

Come on now.

He pulled out further into the other lane and pressed on the accelerator but it was failing. Perhaps a wire had overheated. Perhaps some of the electrical tape had come undone or the rubber tubing melted. The young farmer took a look over his left shoulder behind him and saw nothing – the Master was almost alongside him and below the trailer now – then he pulled out into the opposite lane to make a broad sweeping turn into a field on his left. The huge tractor wheel was close, then closer, and the Master shouted and tried to pull further over, the hedges whipping against the car now, but the wheel kept coming and now bang! It hit against the side of the yellow car and the trailer followed it scraping and shoving the car further over. And just then, now coming around the bend towards them was a huge lorry blasting once, twice its horn and the Master shouted out O *God no* and then he spun the steering-wheel full over thinking to hit the wall was better than to hit the lorry. And there was another blast, and the lorry was impossibly high and huge and upon them and smashing into the turning tractor's trailer and making it seem like matchsticks and the noise of cracking and crunching and the squealing of the brakes and the tractor being dragged backwards and sideways and the old car flying straight into a stone wall and the old man who was its driver thrown against the windshield, his head popping back from where the glass shattered and the blood streamed in a jagged river from his forehead. O *God no*. He blinked blood and tried to raise his hand and he couldn't and realized for just one instant that he was on the bridge of dying. And his last thought was that he did not want to cross over, and he called out the boy's name, though none could hear.

And then, no more.

Out of the bushes a lone butterfly flew.

TEN

I must be mad.

Sister Bridget sat on the bus and considered whether or not she had lost her mind. The boy was sitting beside her, his head leaning hard against the window, his eyes closed. He may have been sleeping or not, Bridget couldn't be sure. The evening had fallen and they were speeding along a dual carriageway across Aberconwy and Colwyn and through the edge of the Cambrian Mountains. The bus was a London express and would pass by Birmingham where Bridget was expected at work in the morning. But she had made a decision even before leaving the ferry, and now was coming to terms with it. This was the way it always was with her: she jumped into things and then looked down to see what her feet were stuck in.

Something about the boy. There is something about him. Jay? J?

She couldn't define it, but that hadn't mattered so much at the time. All she knew was that the right thing to do was postpone returning to the convent that evening and shadow him to London. She could go back to Birmingham tomorrow once she saw him safely home to his father. But even as she reasoned this she felt *there is something here, something isn't quite right.*

That he was travelling on his own may not have been so mysterious. Lots of children were independent now and thought nothing of taking buses and trains on their own. Besides, with so many fractured families now, thought Bridget, it was probably perfectly normal to be moving from one parent to another, one life to the next and back again all the time. So many children live in a kind of transit now. But still, how old could this boy be? And there was more to it than just that. On the ferry he had seemed so deeply thoughtful, as if he were studying for a difficult exam and no matter how long and hard he pored over the text he didn't believe he could pass. *He is troubled.* It was as simple as that. She would just watch over him for a bit.

We are each other's angels, Mother Clare had said. *And so, who knows?*

There was another reason, but it lay beyond her words. Inside her now Bridget carried the fresh wound of not having been there for her father, of his slipping away without her. She had a need to help, to be there for someone, and could heal herself by doing so.

Sister Bridget had quietened the voice inside her that had told her she was mad. The bus sped on and soon the darkness consumed the landscape and there was only the blur of blue and black. Cars followed the beams of their headlamps and came alongside for moments and then sped on. Bridget stared out and bit at her right thumbnail. She watched the road signs for Shrewsbury and Wolverhampton pass, and before long they were going around the yellow glow of night-time Birmingham. *Sorry Sisters.* Briefly there crossed her mind the image of her returning, her arrival back inside the huge machine that was that city. She saw herself making her way back to the old convent, opening the heavy gate. She pictured herself walking down the avenue where the gravel had worn away and the weeds made a speckled carpet, the doorbell that rang so shrilly through the downstairs rooms and her waiting for one of the elderly nuns to come. She sensed her dread of stepping inside the dreary hall and being sympathized with. 'We've all been praying for you, Sister.' She imagined herself smiling and saying that she was fine, and then going up the stairs to the third door on the left. There would be no sound in the old building, the other nuns asleep or in prayer. Her hand would turn the loose-fitting brass handle and she would open the door and be again in her bare room with its narrow lumpy bed and picture of the Holy Family. She would put down her case and take off her coat and hang it on the hook on the back of the door. Then she would kneel down and say her prayers.

All of this Bridget could see as clearly as if it were happening. And it filled her with nothing but sadness. This was not the life she had imagined God wanted for her, praying to him from the backside of a door.

She laid her head back on the headrest now. She thought of her father and of his spirit finding its way down through the skies to the bus. She saw him the way he looked when she was thirteen years of age and he was a strong apple-cheeked farmer in brown trousers and shirtsleeves carrying a bucket of newly-dug potatoes into the kitchen. She saw his face gently smiling, 'Another good year, eh?' and 'How's the best girl in the world?' She saw him as a man who never became upset with how things turned out, it was always another good year to him, and she missed him now for his wisdom and for all the times she had never considered that one day he would be gone.

Stay with me, father. You will guide me, won't you? It was the simplest kind of prayer, but Bridget made it with all her heart.

Signs for Warwick, Banbury, Oxford passed, and still the boy slept in his seat beside her. Though his dreams made him fitful she was glad for his rest. It was not until they were coming in along the great outer reaches of London that he woke.

'Well, we're nearly there.'

The boy blinked at her and the yellow glow of the city.

'London,' she reminded him, 'nearly there.'

'Yes.'

Bridget waited a few moments while the boy stretched out the ache in his neck, then she offered him a chocolate bar.

'No thank you.'

'Go ahead, really. You must be hungry. I've eaten two while you slept. If you don't have one I'll feel like a big pig.'

He took it from her, peeled the wrapping and ate it quickly.

'You've been in London to visit your father before?'

The chocolate was thick and cloying in his mouth and he used it as an excuse to delay answering. He nodded.

I don't believe you. What is the story here? What are you hiding? Don't be afraid of me.

'He works at the BBC,' said the boy.

'Oh, I see.'

'He'll be there.'

'Maybe not yet. It's still half-night,' Bridget said.

'He will.' The boy looked away out of the window.

At last the bus arrived in the terminal, the passengers stirred and moved like weary ghosts quietly down the aisle to the exit. Bridget indicated for the boy to go ahead of her. When they stepped on to the tarmac she saw in his eyes that he had no idea of where to go. He had never been there before, she was certain. He was trying to disguise this, but his face betrayed him.

'I always hate when you arrive at such an awful hour, don't you?' Bridget asked. 'Your father won't even be awake yet, not even nuns are. I suspect we should both sit and have coffee somewhere and just wait a bit, don't you?'

It was a risk, she knew. And so she did not act too surprised when the boy told her he couldn't delay.

'I see,' she said, 'well, perhaps I should come with you.'

'No. No thank you.'

'You're sure?'

'Yes.'

'I see, well, it's been lovely travelling with you.'

'You too.'

She offered him her hand and while she held his she again tried to make him understand that he need not fear her. She applied what she hoped was the pressure of love, and watched the boy's face closely to see if he understood. But his hand was weak and his eyes were fixed, as though he was seeing something else that frightened him.

Then he was gone.

Bridget watched him walk away beneath the yellow lights, his small figure disappearing into the crowds. *Stop. Stop and turn back. Say that you've changed your mind. Stop. Come on. Make him stop. Please.*

But the prayer didn't work and the boy didn't stop and Bridget's brow furrowed like a field. *What? What's the right thing to do?*

There was an announcement, a bus leaving for Birmingham. Figures, grey and brown, low-faced men and women, soft-footed phantoms, slid from shadows and filed towards buses. None spoke. In the weird light of that place, between night and day, there was a sour air of disappointed dream, of unwelcome but necessary journeys. Beneath the high girders that supported the metal roof was a sense of caged company, a drifting collection of people burdened with the need to be elsewhere. A man with a shallow beard and sad bulbous eyes shambled past spilling a steady drool of curses from the corner of his mouth. A woman, whose face was puffed and raw-looking with crying, walked by as if in a bad dream, carrying four blue plastic bags stuffed with clothes.

The needy were everywhere, Bridget thought. Everywhere she looked, in every face there was grief and loss and the need for love. So how could she decide? How could she know what was the right thing to do, who was the right one to help?

Help me.

With every instant the boy was further away.

Halfway to her bus, and without the slightest warning, the woman with the four plastic bags collapsed on to the ground. She did not fall over, but rather slid down softly as though some invisible hand had run a sharp knife through the strings above her. She made no sound. Her head lowered, her bags fallen with balled socks, sweater sleeves, underwear, spilling, she was no more than a half-dark bundle that passengers edged around. None stopped for her. Bus engines hummed, airbrakes hissed and electric doors opened as other journeys ended and more emptied into London.

It was only an instant, a fragment of what happened moment after moment each day in any city. But in Bridget's mind it was like a framed black-and-white photograph of a foreign place where someone was suffering. Where when you saw the photograph you felt small and sad and powerless so that you wanted to pick it up and smash it and pull the shards of glass away with your fingers so that you might free in some small way those trapped there.

Bridget looked into the space where the boy had gone. Then she hurried in the opposite direction towards the fallen woman.

ELEVEN

The morning that rose over the city of London was soft and mild, and the light in the sky had the pale consistency of milk drops clouding water. Some mornings you can believe there is kindness in the air, that the day is a gift given, and in the early hours of this one there was just such a quality. The dark retreated speedily. Street-sweeping machines had gathered up the remains of yesterday and in this brief time between waking and business the city was strangely beautiful. Buildings of stone and glass stood as if they were statues certain of their own importance. The boy had only seen such places in books, and now walked down streets with the unsettling sense of having stepped inside the pages. He looked at everything and then tried not to. Still the hooks of his eyes kept catching on details, the great blocks of sandstone in an imperial bank, polished brass nameplates, 'Archibald Price & Co', 'Holstein, Barrington & Barnes', sheer high walls of reflecting glass, even the perfectly rectangular cut of the paving stones beneath him. All astonished him.

I am here. London.
Say it. London. Transported.
Ported from Latin carried I think. Trans across.

Transported to London. Here. I am here.

In pale pinkish light he walked from the bus terminus in awe. At first there were so few others moving in the street that he thought it was like a street in a dream where you have no body, only eyes, and the camera of you is desperately searching for something but you are not sure what.

He had a free map of the city and knew vaguely where he was headed. But he had no sense yet of the scale, how long the streets were, or how distant one part of London was from the next.

He walked. And as he walked he tried not to keep thinking of the Master or the trouble he had caused, but only of the need he had to find an answer. He likened himself to a mathematical problem. He was a mass of figures, of numbers and letters, Xs and Ys that had to pass through various complex operations before the solution could be found.

Once you work it out.

Once you know A, say, equals B and C equals D and so on.

It will all work out.

But the next part of the solution to the equation was to find his father.

Simple as that.

Rocheford Street. Harrington Place. Lemon Mews. The names of the places themselves were like characters in a book.

And perhaps it would all turn out as it did in books. Perhaps it was to be a simple two- or three-day tale of adventure, and soon the boy would be back home with the Master. It seemed so, because of the beauty of the morning, because of

Light catching glass prisms.

Elegant those buildings so.

And grand-looking taxis.

Entranceway with twin bay trees.

Tophat hotel porter.

Toon & Huntley, Gentlemen's Outfitters.

At last the streets woke around him, and the pavements began to liven up with men and women heading to work. At corner stop-lights crowds gathered in eager anticipation of a simple crossing to the other side. In a way it was marvellous. The boy caught the smells of morning showers and shampoo and shoe polish and perfume and smoke and after-shave.

The boy walked as the morning rose. When he neared the point on the map marked with the BBC building at Shepherd's Bush, his chest tightened. He slowed down for what seemed the first time since he had strode out of the church at his Confirmation.

Was this it?

In a moment will I meet him?

And say what?

You are my father and you never knew because my mother never told you but why did you not love her enough? If you loved her enough you would have gone after her and found her and found that I was to be born.

He had not taken the time to really figure this out. He had been *propelled*, he remembered thinking. All of the miles that lay behind him were now coming to an end and suddenly he felt as though there was a weight pressing.

He slowed down. He could see the building straight ahead of him with scaffolding rising around it and stone-cleaners working. Then he stopped short and a man with a backpack bumped against him and the boy apologized and stepped in towards the wall to let him pass but the man was already gone. Standing, the boy struggled to slow his heart. A pulse beat furiously at the base of his throat. There were beads of sweat along his forehead. His upper lip was dry, his whole body weak.

And then the strangest thing. He seemed to himself like a figure in slow motion. For just when he should have stepped forward, just when he had arrived at his destination, he had the sense of time slowing and stretching, as if a hairline fracture opened in the mechanism of all clocks and the steps he began to take carried him no distance at all. The instant would become a forever in his mind. He was walking towards the building. Everything else was perfectly normal and nothing he sensed betrayed the outrageous thing that was coming, a calamity without premonition or alarm. It was a scene in a film where the soundtrack slowed to a drawled-out whrrr and clrrr of sound and the passers-by slow-stepped and slow-stepped . . .

TWELVE

Many days later, when he was travelling on a bus through a desert far away, the boy would remember how he had looked straight up into the sky just a moment before. He would remember it was a blue sky, and that he had offered up a small prayer and that it was not exactly to God but to the Master. *Send me a sign.* He had prayed to the Master to help him because he hadn't felt that he would be able to continue without help. He had felt the way you might feel when you have raced forward without thinking and suddenly arrive on the lip of a huge abyss. Suddenly there was right in front of you a great hole of darkness that you could not jump across and in an instant you would in fact fall headlong into it. He remembered how he had stood against the wall of the building feeling weak, how he had pressed his back to the stone for reassurance. He remembered being frightened. But the blue of the sky had been so perfect. The sun had burned off a thin layer of cloud and everything was lit and lovely and his prayer for help had flown like a white paper plane into the blue.

Later, in the bus crossing the desert, he would wonder if there had been an answer to the prayer. He would wonder if something had come out from the blue sky to keep him there against the wall and not move him forward the last few yards to the BBC building at Shepherd's Bush.

Because otherwise I would be dead.

The noise was the thing that came first. It was enormous. A sound that was nothing like the words *bang* and *crash*. For these were outside of you, these were sounds you heard. Instead this was something ten thousand times bigger. It was like a vast urgent rip in the world itself, a huge violent burst of noise that tore up the sky as if it were nothing but blue cloth. The noise made shredded ribbons of it. Gigantically it boomed. The boy's head was thrown forwards and backwards and hit against the stone wall. His ears were deafened. A great sea rushed into his head. And he was trying to understand what had happened, and his head was hurt and at first, in the very first instant afterwards, he was only trying to understand how the hurt had happened. He had touched the back of his head instinctively and there was blood on his fingers. There was more blood than he had seen before, and some part of his brain was stuck on this, how thick and dark, almost black, was the blood on his hand.

So it was further moments, further broken fragments of time before his brain could take in the scene around him.

Glass. How the glass flew out as the windows blew asunder. Glass flying sideways like water flowing from a world turned on its side. Scaffolding tossed away like a work of matchsticks, and men flying backwards through the air, their wingless flight and fall. How one man hit the ground and his head snapped back and his yellow helmet flew off and spun like a top. Another stood, blood-faced and dazed with half a dozen shards of glass in his eye and cheek. He reached up his hand and then fell to the pavement. There was smoke. Thick and black and curling, as though some great and fierce creature or spirit had been released from long imprisonment and now moved and roared in the shape of tongues of smoke. They came in long angry twists, and in the windless air hung like banners of an army with invisible soldiers. Cars in the street crashed. Heads thumped off windscreens and popped back leaving the glass like shattered spider-webs. A double-decker bus braked and pulled to the right, angled and toppled over, sliding into the stopped traffic and knocking car into car as though these were weightless things.

There were screams, though the boy could not hear them, figures with their mouths open wide running as if from awful dentistry. There was a woman with her whole body curved over like a C sheltering the child she was holding. Then from the building itself there were men and woman running in wild patterns into the smoke. They ran and were suddenly blinded and stumbled over and were like the fallen on a battlefield.

The boy had stepped forward and put his hands to his ears and tapped them. But he heard nothing, just the sea that had filled his head. On the fingers of each hand there was blood. He pressed his hands back against his ears and held them there to see if it would stop. The smoke had encircled everything and he could see only a few feet in front of him. Figures like phantoms appeared and disappeared. Their faces blackened, clothes torn, they ran by mute and open-mouthed. From somewhere above in the shattered building papers flew, rectangles of white descending as weird snow into the street. There were flickering lights of ambulances and police cars and fire engines with sirens he could not hear. When he walked forward there was glass beneath his shoes. Scarves of smoke bound everything. His eyes stung. He shouted loudly to hear himself but there was no sound, only the empty frequency, so he brought his hands to his ears again and tapped on them but the blood was oozing and sticky and when he saw it he felt the life bleeding out of him. The shock passed like a clean knife across the base of his throat and sliced his air. He gasped and fell down in the street.

*　　*　　*

109

He woke in a white space. He did not know how he got there.

He did not know if it was a place in a dream or not.

There was no sound, only the sea in his head.

He opened his eyes for a moment, then closed them and fell again from the white place to somewhere where all he saw was an old man with a bleeding heart. The boy couldn't quite see his face. He couldn't tell if he knew him or not. The man's face was turned away in pain and though the boy tried to reach for him in his dream always the old man was just too far away.

He opened his eyes and there were needles pressing in through his ears. He raised his hands to push them away but they were not there. Only the pain was. He shouted out but the sound was sucked away somewhere by the sea so he could not hear it, and he shut his eyes and asked, *Am I dead?*

There was no answer. In his head the pain continued. It hurt in a place he could not reach. He had brought up his hands and banged them against the sides of his head to see if he could knock it out and he had cried out the silent cries he made that were like strange birds that became invisible the moment they flew out of his mouth.

A woman in white appeared and held his hands from hitting his head and made words with her mouth that were like the words of fishes in the sea.

'My ears, my ears!' the boy had shouted. Or this was what he thought he shouted. The sounds were blurred together. The woman in white nodded and rubbed some liquid on the back of his hand and raised a needle, and the boy fell from there again.

He tumbled down through dreams of all kinds. He saw the old man turned away and blood flowing and the glass that was like drops of water falling sideways. The smoke in his dreams was like great lengths of black cloth. He was caught in it and fell and rolled, and saw fly past him the bulky figure

110

of the bishop, the vicious man in the night, the lorry of Ben Dack, the twins on the ferry, the woman bent like a C.

And then the pain came back like needles piercing his head. The boy cried out again and opened his eyes.

And Sister Bridget was standing beside him.

THIRTEEN

'There, there now, shshsh,' Bridget said, though she had been told the boy could not hear her.

She knew. She knew when she heard of the explosion at the BBC buildings that he was there. She knew and had hurried there directly and come to the place where the police had run a yellow tape, stopping anyone from getting closer. She had prayed then. She had prayed not just for the boy but for everyone because the gaping hole in the building was so shocking with the glass everywhere and the smoke still hanging in the air. There had been no sign of the boy. Ambulances had already transported the victims. What was left was an aftermath, like a print of anger. Television reporters spoke to cameras. People stood along the yellow tape and stared.

'I can't believe this,' an old man said. 'I just can't believe it.'

Sister Bridget had enquired where the ambulances had taken the victims. She was given the names of five different London hospitals. It was in the fifth that she found the boy.

'Shsh, don't try to speak,' she said and put her finger to her lips and then reached out to touch the bandaged side of his head. 'You're going to be all right,' she said, 'you're going to be all right.'

The boy made a puzzle of his face trying to understand what he couldn't hear.

'Oh dear, you're such a dolt sometimes, Bridget,' she muttered and searched in her handbag for a pen and small notebook. On a page she wrote:

I am so pleased to see you.

And with a quivering hand she held it out for the boy to read.

He nodded slightly. She wrote:

Your hearing will come back, the doctor says. You are not to worry.

And again she held out the page and showed him.

'Wha . . . at?' His voice was not his own voice, but a loud distortion.

A bomb. There was a terrorist bomb. I'm afraid people were killed. You were very lucky to be saved.

The boy closed his eyes and turned his head into the pillow.

Tell me a phone number back home to call.

Bridget held out to him the notebook and the pen. The boy did not move for some moments. Then, very slowly, he raised a hand and took the pen, and, while Bridget held the notebook, he wrote the Master's phone number and his name: Joe Carpenter.

Thank you. I'll be back. Rest.

Sister Bridget went down the white hospital corridors to Reception and from there was directed to a public phone. She had to wait while a small queue of the distressed made calls. At last she dialled the number and waited and listened while in the cottage in County Clare the phone rang and rang.

She hung up and stepped away and back to the end of the queue to try again. The second time the same thing happened. The ringing pulsed two beats, then two beats again. But there was no answer.

She came back to the boy.

No one home. You're sure this is the number?

He nodded.

Never mind. I'll phone again in a little while.

Then the boy closed his eyes and Bridget was not sure if he was asleep or just weighed with sadness but she did not disturb him. She watched over him. She let her eyes drift to the window where luminous white clouds moved across the blue May sky. How innocent they seemed. How undisturbed the world turned despite the horrors of the explosion. Birds flew and sang on the hospital's window ledges. Beyond, in the sunlit afternoon children were kicking balls in parks whose grass was greening sweetly. Bridget thought again of May afternoons long ago, of her father in the fields, waist-high to the hay, running his hand over it and calculating how long before it would need to be mown. She slipped back into summers that lingered in her memory, when the sun was warm and the fact that it shone at all was reason enough to be happy. She remembered the hay-making, bringing a milk-bottle of tea with a cloth top and a fresh tea-towel full of ham sandwiches out to her father in the fallen meadow. She had run barefoot across the stippled field, the ground beneath her prickling her feet, her father's hand just landing lightly on the top of her head and his smile. *Dad.*

Then the boy twisted sharply in his blanket and Bridget sat up and leaned over him. He was dreaming. He kicked at the cover and made a moaning sound. His head was hot when she felt it.

'Shshsh,' she said, 'shshsh,' though she knew he could not hear. Like a swimmer carried on a wave, the boy drifted away and was quiet again.

An hour passed. Bridget went away and in vain tried the phone again. She bought a newspaper at the small hospital shop and came back to read it by his bedside. 'THE HAND

OF GOD?' asked a huge headline over a photograph of the devastated building with bodies lying in the street. Religious extremists, the article said, were to blame.

By early evening the boy woke. Sister Bridget had been to try the phone four times by then without success.

I'm sure I'll get through later.

The boy looked at the newspaper on her lap.

'It's awful,' Bridget said. But the boy indicated that he wanted to look and so she held the pages for him and he read.

It'll be all right, she wrote.

But she knew she had no evidence of this, and the boy turned away.

He slept. She sat in the chair beside him throughout the night, but for the moments when she went and tried the phone.

The following day the boy was awake hardly at all. The pains in his ears were worse and the doctor was called and changed the dosage of painkiller so the boy slept or slipped away on a tide of medicine and sorrow.

Sister Bridget sat like a statue or a saint. A nurse from Mayo called Nora brought her sandwiches and biscuits and milky tea with no sugar. Once, in the second night, the boy woke and with eyes wide said loudly the word, 'Father'.

She wrote on the notebook:

What is his name?

The boy hesitated. His face froze in the thin light that came from the monitor over his bed. Then he took the pen and wrote:

I DON'T KNOW.

His eyes did not leave Bridget's face as she read the three words. She looked at him the way you look at a jigsaw puzzle when you have suddenly seen how one of the corners fits. *What an idiot you are, Sister. What a complete idiot.* She wrote:

How can we find him?

The boy took the pen and with a rapid movement under-
lined the three words:

I DON'T KNOW.

Then he lay back on the pillow and the sea in his head took
him away once more leaving Sister Bridget in a complete state
of unknowing.

At noon the day after that, Nora brought Sister Bridget a
local Irish newspaper left by one of the patients. The boy was
awake. The bandages over his ears had been changed and he
looked fresher and the doctor said his wounds were healing.
His eyes were bright and clear, and Bridget thought *I was
right, things are going to be all right. You see. Have a little
faith, dear one.*

She leaned forward over the bed and opened the newspaper
wide so that the boy could read the pages on one side while
she read from the others.

*You see, everything will be fine. Just give him time. First
things first. Then we can sort out this business with the missing
father.*

Then suddenly the boy cried out. He hit the newspaper hard
and it buckled forward and Bridget jumped up in alarm.

'What? What is it? What's the . . .'

The boy hit his hand on the newspaper and wailed out, a
long piercing shriek of grief.

Bridget was beside herself. 'Nurse! Nurse!'

O God, stop. What is it, what is it?

The boy pressed back his head and arched his back and the
long fierce red ribbon of sound continued. He thrashed his
head back and over, alarming the nurses who came running.
The corridor sounded with their slapping rubber soles. But
before the nurses even arrived the boy had hit out at the newspaper again and Bridget's eye had followed to the photograph
and its caption.

There, in black-and-white was a picture of an old car crashed into a stone wall. Above it, the headline, 'FATAL ACCIDENT, MONASTEREVIN'.

Sister Bridget read only the first words. 'An elderly man was fatally injured . . .' Then she looked up to where the boy's eyes met hers. His tears were thick and falling.

O God O God O God.

Before the nurse had finished his injection, he wrote four words.

THE MASTER . . . MY GRANDFATHER.

Then his eyes closed and he went away with the sea again.

FOURTEEN

Dead.
Master is dead.
Because of me.

FIFTEEN

The boy fell back against the pillow and shut his eyes. It was as if an iron door had closed, trapping inside a great poisonous cloud of grief. Sister Bridget struggled to breathe.

Why? Why this? Why now?

All of her prayers were questions.

Why to this boy?

She bowed her head. The light of the day passed into afternoon and evening. And when at last the first raw hurt had passed she began to find in herself a resolve to do something. The way we defeat sorrow is action, she remembered Sister Agnes saying once.

I will help him find his father. That's what I will do. That's what I am supposed to do. Yes.

In the darkness, her body stiff and aching from many hours in the chair, she prayed the oldest prayer, the 'Our Father'. When she finished she began again so that the last phrase joined the first until the prayers were like rings thrown up into the invisible.

At dawn the boy opened his eyes. From the window above him the palest light was leaking. Sister Bridget reached out and put her hand upon his forehead. Nothing more. The boy

121

lay still in the grey silence with the nun watching over him, as though they were travellers paused on the furthermost edge of the world.

During the boy's waking moments over the next two days, Bridget gradually began to find the way forward. She wrote questions for him on her notebook. At first he would not answer at all, but stared at the words as if they were a puzzle or the answers were irrelevant now. When at last he began to reply he did so sometimes by saying just a few loud words, sometimes by taking the pen and writing. From these she learned fragments of his story and of Joe Carpenter, the Master. She learned of the day of un-Confirmation as he called it, of the burning of the letter from his dead mother, of the sudden decision to leave in the night and the journey that had brought him to within fifty yards of the BBC.

God spared you, she wrote.

The boy took the pen: I DON'T BELIEVE IN GOD.

He watched her face for a sign of anger or disagreement but there was none. IF I DID I WOULD BELIEVE HE WAS PUNISHING ME.

Bridget knew enough not to argue. She let her kind eyes hold him for a few moments until he looked away. She wrote:

Besides your father, is there no one else?

The boy looked directly at her then shook his head. With the pen he dug at the page to write:

THE MASTER IS DEAD! EVERYONE I KNOW DIES.

Bridget had no answers. She had sat for a time with the cold company of feeling useless. She could not repair what was broken, although in her spirit this was her strongest desire. She wanted to direct the powers of God herself, to be able to call upon Him in whatever corner of the heavens He was and say, 'Look upon this boy'. And if God was unavailable, Bridget wanted some portion of His influence to bring about an instance of goodness, some beginning of healing. This was the essence of her character. It was Bridget's greatest challenge that the world constantly disappointed her hopes for it, so she found herself time and again wanting God to come down and fix it. When He failed to do so she forgave Him, but sought to bring about some temporary remedy herself, something that would hold things in place until He came. So, in the grey light of the hospital, some hours after sitting with the chill realization that for the boy there was no one but her, she abruptly decided to go to the BBC herself.

The piece of this man's name that you know is 'AH . . . SH'?

Very slightly, the boy nodded.

I will be back for you.

When she walked down the stairs and through the doors into the street and daylight hit her eyes Bridget realized it had been nearly a week since she had been outside. Straight away she sensed or imagined a difference. Though in the aftermath of the bombing people had returned to the ordinariness of their days – they drove to work or waited for buses, they beat old routes along the footpaths, to and from the Underground they descended and rose again – there was in each face an unmistakable wariness. It was as if during the days and nights she had spent in the hospital an invisible enemy had invaded, and with it now all were at war. The enemy was everywhere and nowhere. He might be that man ahead of you anxiously looking around in the queue. He might be your taxi driver, his ally the newspaper man at the kiosk. The enemy could be that woman carrying a large handbag and pretending to be a nun. No one could be presumed innocent. Down upon the heads of every man and woman in every street, in every office, shop and pub, had fallen a stain of distrust. This was the real damage of the bomb. There was no faith now in another's goodness, but instead, in the eyes that met your eyes, fear.

Sister Bridget sensed it at once. London was not London, but a city imagined in a science-fiction novel populated by figures of wordless nervy watchfulness. The sound of a siren pierced to your heart. Some stopped and looked on the skyline for smoke, for a sign, then hurried on with eyes down not wanting to let on there had been a flicker of fear, that thoughts were of the enemy all the time. This is how it was. With a simple straightforwardness learned from her father, Bridget decided not to surrender but to meet the eyes of everyone and smile and say a cheery 'good morning' or 'hello there'.

Best to show you have no fear. I have no fear. Not really. Not exactly fear anyway.

Who's going to blow me up?

And if they do, if I just happen to be there at the wrong time because that would be just like me then I'll suppose it's to be for the best. Not that I can understand that here and now, but no doubt I will at some stage later on. That's it. Later on, it'll all make sense.

So.

'Hello there.' Brightly she greeted a businessman who started with surprise and dodged across the street through the cars.

Down the footpath a pair of young policemen patrolled. Beneath their helmets their eyes were small and apprehensive.

This enemy can't be arrested. Everyone looks suspicious now. You might as well be trying to catch people's thoughts, or beliefs.

In brown sensible shoes Sister Bridget strode purposefully on her mission for the boy. At one point she turned into a street and walked directly into a protest march on behalf of London's Muslim population. Banners and posters claimed unfair treatment. 'Imprisonment Without Charge' read one,

'Discrimination against Muslims!' Others were simply single words: 'Harassment!' 'Justice!' 'Persecution!'

Oh dear.

There is nothing to be afraid of. There is absolutely nothing to be afraid of.

Still she was afraid. At last she approached the BBC building at Shepherd's Bush where a great hole gaped, and streams of yellow tape tied off the empty space where sixteen people had died. An ethereal sadness lingered. The building itself was closed. But there was a sign saying that the offices had moved to an address just down the street. OPEN FOR NORMAL BUSINESS, it read.

Bridget arrived at Reception in the makeshift office where a very properly dressed elderly man sat with his name, 'Oliver Hazelworth', plastic-coated on a chain.

'Good morning,' she smiled.

'Good morning, yes?'

'My name is Sister Bridget.'

'Yes?'

'I have been sent by a young boy whom I am looking after at present. He is in hospital. He was injured in the explosion.'

'Ah.' Oliver Hazelworth's face softened. 'Is he all right?'

'Oh well, he has no hearing at the moment. But the doctors think it will come back. Well the thing is, he is trying to track down someone, a relative.'

'I see.'

'And, it's someone who works at the BBC, but I'm such a complete fool I've forgotten the name. It's a man, a correspondent. His name begins with Ah-something Sh-something.'

'Ah-something Sh-something?' The man smiled as if it were a joke.

'Yes. It's my fault completely but . . .' Bridget made what she trusted was her hopeless face.

Oliver Hazelworth looked at it for a moment only, then

began scrolling with considerable slowness and care through a list of names on his computer.

'Ah . . . Sh. You're sure? Not An, not Anthony Shaw?'

'No, no. Ah. I'm sure of that much.' Without her realizing, Bridget's hand went to the cross at her neck.

Come on, come on, please.

'No. There's no . . . it's surname Sh, yes? Because there isn't really anything.'

'Yes, it's a surname.'

He moved the mouse so the screen scrolled again while slowly he shook his head.

'A correspondent?'

As though it were golden liquid, Bridget felt the hope leak out of her.

'No, I'm sorry,' the man said. 'No correspondent Ah-Sh.'

'Perhaps it's on another list?'

'No, I have all of them listed here. Sorry.'

Sister Bridget didn't move. There was nowhere to go now but back to tell the boy, and she couldn't do that. The cross dug into the palm of her hand.

'This is very important,' she said.

'I'm not sure what I can do, dear. If you came back with the full name.'

'He doesn't know the full name. He knows it's a correspondent for the BBC. He knows it is the only person left alive in the world with a connection to him.'

There was a pause, a moment flattened by the weight of desperation, then a flash of inspiration.

'He may not be a correspondent now,' Bridget said, 'but he was at one time.'

'I see.' Oliver Hazelworth sat back in his chair. He did not normally work at the reception. The man who did had been killed in the bombing. Now everyone who came through the doors seemed attached to that explosion, witnesses, experts, professors, relatives. Everyone Oliver Hazelworth saw had the same urgent burning in their eyes. For them all the bombing was not over, but would carry on, and for some never end. This profoundly struck the old man. The day of his retirement from the BBC had been shattered by the explosion. He had survived in an upstairs office where one wall had been blown away. Now temporarily he worked at reception, hoping he could understand why he had been spared. Oliver Hazelworth brought his hand to his chin and let his eyes look away into the past.

'A correspondent . . . unless . . .'

'Yes?'

'Unless . . . could it be Sharif? Is he Asian?'

'Sharif?'

'Ahmed Sharif. He was BBC once, but he's, you know, not any more, he's freelance now. He's Egyptian, I think. He's the one did those pieces on the terrorist thing. Back oh, well, a fair while now. You know. Vanishes for months at a time, infiltrating some group or other.'

'Do you have any contact for him?'

'No. I'm sorry. You've little chance of finding him. He's underground, dear. Let me see, well, yes, he was, hold on, what was it, something in Paris. Some mosque where they were supposed to be preaching terror, or something. That was his last piece if I remember correctly. Last thing I heard about. Yes. Yes, that's right. North suburbs of Paris, I remember because I was there one time myself as a student.'

'How old a man would you say he was?'

'Must be what, about late thirties.'

Briefly the vague figure of this man flitted in her mind. Then Oliver Hazelworth wrote down the name of the mosque and Bridget thanked him.

'Of course it may not be him at all. But if you get the right name . . .'

'I know. Yes. Thank you.'

When she came out into the street two ambulances with their sirens wailing raced by. Squad cars followed leaving behind the fumes of foreboding. The world was suddenly rotten with fear, Bridget thought. And she lifted her chin and tightened her lips, as though she wore a helmet or needed protection from the despair raining down.

SIXTEEN

'I can hear.'

'What?'

'I can hear you. I can hear the birds.' The boy raised his hands to protect his ears, for inside his head his own voice boomed. 'Did you find him?'

All the way back to the hospital Bridget had rehearsed, but looking at the peculiar mix of fear and hope in the boy's face, she lost the words. Instead she blurted. 'He wasn't there. It may not be him anyway. There's no way to know.'

'What's his name?'

'Well, as I said, there's no way to be sure even if . . . but your hearing, that's wonderful, that's more . . .'

'Tell me.'

She looked at the round brown eyes fixed on her. She was not sure how the boy would take it. She was not sure of anything.

'His name? Please.'

'Well, this man's name is Sharif, Ahmed Sharif.'

There was a sudden gap in time and the name itself became an actual man and he then entered the hospital room and stood between the nun and the boy. Through his name the boy looked at him. The dazzle of the afternoon light in the window, the trilling birdsong, the scent that climbed from the rose garden below, even the kind face of the woman by his bed, were all erased from the boy as he stared into the space where the name Ahmed Sharif now dwelled.

'Are you all right?'

Bridget poured him a glass of water. But the boy lay absolutely still in a pose of arrest.

'It's silly to think too much about it anyway. Because as I said it may not be him at all. It was just the only name they had that began Ah-Sh. And besides, the man you are looking for may have left the BBC long ago. Might be Shaw or something,' she said and then wished that she hadn't.

'What does Ahmed Sharif do?'

She told the boy what she knew.

'It's him.'

'It mightn't be him. There's no way to . . .'

'It is him. Look at me. I am an Arab.'

'No, you're . . . you're Irish.'

'I am the child of an Irish mother and an Arab father.' The boy's voice was firm. 'He's the one. He's the one I have to find.'

'But, Jay, you don't *know*.'

'I do.'

'How?'

'I just do.'

'That doesn't make sense.'

'No. It doesn't. I know. But not everything does. Can you explain anything that has happened? Can you explain it?'

'You don't know where he is.'

'He might still be in Paris. I'm going there. To this mosque. I'll search on the Internet. I'll find him. I will.' The boy's voice quickened. His eyes were bright, electric with desperation and resolve.

'But how can you?'

'How can I not?'

He moved the covers of the bed aside and took out his clothes from the bedside locker. Bridget had to look away. With her eyes on the window, she tried to sound reasonable.

'But we really don't know even if it is him.'

'I'll never know if I stay here. I have to just go.'

She turned around to him. 'But he may be impossible to find.'

'You believe in the impossible.' He pointed to her cross.

'But, but . . . Paris is not only enormous but it's miles away from here. Besides you have nothing to go on, and you told me you have only a little money.'

'I have enough to get to Paris which isn't all that far really. Just a train journey. That's all I need.'

The boy was dressed now. He had taken out his small backpack and checked it.

'Thank you for everything,' he said.

'But you can't just walk out. The doctors have to sign papers, you have to . . .' Bridget stopped herself. That's just what he was going to do, walk out of there. And before she had taken time to consider, she said: 'I am going with you.'

The boy looked at her.

'I am not coming back if I don't find him there,' he said. 'I'm going on.'

'I'm going with you,' Bridget said again, as if testing the words to see if they could be true.

'You're sure?'

'I'm sure.'

'Thank you,' said the boy.

'No need, ' Sister Bridget told him, 'it's what God wants me to do for you. Especially since now you don't believe in Him.'

'Or Her.'

'Yes, well. We'll discuss that later. And also where you stand on angels.'

'Angels were fat babies with wings. The last ones anyone saw were in the Renaissance, weren't they?'

'The Renaissance?'

'There was a book the Master got me one time.'

'That man has a lot to answer for.'

And so, within a whirling few minutes, a decision had been made, and the nun and the boy slipped from the hospital down the back stairs. At Bridget's insistence they left a note on the bed.

MY HEARING HAS RETURNED. THANK YOU. I HAVE TO GO TO FIND SOMEONE.

'Good manners,' Bridget said. 'Always important.' Then she went out into the corridor to check on the movement of the nurses. They were watching the television. She beckoned the boy, and he got in front of her, and though she was neither tall nor wide, Bridget thought she could hide him so.

'If someone sees us and calls us back . . .' she began.

'We run,' said the boy.

'I'm not very good at running.'

'I'm worse.'

There was no need. They made the door to the back stairs unseen except for the steady eye of the surveillance camera. Once through the door they raced wildly down the steps until they arrived breathlessly in the front lobby across which they tried to stroll as calmly as possible. Then they were out in the city once again. They walked quickly to the Underground. By the entranceway there was a man selling newspapers. 'WAR ON TERROR' was the huge headline.

The boy shook his head, but said nothing. When they were further on, Sister Bridget thought she should assure him in some way; 'This war on terror,' she began.

'You can't wage war on a noun,' the boy said. 'That's what the Master would say.'

Sister Bridget looked at him.

'And he would be right. How can you win? One day will they say there is no more terror in the world?' The boy shrugged his shoulders and they moved on.

They descended beneath the city. In the Underground passageways people seemed even brusquer than before. They wore masks with far-away looks. As if clothed in bulky suits of fear they could not stand too near each other on the platform, but edged away allowing a space for anxiety. The nun hoped the boy did not feel this. She hoped she provided some degree of security for him, but she wasn't sure. A nun in brown shoes, navy-blue skirt, cream blouse, grey cardigan; how fierce a protector could she be?

They stopped at an Underground map. She was unused to it and was still trying to unravel the lines, when the boy ran his finger along the route.

'This way,' he said.

'Wait, wait a minute. Here, I have something to do.' She crossed over to a small kiosk and bought a card and a stamp. On it she wrote a hurried message to the convent.

Delayed returning. I have something to take care of for a few days. God bless all. Sister Bridget.

She slipped the card in the box.

'It may take longer than a few days,' the boy said.

'You don't have any faith at all, do you?' Bridget smiled. 'Come on.'

They rode the Underground train in silence, their own faces peering back at them from the dark windows.

An hour later, after some discussion, and counting of money, they had bought one-way train tickets to Paris. Crossing the concourse on the way to the platform, Bridget stopped as though she had suddenly remembered something.

'What is it?' The boy turned back to her.

'I can't believe this is happening,' she said.

A thin smile played on the boy's lips. 'That's what I am here for,' he said.

'What?'

'To help you believe. Come on.'

SEVENTEEN

Before the train left the station armed policemen moved watchfully through the carriages. Wordlessly, they scrutinized each of the passengers, scanning faces into memory where an impossible crosscheck was to occur. Behind them they left a parcel of disquiet in each carriage. The passengers sat grim-faced and vaguely claustrophobic. They clutched their knees, and looked out of the window.

'Well it's right, it's because there could be a bomb,' a cheery old woman said and smiled.

It was only when the train was cleared to depart, and pulled away with slight swaying and soft clacking, that the passengers seemed to find some relief.

To feel the rhythm the boy sat with his head against the window. There was little to see. Soon the train would enter the long tunnel beneath the sea and arrive in France. He didn't want things to see anyway. He wanted to think.

Ahmed Sharif. Who are you? Where are you right now?

Am I the son of Ahmed Sharif?

As soon as I heard the name I knew it was you. I recognized it. I recognized it though I had never heard it before. Maybe it was an imprint in me. Maybe such things exist.

135

*Maybe it's like starlings returning to the barn where the Master
says their great-grandfathers sang.*

Ahmed Sharif. Ahmed Sharif. Ahmedsharifahmedsharif.

*If I say your name often enough will you hear it? Will you
know that I am coming?*

Ahmedsharifahmedsharifahmedsharif.

I will find you.

Because there is no one else.

Because otherwise there is nothing.

Because that is my deal.

In case You have forgotten.

The train raced through the neon tunnel. The boy thought
of his mother and her meeting this Egyptian in England.
From the pages of *David Copperfield* he took out the letter.

That's what she meant. Different worlds.

Outside the faith. That's what it's called.

*I don't believe there are any different worlds. There is only
this one with everybody in it.*

I am Egyptian-Irish.

That is who I am.

I am sun and rain.

I am sand and field.

I am Muslim-Christian.

After a time he took out his journal and wrote:

> Ahmed Sharif. If Shar Med Ah.
> Sharif. Sharp-sound. Knife-edge. Sharif.
> Ahmed Sharif, where are you?
> I, your son, am coming to tell you that I exist.
> Do you know already?
> Can you feel it? Can you imagine me?
> I will see you and I will say 'Father'.
> Then what will you say?

*   *   *

136

The train sped on through the illuminated undersea.

'I don't like it very much, do you?' Bridget asked. 'The train, going under the sea?'

The boy shook his head.

'If you'd like to talk, I mean I know so much has happened for you and I always find at first when anything happens to me there is only the shock. I can't quite figure out what I think about anything. There's just this sense, you know, that *something has happened*. And that it's part of things now, but just what I think of it, how I fit it into everything, doesn't come until quite a bit later.' Bridget paused, and looked at the boy who had turned back to stare at the nothing out of the window. 'Anyway, what I want to say is, that quite a lot has happened to you in the last little while and if you'd like to talk about it I'm here to listen.'

'I don't want to talk about it.'

'No, that's fine. That's perfectly fine. Just, when, I mean if, then, well, you know.' She raised her pale hands from her lap and let them fall lifelessly. 'Rabbiting again Bridget, as Mother Clare says.'

'No, it's fine. It's just that I don't know,' said the boy, and then after a beat, 'the Master's dead.'

Bridget bit down on her lower lip.

'He's dead.'

'I know.' She placed her right hand over his. He looked away. The nowhere where they were flew past.

'I wish I had met him, the Master,' Bridget said softly. 'He sounds a wonderful man.'

Like a current of air blown through a tube, the train tunelessly flew. The boy and the boy's face in the window remained, the eyes looking back at him as they had in the bathroom mirror the morning of his un-Confirmation. He did not turn back to Bridget, but he said: 'He was always there for as long as I remember. I never really thought of there ever being any life without him. He was the Master, he was my teacher in school, but he was also there when I came home. *There*. Sort of like, I don't know, like someone who is always around. Not that he was the kind who'd be looking over your shoulder, or following you about and worrying. He wasn't like that. He would be off in one corner of the cottage reading a book on something, maybe poetry or history or something, and falling asleep in the chair as often as not, and I'd be coming and going doing whatever I was doing, and he'd just be there, you know?'

The boy turned to Bridget, his eyes polished with grief.

'After his wife died, he was sort of mother and father to me. He wanted to show that we could manage ourselves, that we'd be all right, and he bought this big old cookbook and set it up on the table and bought in ingredients for whatever the recipe called for. And one day we had whatever was on page fourteen, and the next day page fifteen, until we worked our way through about a hundred pages and came to Fried Calf's Liver with Puréed Lima Beans and Celery Sauce. He looked at me and at the photograph of the dish and said: "Maybe it's time I taught you about the editorial prerogative." And we began skipping after that.

'We flew kites together, up on the big hill. He loved kites, and I did too. He used to say there was something special about a kite. He shouldn't wonder he said if there wasn't some religion that had kites at its centre. Something to do with the way they are off in the sky but still connected to the ground. We'd go flying them, and be up there on the hill and hardly say a word to each other. But be somehow happy all the same, you know?'

'Yes.'

'He gave me books on everything. One time he brought home this big box of old copies of *National Geographic* magazine, and after that there were some everywhere, in the kitchen, in the bathroom, everywhere. And he was reading them and I was reading them and he'd say, "Peru looks interesting," or "You'll get to Africa one day, I hope." And I would tell him I would.'

The boy pressed his lips together on the memory. He turned back to the window.

'He was a wonderful man,' Bridget said, 'and would be very proud of you.'

The boy did not answer.

After a while he slept. What dreams he had made him shudder but not waken. He was like a figure pulled by strings. Once he kicked at some pursuing spectre and pulled his head about so that Bridget saw his face, shut-eyed and distorted with a grimace and she wondered should she wake him. But the moment passed and she let him sleep, unsure that his waking world was better than the one he dreamed. Instead she prayed for him, and for their safety, and then for the victims of the bomb. Finally, she prayed for the Master. For although she had not met him, nor seen his picture, she felt a strange sense of his nearness, and could imagine something of his life with this extraordinary boy.

The train surfaced in the brightness of France. Perfectly flat fields spread out on either side. They were empty of animals or machinery, and seemed almost unnatural to Bridget in their symmetry and order. She had never been this far away before, and suddenly there came another wave of concern.

And what now?

You are the grown-up here. What is the plan?

To arrive in Paris and then what? How will we find him? How will we even begin? Where will we stay?

You haven't the first notion, have you?

What kind of help is that?

Bridget, Bridget. Come on.

A claw of panic seized her. She felt her face film with clammy sweat, as though facing an examination for which she had not only not prepared, she could not even remember the subject. Quickly she stood up, and moved down the carriage to the toilet. Inside, she ran the cold water and splashed it several times on her face before bringing her eyes to the mirror.

All right now. Come on.

Come on. Stop this.

Have a little faith. Have a little faith will you?

It will be all right.

Nothing worse is going to happen to the boy. He will be all right now.

She shut her eyes.

You won't let anything else bad happen to him, will You? You won't, please?

Then a thought occurred to her. *What saint's day is this? Bridget, you should know that. You should know it. What saint's day?*

O, Saint Whatever, please, have a word on our behalf.

Her faith in her own prayer was thin and almost the instant that she opened her eyes she feared for the boy left alone in the carriage. She grabbed at the handle and rushed out and along the swaying carriage back to him. The distance seemed so much further now than before. There were the faces of passengers, their eyes turning to see why she was hurrying. The boy, was he all right? *Why did I leave him?* Something could happen. Something could happen so easily. She grabbed the headrests on either side as she stumbled up the carriage. Then she came nearly to her row, and could not see the boy's head and her mouth opened for the cry she was to make and then she saw him. He was still sleeping, and had slid down, his head on her side of the seat. Bridget allowed herself a sigh of relief, then very carefully edged herself in and raised his head on to her lap. When she was sure he was peaceful once more, she softly rummaged in

140

her bag for her diary. She wanted to check which saint's day it was.

Within an hour the train was slowing to move through the densely stacked suburbs of Paris. Buildings with their backsides to the tracks looked grim and forbidding. There was yellow and blue and red graffiti in Arabic, slogans and sayings that might have foretold the end of the world for all Bridget knew. There were tall apartment blocks; some with windows broken, others with brightly coloured washing hanging over small iron balconies. Though she couldn't keep her eyes away from this glimpse of a side of Paris she had not imagined, Bridget saw not a single face. The train slowed further still, and was then as if in procession through this grim place of the poorer Parisian.

The boy was released from his dreams and gave a moan and opened his eyes.

'Where are we?'

'We're there. Or here, which is a kind of nearly there. Take a look.'

The boy rubbed his eyes and turned to the window. He watched, said nothing.

At the outer reaches of the station, they passed in through spaghetti of tracks where old carriages and engines lay rusting. Many of these too were brightly graffitied.

'I think it's quite pretty, really,' Bridget said.

'It's Arabic.'

'Yes.'

'I wish I could read it.'

Bridget smiled at how earnest he was. 'Well, for a long time I have to admit to you that I couldn't tell b's and d's apart, so that when younger I proudly signed myself "dribget", quite a few times. So, I'm sorry I won't be any help.'

At last the train stopped.

'Well?' Bridget asked. 'Will we go with your plan or my plan? Mine is to go to a convent I found listed here in the back of my Sisters of Mercy diary, and see what the quality of mercy is like in Paris.'

'Let's follow your plan.'

'All right then.'

The station was enormous, the roof high, the concourse huge, a bedlam of people moving back and forth.

'Oh by the way, happy Saint Augustine's Day,' Bridget said.

'I don't believe in saints.'

'Of course, sorry. Sorry Saint Augustine, he doesn't believe in you,' Bridget said to the high roofspace. Then she turned to the boy, 'I think it's all right, as long as he believes in us. He's the one saves people. We don't have to save him.'

The boy smiled at her. 'I almost don't want to move from here,' he said.

'I know.'

There was another instant then in which they stood on the platform and the noise of people and engines, of haste and hope and determination, of all human endeavour, of time itself ticking relentlessly towards some appointed second, came and washed about them. In that moment, for no reason, the boy looked up into the arching girders of the roof. How the light played there – a sunbeam caught in the iron architecture made a pattern like a giant butterfly overhead. The boy saw it. The nun looked at him looking upwards but didn't see what he did.

There was a moment and then another, and another still. Then the boy said, 'All right.'

And they stepped forward, not yet knowing the delay had saved their lives.

EIGHTEEN

Because he was married to a saint by the name of Josie, and because on Saturdays Josie devoted herself to volunteer visits to elderly patients in long-term care, Ben Dack often found himself accompanying her. He would carry the laden basket of cakes she made, sultana-scones, nut-o-choc biscuits, apple and rhubarb tartlets, and such. Then when she went to call on some of her elderly ladies he would wander off along the corridors of the Ennis General Hospital with bags of mints and liquorice in case there was anyone who needed company. His short round figure and ready smile were familiar to all of the nurses, and sometimes they made suggestions about a patient whose spirit was low, or was a long time without visitors.

'The human voice is a powerful medicine, powerful,' Ben Dack would say, and head off towards whomever the nurse indicated.

On this Saturday afternoon, whether by chance or design, one of the nurses who was remembering the last days of her own grandfather, suggested he visit the man who had been in the newspaper.

'The miracle,' she called him. 'Well, sort of.'

Ben didn't understand.

'You know the man who died, Mr Carpenter. Who was in the paper, the car crash.' The nurse was proud of the celebrity. 'He's, you know . . . he came back. After being dead. He was revived but he's in a deep coma. He can't make a sound or anything, but I thought, well, maybe you could speak to him. Maybe he could hear something. You don't have to if you don't want to. My grandfather, well, he . . .' She didn't finish.

'No no, of course. Of course Ben Dack will talk to him. Point me the way.'

The nurse took his arm and squeezed it, as though it was a favour he was doing her, or balancing some account in goodness on her behalf. Then she showed him the way along several corridors to a closed door in a silent part of the hospital.

'Thank you,' said the nurse. 'Maybe if you just talk to him,' then she turned and was gone.

Ben stepped into the room where the air was strangely cool and still. In the faint light there was a single bed and in it the body of a man. His face was lost in bandages. There were many machines. A hiss and suck sounded repeatedly, and seemed in the labour of its workings like some newly invented valve. Hiss and suck and then a terrible pause in which it seemed the machine itself had failed, and then the hiss again. Pale glowing came from a monitor where green and red lines moved in a slow graphing of the man's life force. The whole place was like the sad solitary domain of some lesser kind of existence, one without the ability to move or talk or even breathe. When Ben Dack stepped inside the door he was momentarily overwhelmed. He could hardly breathe himself, and gave a little tug with both hands to open further the collar of his plaid shirt.

The hiss and suck sounded.

He swallowed hard.

'Dear God,' he said.

He stood waiting to know how to continue. His eyes took in other details. The legs of the man in white plaster casts, the neck-brace, the way the bandages encased his face and left only the narrowest opening where a mouthpiece was inserted. The thin refined air smelled like that of a deep cave. Despite the small constant noises of the machines, the sense he had was of profound silence. It was as if this man had fallen off the world, but at the last moment had landed on this thinnest ledge where now just barely he lingered. It was a place of great loneliness.

Ben remembered one of the newspaper headlines. 'THE MAN WHO WAS DEAD'. He remembered coming past the crash scene on the road himself and seeing the old car crushed into the stone wall and the shudder he gave passing a place where a life ended. He remembered the evening paper announcing the fatality, followed by the astonishment the next morning when the news broke that the dead man had started breathing. The doctors' statements, the enquiry, the whole story ran again in Ben Dack's mind right up to the latest discussions on the radio. There a medical expert had pointed out that to all extents and purposes the man was in fact still dead, that he now showed no brain activity, had only breathed on his own for a short time, and now could only do so with assistance. He should be allowed to go, this professor said. His life was over. There had followed a flurry of phone calls, and voices arguing both sides. But after the initial interest, the heat of the argument had passed, the calls had stopped coming, and the discussion had returned to high petrol prices.

Now, here, away from all that, was the man himself, a bandaged figure in the bed.

Without stepping forward Ben Dack pushed up the sleeves of his shirt. Slowly they slid down again. He tried to breathe deeply the thin cool air. In his hand he held two bags of mints and liquorice.

'Dear God tonight,' he muttered under his breath, and then he approached the bed. Next to it was a chair with newspapers where a nurse must have sat watching over the patient.

'Well now, Mr Carpenter, mind if I sit down, you don't, the legs you see, aren't the greatest, not that there's that great amount of them in the first place, and then of course I'm in the lorry you know driving back and forth across the country all the day and they don't get that used to holding me up which is a bad thing of course and of course Josie, that's the saint I'm married to, she's downstairs in the long-terms, says it'll get you in the end, indeed it will, but you know yourself, so anyway, what can you do about it, right?' He lifted the newspapers and then the chair so it would not make a noise, and he sat down. 'Oh that's grand, that's grand altogether, a comfortable chair is a great thing.'

Ben Dack settled himself down and slapped his two hands on his thighs as though in front of him an important football match was just beginning.

'So? So you know, I suppose, that you're the miracle man?'

Hiss.

Pause.

And then suck.

For the first time Ben allowed himself to turn and look directly at the man's eyes which were open and still and looking upwards as if towards an impossible place far above.

Hiss.

Pause.

And then suck.

'I come often enough because of Josie, you see, that's how it is when you're married to a saint. You've no choice. You're pulled along as it were, get a bit of a drag into the wake of her goodness you see, and what harm but do a bit of good yourself. Usually you see it's the mints and liquorice with me, and just chatting away because some lads would have no visitors at

146

all and be just sitting there with nothing to do and they'd be happy enough to hear another voice talking and maybe sometimes old lads you wouldn't expect, old lads who you would think would not even be listening to you would suddenly start talking. They would. Many's the time it happened. The next thing you know an old lad would butt in and add his opinion or some memory that had dislodged itself in his mind would come floating along and he'd launch off into some story of his schooldays or the war or something of that class. Indeed. That's the way of it. Many's the time.'

Hiss.

Pause.

And then suck.

'Some lads of course would be quite down in themselves. Down deep, and would be afraid. There's a lot of fear in hospitals. There is. Fear of the body mostly, I'd say, of not getting well and never getting out of here and . . .' Ben caught himself when he realized what he was saying. Though there was not the slightest movement from the man in the bed, the slightest sign that anything Ben said was even heard, he made a grimace of regret and brought the tips of his fingers to his lips as if pressing the words back in.

Ben sat. The man lay there, his eyes wide open, the machines opening and closing his lungs.

Ben was lost. This was a greater challenge than he had imagined.

Hiss.

Pause.

And then suck.

Normally, when he sat at hospital beds, even if the patient didn't seem to be listening, Ben always knew he was *heard*. He could believe that he was making some difference even if there was no sign of it. But here, how could he believe this man in the bed could hear him? It was like talking to the darkness.

Hiss.

Pause.

And then suck.

There was only the struggle in Ben Dack and the noise of the machines.

Then he turned himself in to the bed, and leaned over so he rested his weight on one elbow and could look directly into the still eyes of the man. He looked into them the way a fisherman looked into a deep pool. He brought his face so close that his breath warmed the other, and the smell of his clothes and the very texture of his life could have been felt and been a message of sorts sent across a great distance into the unknown.

And so, near as breath, and looking into the eyes of the man, Ben let his words out like a long line, unravelling down into the still water.

'Mr Carpenter, I am going to be talking, and sometimes I am going to say things I shouldn't and I'm sorry if I hurt your feelings by what I'm saying at any time, 'tisn't my intention, you know that, and Josie will vouch for me there, she'll be the first to tell you it's often Ben Dack says the wrong thing and the words come out of his mouth before he has the brain switched on. But I'll try and do my best as the fella says and I'll come and visit and tell you what's going on if you like and maybe it'll be something. You know. Maybe it'll be worthwhile. There's terrible things going on right now you see, the bomb in London, and others this morning in Paris, and I'll let you know about anything like that, and well, maybe I could drop you in a transistor radio I have and they'd let you have that on too. Because I can only come by on weekends you see. I'd be up and down the country the rest of the time. How does that sound?'

Hiss.

Pause.

And suck.

Ben Dack waited. He expected no response. The response

148

was inside himself. When he was happy that he had heard it, he smiled and leaned back from his closeness to the man in the bed.

'Right so, that's agreed,' he said, and then, looking down at the newspapers, had a sudden thought. 'Now, you know, of course, you're a bit of a celebrity? You are, you are indeed.' He flicked through the pages of a newspaper. 'Hold on, hold on, here we go. "Funeral Cancelled", I like that. "The small village of Killsheen was just coming to terms with the tragic death of its National School principal" – there's a picture of you there, from your driving licence I'd say, not the best but never mind – "when the news broke that he had in fact come back from the dead. 'It was a great shock,' local curate Father Paul said. Duggan's Undertakers had already readied a plot in the graveyard behind the church. A band of young tin whistle players, all taught by the principal, were preparing a guard of honour from the church gates to the main aisle where Mrs Delia Conway, organist, was to lead the village choir in 'Ever with Thee.' A small number of the local Tidy Towns Committee had re-dressed window boxes throughout the main street with pansies and marigolds."'

Ben Dack gave a chuckle and lowered the paper. 'Pansies and marigolds! Would have been a fine thing, your funeral, I'd say. It says here that the bishop might have come, what about that?'

From the figure in the bed there was no response.

'Well, first things first, in the paper here it says that you liked to be called the Master.' Ben smiled again. 'I like that,' he said. 'The Master, it is, so. Nice to meet you, Master.'

Hiss.

Pause.

And suck.

149

NINETEEN

They were on the ground. There were people everywhere on the ground, stirring slightly or lying perfectly still, as though they were no more than leaves taken down in the first sudden arrival of autumn. Everywhere they were scattered, curled men and women and children, forms, figures fallen beneath some force of super-gravity that would not allow them to stand. After the boom the echo resounded in every brain. They had been knocked down by a noise, by the wordless roar of a beast the newspapers called Terror. The sound of the bomb alone had brought two hundred to their knees along the platform, others in the main concourse where the beast had reared were not yet discovered dead. Like a child abandoned and desperate for attention an alarm shrieked. There was smoke and the fizz of live electricity and the strange twisted smell of burning and ammonia travelling through the station as if these were the proclamation that the beast had been present.

The boy was on the ground, the nun beside him.

Shock and fear and a tangle of things that could not be named lay on the ground beside them. They lay in weird poses, lifeless as laundry. Above them neon lights popped. In delayed response glass crashed. Then, as though a switch had been thrown, life returned. From fallen figures there came murmuring, groans and cries. Voices in many languages sounded. The bombed station became suddenly an Everywhere. The world was there and it was wounded badly. A man stood up unaware of the blood coming from his head. Two Japanese girls began to crawl forward. A woman of sixty, her glasses a mad wire bicycle gone over the hill of her nose, pawed the ground for something she had lost.

At last the boy came to himself. He had not been sure whether the bomb had been real or was a dream of the London explosion revisiting his tired mind. When he opened his eyes it was his own hand he saw, and this he looked at for some moments as if it were a piece in a puzzle. It lay inert, a strange thing, outreached and still, the fingers opened for a handshake. *With whom? With what?* His head against the cold of the platform, his brown eyes looked at the hand and nothing else. So intent was his focus in those moments that he might have been one newly arrived on the planet, and never before studied the thing with fingers.

Then he heard his breath. He heard the sound of it somewhere inside the back of his ears. It was the breathing of someone who has run too fast. In the cage of the chest the heart hurts and the air is a hiss and pause and suck and does not seem to be enough. The boy lay, and in the line of his vision above he could no longer make out the last thing he had been looking at, the butterfly shape.

The world flickered back to life in fast-forward. Suddenly there was pandemonium. Passengers were up and running and shouting. A woman was fighting with the spilled contents of her suitcase while a man was dragging her away. Down in the tracks an elderly man was moving towards an open cello case, the instrument some yards further on, the scroll-head broken free and held loosely by the strings. Everywhere people were running, pushing, helping no one. In the main concourse a bomb had exploded. Those on the platforms had been saved.

'Bridget, Sister Bridget, come on.'

'My God.'

'Come on, we have to run.'

The boy took her hand and held it. There were people passing, pushing around them.

Bridget's eyes were opened wide, blue as the sea in sunlight. She was like a clockwork figure or a saint stopped amidst chaos.

'That was a bomb,' she said.

'Yes. Yes, come on, we should get out of here.'

'There will be people who will need help.' She didn't move.

'There could be another bomb.'

'Then it will blow me up,' she said. 'Wait outside for me, directly across the street.'

'I'm not leaving you.'

'Please.'

'No.'

'I have to do something. I can't just walk away.' She spoke with strange calm, her expression remarkably serene, as if just then she had come across a pointer to the meaning of her life. 'Please wait outside for me,' she said again, and then turned from the boy and went to help the old man with his broken cello.

The boy left her. He moved into a concourse where in its aftermath the beast had left hanging banners of thick black smoke, curls and flourishes like writing in a foreign language. There was a blackened hole where a newspaper kiosk had been. There was a glittering floor of glass. Various sirens and alarms rang. Police and firefighters arrived, and only moments after them, television crews. Between the bomb and its reporting were minutes, no more.

He came outside into the streets of Paris for the first time.

For the first time he saw the grey rooftops and the elegant old white-golden buildings. There was an innocent blue sky, poplar trees with glossy leaves shimmering. There might have been birds, there might have been the pastel colours of fashionable men and women strolling, there might have been the light soft music of spoken French. But instead there was only chaos. In the streets cars had been abandoned. Doors were left open, engines running. Drivers who had stayed in traffic pumped their horns to no effect. Their doors locked, their windows shut, they peered from inside the windscreens like insects trapped in a glass. Everywhere people were running. Breathless stragglers cried out after friends who were swifter. Two back-packers with small Dutch flags jogged up the centre of the street like paratroopers. A beautiful woman in a grey suit stood perfectly still and smoked a cigarette, one of her shoes missing.

The boy crossed the street to a bank and looked back at the station.

Don't let it happen. Don't.

He stared his prayer at the building where the smoke hung, a black flag.

Don't let anything happen to her. Are You listening to me?

It was fifteen minutes later when Sister Bridget appeared.

'Oh God, oh dear.' She opened her arms and embraced the boy. 'Are you all right?'

'Yes, yes, I'm fine.'

She held on to him. 'Thank God.' When she let him go there was a new look in her eyes. The boy remarked it; the nun seemed older, but less uncertain. Her hands still on his shoulders she held him back from her. 'Well, strange boy, we are still alive,' she said. 'You've been spared again.'

'Why?'

Bridget couldn't think of an answer. 'Come on.'

The plan had been to take the Métro to Châtelet and then walk, but from beneath the city hundreds had fled into daylight, and the Métro was closed. The streets were brisk with the flux of fear. Down every street, in every direction people were hurrying. It was as if a general announcement had been made and the entire population of the city was now fleeing homeward. In their own homes, with the doors locked, they would feel safe. Sister Bridget reached and clasped the boy's hand. He stiffened, too old to be held like a child.

'For my sake,' she said.

So he allowed it, and they made their way as quickly as possible through the mayhem. Here were mothers racing to get their children from school; here were those emptied from offices; those elbowing and shouldering, ladies carrying high-heels and running barefoot; men in executive suits trying to retain an air of indifference, but hurrying nonetheless. Thousands jammed the mobile phone lines, shimmying between the ranks with phone to ear; here were all the languages of the world, a gabble of words untranslatable except for their tone, urgent and afraid; here at street corners red lights stopped nothing. The crowds flowed on and dispersed and joined with others until it seemed the buildings themselves must give under the pressure of the exodus. Nor was there calm or kindness. With a metallic clanking shutters came down on shop windows. Visions of fine fashions or furniture were shut off, the face of Paris blinded. Salesmen stared momentarily through glass doors at the massed crowds then locked their shops and ran. Alarms rang. In the distance too sounded the church bells. They tolled deep and full and to the boy had a sense medieval, as though they clanged to warn of plague.

He hardly saw the streets they moved through. The broad Boulevard Haussmann was crammed with cars and eddies of people going in many directions.

'All of this from the explosion in the station,' said Sister Bridget, 'it's too much. Something else is happening. There's something going on. All these people. It doesn't quite make sense.'

It was true. The mass moving eastward along the boulevard soon met an equal throng heading west. They pushed through each other. The boy and the nun tried to find a lesser street to take, but soon this too was flowing with people.

Through the district of Le Marais with its elegant old townhouses to the Place de la Bastille, Sister Bridget and the boy hurried hand-in-hand. They had no map, but the boy knew the city from an old Michelin guidebook the Master had given him one time, which like all other books he had devoured and its information now unfolded for him.

'This way, down this one.' He tugged the nun. She had no reason to doubt him.

They crossed the River Seine and entered the narrow crowded streets of the Île Saint Louis. Both sides of the riverbank walks were packed with heads and bodies. Where were they going? Where was there to go? They left the island and entered the Latin Quarter.

'Nearly there, I think.'

'I don't understand. I just don't understand why so many are . . .' Bridget said. She tapped a man's shoulder as he was hurrying past her, 'Why, what is, *qu'est-ce que c'est?*'

He did not stop walking. Over his shoulder, he said, '*Bombe, bombe. Islamique.*' And he hurried on.

'Yes but . . .' Bridget looked at the boy. 'This is madness. I want to tell them all to stop, this is exactly what whoever planted the bomb wants. This is . . .'

'Come on, I think it's this way.'

'But don't people see, this is . . .'

The boy pulled her along, in the crowds and through the crowds, among the French and the Arabs and the Indians and the Chinese and the Asians and the Americans and the Northern and the Eastern Europeans, those from places where bombs were everyday occurrences and those who had never heard a gunshot. He brought her along iron railings to a gate on a small street behind the Panthéon.

There was a small white bell.

'What will you say?'

'That we need somewhere for tonight. They are Sisters of Mercy. We need Mercy.' Bridget smiled thinly. She rang the bell. Soon down an overgrown gravel path a nun in a white habit appeared.

'Pardon Sister,' began Bridget, 'we don't speak Fransay, French. Sister Bridget,' she tapped herself on the chest and let a hand rest on her cross.

The nun opened the gate.

Soon they were inside the stone walls of the convent. Bridget went into a room where she spoke with a nun who could understand her. The boy sat outside. He felt the coolness and calm there, how removed and safe it was from all that was going on outside. In the half-light nuns passed but none spoke, their movements along the stone floors so soft they might not have had bodies.

'We can stay,' Sister Bridget said when she came out. 'They were a little worried about you, but . . .'

'They had Mercy.'

'Exactly.'

They were shown up two flights of stairs where the mustard-coloured paint on the walls flaked and drip-stains of uncertain origin looked like old tears. There were diamond-shapes of lead in the windows. At the end of a long corridor they had small separate cells. They thanked the nun who had brought them and for a moment stood still for the first time since the explosion.

'I am not sure if I should tell you,' Bridget said. 'But of course you will find out anyway.'

'Tell me.'

'There was not just one bomb.'

'No?'

'No. The reason there were so many in the streets is there were bombs in all of the main train stations in a ring around Paris. The Gare du Nord, the Gare St-Lazare, the Gare de l'Est, the Gare d'Austerlitz, and the Gare Montparnasse. All at the same time.'

The nun paused.

'They think there could be hundreds dead,' she told him. In her eyes was unutterable sadness. 'I need to pray,' she said.

TWENTY

When the door closed, the boy stood in the narrow cell. He could almost touch the walls on either side. The window opposite was triangular and through it the boy could see treetops from the small convent garden below. A thin grey blanket covered the simple bed.

A moment after Bridget left, only the stillness and silence struck him, as if these were qualities felt in the air or composed a particular scent within the cell. The boy discovered his heart was racing. Only now did what he had seen and heard and felt in the train station and the streets outside return to him. Up until then there had only been the prime concern of safety, of finding the convent and a place where they could close the door on the world outside. But now, in the first moments inside the tremendous quiet of the convent, the boy's mind threw back to him images of chaos. He sat on the bed.

We were like a herd.
Like nothing mattered but yourself.
People trampling on top of others.
And me too.
He remembered some he had seen fall in the rush. He

159

remembered seeing bodies on the ground in the Gare du Nord. He had just left them there.

I should have stopped. Sister Bridget was right.

I should have tried to help.

But I couldn't.

I couldn't.

On the Boulevard Haussmann had he trod on someone's glasses? What was the crackling beneath his feet that only now came back to him? And that lump, was that, were they, *legs,* he had stepped over? Had he really shoved a woman and pulled someone back when he feared that Bridget's hand was about to let go?

What are we? What am I? How can I be anything when I just cared about myself?

Revulsion rose in his gorge and he gagged once, twice, and stood up sharply thinking he would throw up. He pressed his face to the small opening in the window and sucked in the air.

Breathe. Breathe. O God.

The old glass was cool against his forehead, the Maytime air of Paris impossibly sweet. Birds lined rooftops and watched. The sky was a pale blue, its blueness thinned with white, and in desperation the boy looked to it now as though it were an opaque glass and behind it there might be something. The boy knew the theory of evolution, he knew the order of the great discoveries of the world, he knew of Galileo and of Copernicus and of Kepler and of Newton. He knew of Einstein and also Oppenheimer and had read in library books the exact order and explanation of all that could be explained in the cosmos. He could tell you there were black holes and what they were, inform you of new theories published in *National Geographic*, of gaps in the Time-Space continuum, of cosmic dust, of particle storms. There was little the boy could not tell you, and do it accurately and with a tone not of awe or excitement but matter-of-fact: these things are. He knew. He knew enough to know the cause and effect of so many things, the rational and logical proceedings by which one thing became another. To him it was as if the universe from the very beginning of Time was a vast and elaborate game of Connexions and there was no such thing as mystery or miracle, only a Connexion that had not yet been found in the bottom of the box. He knew all of this. And yet, as he leaned forward against the window and sucked the air and studied the blue-white of the sky, he wanted something else.

He wanted help. He wanted a sign. And he wanted forgiveness.

Birds on the rooftops watched him, that brown-skinned face, one side flat against the glass.

Time passed.

But the sky revealed nothing.

The boy bowed his head and wept. He wept for himself and for the Master. He wept for the warmth and the company and the love he felt for the old man in his worn tweed jacket, he wept for all the memories they had shared together, and for the life they had had in the cottage and that was now gone for ever. He wept for the loss of himself, for the boy he had been and could never be again, and for the place he found himself now where he was neither one thing nor the other. He was neither a boy nor a man. He was this thing with great intelligence but no idea how to use it. What use was it to be smart? What did it matter? The world didn't care but blew up the clever and the foolish alike. The world didn't Connect.

In the cool dim cell the boy held his arms about himself as though he were two people. Very gently he rocked back and forth on the edge of the bed and shut his eyes. The rolling motion was soothing, and made everything slip softly away. It gave him that most ancient first comfort, of being carried by his mother. And as he rocked he had the illusion of travelling so in perfect safety in a world calm and warm and dreamlike.

'You're all right.'

The Master's voice startled him. The boy opened his eyes and saw the familiar figure, looking thinner but otherwise just as he had been.

'This is a small enough place, isn't it? Tidy,' the Master said, as he looked around the cell. He angled himself at the window, then said, 'Well, now, you're all right, that's the main thing.'

'How are you here?'

'I'm always here, J.'

'But you're dead.'

'Now, don't start that. Look, some things don't make sense. That's all.'

The Master scratched at the tuft of his hair and then pressed and patted it with the palm of his hand to no effect. His face crinkled. 'I made a terrible mistake with you, you know.'

'What?'

'You see, you were a smart little fellow. Right from day one. And your mum was smart too of course. And, well, because I was the Master in the school everyone expected that you would be brighter somehow than anyone else. Having the benefit of me, you see, twenty-four hours, as it were. Which of course is all nonsense, but people are people and will think what they think. In any case, with you, you were special straight away. I believe if you were born into a house where there was not a book or a newspaper that your intelligence would have found a way to knowledge. That's just the way, like a spring rising in the ground and the water finding a route. But anyway, I went the other way. I brought home the books. I let you find out everything. And as you grew you knew everything. More than anyone I know. Including myself. But I neglected everything else.'

162

'What else?'

'What doesn't fit. What makes no sense. Like this, like me being here.'

The boy looked at the old man and wanted to be held against his chest.

'There's more in the world than can be explained,' said the Master, 'you're finding that out now.'

'Why am I alive?'

'Exactly.'

'That's not an answer.'

'Sometimes finding the right question is more important than finding the answer.'

'If there is God why is He letting this happen? If there is Allah why is He letting this happen? Are we just alone?'

Outside the door to the cell, Sister Bridget raised her hand to knock, and then heard the boy talking. He asked a question, and then paused as though listening to an answer. Then she heard him ask another. She stayed fifteen minutes listening while the boy interrogated the air. She did not hear any other voice.

'God help us,' she murmured. Then she went away.

TWENTY-ONE

Later that evening Sister Bridget returned to the boy's cell with a tray of food. From the corridor outside she could hear music. The low sad notes of a slow air sounded, and once she had realized that it was the boy playing his flute, she hesitated to disturb him. She waited some time, listening. The music escaped from behind the heavy wooden door and floated in the dim spaces of the convent corridor. It was music old as Ireland and in the haunting of its melody impossible not to imagine the hills and fields, the green and dripping places, the mucked corners behind the hedgerows where the cattle stood for shelter, the lone hare running. She had listened in a kind of dream until the boy ended the air, then she knocked.

'You play very well,' she said, bringing in the tray and trying to appear as though everything was still normal in the world.

'The Master taught me,' said the boy.

'He taught you very well.'

'When I play it I think of him.'

'Of course.' Bridget paused. She was not sure if the boy wanted to say more. She watched as he put the flute on the bed. 'I am sorry to have disturbed you,' she said, 'but I wanted to make sure you had some food. I thought it would be a little awkward for you to come down and join all the nuns in the refectory, so, here's the best of what's on offer.'

She handed him the tray.

'Are you all right?' the boy asked.

'Oh yes, I'm fine.'

'You seem different.'

'Do I?'

'Sort of.'

'Well, I suppose we may all be a bit different from now on. It's been a shock. I'm not sure any of us can really take in what's happening. But yes, maybe I'm asking myself lots of questions now.'

'Like what?'

'Like what I should be doing.' Bridget looked directly at the boy, but didn't say more. She didn't say that his being at the scene of two bombings had struck her as more than weird coincidence, that she felt his vulnerability and had a sense of her inadequacy as a white knight protecting him. She didn't say that in her mind now was a grey legion of fears, moving stealthily forward to the place where she could become paralysed and able to do nothing. Against them she fought silently, erecting barriers of hope and resolve. She was filled with concern for all, but especially for him, for this boy who had again come so close to death. About him there was mystery. She shrugged. 'For now the main thing is that we are fine and safe here,' she said. 'You should eat and get some sleep. We'll talk in the morning.'

Bridget closed the cell door carefully behind her and went downstairs. She did not want to eat, and instead made her way to a small lounge where she had seen a television. There in the company of a semi-circle of silent nuns she watched the news with a kind of grim fascination. How unbelievable it seemed. How hard it was to accept that this was real, that just beyond the gates of the convent there was this chaos, that there was the Gare du Nord, the Gare d'Austerlitz, smoke billowing from them. She watched the strange collage of amateur video, news-reporters, studio experts, analysts, and reruns of the explosions. She and the other nuns watched without comment. They sat the way people sit watching a film where the plot has such a hold that no one dares rise from their seat, where the question is, *How will it end?*

Only this is not a film, this is how it is.

There was a report from London, but it was in French and Bridget could not understand it. There were faces of Asian men shown, but she was not sure whether these were suspects or had been killed. There was footage from an Arabic television station and what appeared to be a statement from a group of Islamic extremists claiming responsibility. Then back to the shots of the explosions on closed circuit television. They were shown over and over again. Each time they were repeated it was as if some desperate effort was being made to establish to the unbelieving that this had actually happened. Look, it seemed to say, we will show you again. Here is the bomb going off, here are the crowds running through the streets of Paris. Here are the fallen, the injured and the dead. Here are shots of ambulances racing. Here is footage shot from a shoulder-held camera as our reporter is running for his life, you can hear the screams and the sirens. Here are the professors explaining it all, the ones from the Centres for Cultural Studies, the ones from the Institute for Studies in Contemporary Terrorism. And again, here are the train stations exploding from a different angle. We leave you with this image as we go to a commercial break.

The nuns sit silent as stones.

When the broadcast returns they hear the frantic garbled words of eyewitnesses. Here behind the head of a woman is a camera shot of smoke rising sinisterly. While she speaks the director cuts to a helicopter view of the pandemonium in the streets where the people seem like insects. Then there is a government spokesman urging calm, but his eyes seem fearful and his hands keep rising into the screen as though hopelessly fanning at flames. There is a head of police in uniform, then some sort of medical officer, and a phone number for enquiries about the injured and the dead. The city is under attack, Bridget understands one of the men to say. And then the broadcast is back to amateur shots of the bombs exploding once more. The nuns watching seem not to realize they have seen all there is to see, and they stay in their seats to watch it again. Perhaps they still do not believe this is what has happened outside the railings of their convent. Perhaps their seclusion is so great that the television screen shows them another world entirely, one they have prayed does not exist. And so perhaps the images of the bombing, of the cruelty and intolerance and hatred *out there,* shatter the stone-like certainty of their faith that God is good and like a wide-winged angel looking down benignly on the world.

Sister Bridget sat for an hour and then rose and slipped away without a word. She went through the cool stone corridors to the small chapel she had seen off the main hallway. She bowed and blessed herself and went inside. The pews were empty. Through stained-glass windows thin coloured light fell. She knelt not far from the altar and prayed.

As always, she prayed as though God were a personal friend, as though He were right beside her, kneeling too and listening to every word.

I know You know what is happening. I know to You it must make sense. It must have meaning, but I am lost. Help me to understand. What am I supposed to do? I am afraid. I am not able for this. I am Sister Bridget, You know, the one who thought You wanted her to save the world one time, and then You got her that job in Birmingham. So, I think maybe now You knew best, and yet here I am with this boy on this hopeless search and I don't know, I don't know if this is what

I am meant to be doing or not, and I don't know why these bombings are happening now and I am in the dark. I am just in such dark. I need Your help. Please God.

Silently she said the last words, and then she bowed her head and waited for her friend to help her.

She did believe He was there. She did believe that praying was the word for talking to God, only that He did not pray back. He communicated in other ways, for as Mother Clare had said once, 'He has all the languages of the world, and I mean also those of light, of shadow, of sunrise, of sunset, of music and laughter. Tell me you haven't heard Him in autumn trees, in April rain, in Mozart.' It was something Bridget always remembered. The old nun's face in a thousand wrinkles and her small green eyes twinkling. 'I have even heard Him in an abundance of blackberries,' the wise nun added, bringing her tiny twig-like fingers to her mouth and making a small bird-like laughter.

So, as Bridget knelt in the small chapel in Paris, she listened for responses in all languages. She looked at the statues on the altar, she looked at the Christ hanging on the cross. She looked at the fresh flowers that had been picked that morning arranged in two vases either side of the tabernacle. There was absolute silence. The last light faded, and the stained-glass windows darkened. Before a statue of Saint Francis, in two small metal trays, a few tea-candles burned. Their flames were perfectly still.

Bridget waited.

I know You are there.

I know You are listening to me.

She kept her eyes on the flames now. She stared at them and willed them to move. She wanted even the slightest flicker. Anything could be a sign.

I am really lost.

Help me.

169

I am afraid.

Help me.

Above the candles the figure of Saint Francis had his arms reaching outwards. On his right hand there was a small bird. On the saint's face there was the thinnest smile, the smile of knowing. The saint in his statue seemed to be saying he understood the place of everything in the world, even this small bird. Of all things in the chapel Bridget felt her attention drawn there. She watched the statue for a sign, she watched the candles to see if they would flicker.

Anything.

Please.

The chapel was still and silent as a tomb, the world outside far away. Perhaps an hour passed. Or perhaps longer. It didn't matter. It didn't matter, for Bridget's devotion was such that she did not notice the movement of time there. It might have been one of those scenes in the small hours of the morning, when great friends sit in each other's company, quiet and comfortable and awake on the island of their own friendship. Only Bridget wanted the quiet to pass. She wanted counsel. From her friend she wanted a sign, and so she waited. She waited with her hands held together in a pose of beseeching. She watched the candles burning, the saint's face. She waited so long she forgot herself. She forgot her own body and where she was and the events that had brought her there. She forgot her past, her family. All slipped away from her in the chapel.

She did not know how long it was before the pain in her knees returned her to the real world. They were locked and caused agony and she let out a groan trying to sit up. She rubbed them gingerly, and looked over at Saint Francis.

'Easy for you,' she said. She blessed herself and stood up. The candles had not moved. There had been no visible sign.

TWENTY-TWO

In the morning the boy was awake and sitting on his bed writing in his journal when Sister Bridget arrived with a breakfast of coffee and a length of baguette. She was wearing a nun's habit, and at first the boy was struck by how different she appeared, as though he had forgotten she was a Sister of Mercy.

'Well,' she asked, 'how did you sleep?'

'I dreamed someone was after me. They wanted me dead.'

'Did you see their face?'

'No,' said the boy. 'I think it was God.'

The nun was startled. 'It couldn't be,' she told him, 'you don't believe in Him.'

The boy shrugged. 'That's true,' he said. 'Maybe it was you He was after.'

He sipped at the bitter strong coffee and scowled.

'Nuns' brew,' Bridget apologized. 'So?'

'So?'

'So have you thought about maybe going back?'

'I am not going back.' He tried the coffee again. 'If you want to you can. I can go on by . . .'

'Things are not the same as they were. Everywhere is more

171

dangerous now. I watched the television last night. The world is . . .' Bridget searched for an adequate phrase.

'At war with itself.'

'Well . . .'

'It is. I know it is. But there is nowhere for me to go back to. I'm going on.'

'There must be. You must have friends who will be missing you.'

'I have no friends.'

Something in the way the boy said this made Bridget bite her lower lip. She knew he was going on and she knew she was going with him. 'From what I understand of the news,' she said, 'there are over two hundred people dead. They say they thought Paris would be safe. They thought because of its politics, and because there is a large Muslim population here on the outskirts of the city, because they have lived here peacefully a long time, they didn't think . . .well, things are out of control now.'

'Do they have a computer?'

'What?'

'The convent here, do they have Internet?'

'Yes, I think, in the small library off the main hall.'

'Can I use it?'

Bridget hesitated. She knew the Mother Superior did not want the boy moving about in the convent, that it was a condition of their sheltering them.

'There is Mass at ten,' she said. 'When all the nuns are there, you can slip down and use it. Be back here in forty minutes. Let nobody see you.' She unsnapped the small buckle at her wrist and handed the boy her watch.

'Where will you be?' he asked her.

'Praying to God for you.'

* * *

At ten o' clock exactly, the boy opened the heavy cell door and stepped out into the flagstone corridor. He let the weight of the door take it gently back into place, and then he moved away like a thief, stepping softly, prepared at any moment to run. Down the stairs he heard the faint murmuring of voices from within the chapel. The prayers were like the low hum of an engine, a secret force in the heart of the city. Quickly he slipped past. He made his way into the front hallway and saw the sign 'Bibliothèque'.

The library was pentagonal, with a centre space where chairs and tables were arranged for reading and study. There were rows upon rows of ancient books in French and other languages. It was the kind of place the boy would have loved to spend a day, many days in fact, browsing the shelves, opening books and trying to read even in languages he couldn't understand. He would have loved just being in the presence of all that knowledge. He would have loved the feeling you would get from such company, the feeling that here was the wisdom of the world, here were the stilled and profound minds of serious men and women who had considered things as they were and then written of them. In such a place he would have felt hope for the world. He would have felt the books were a proof of a kind, a testament to things continuing in some way since the very beginning of time, since the first words were scratched out as witness to wonder and beauty.

But now the boy had no such time. He went to the single computer on a small desk. It was turned on. On the screen was an image of the face of Christ and across it was written the name of the convent and its address and a motto in Latin. The boy sat and moved the mouse and found the icon to connect. He clicked and when the window came up for the password it was already asterisked. He clicked again and the computer connected to the Web. The homepage was the Sisters of Mercy worldwide. The boy brought down a search engine and in the white space he typed: AHMED SHARIF and clicked 'GO'.

On Sister Bridget's watch it was ten minutes after ten. They were not yet at the Offertory, he thought. And at once he recalled the last time he had been to Mass and the image of the failed Confirmation came back to him in all its humiliation. He felt his face redden with anger. He stared at the screen while the hour-glass symbol turned.

At last it stopped. Under 'Ahmed Sharif' four thousand entries were listed.

The boy's breath was taken away. At the back of his neck a chill ran. And just when he should have clicked on the first one, just as he had suddenly come this close to the man he was looking for, he hesitated. He stared away across the top of the screen, unable to move on. He stared at the shelves, the ranks of books that explored all aspects of Christianity, of the relationship between man and the divine as it was understood in that order of nuns, and he was as if bound round and round with invisible threads. He couldn't move. In his head, pulsing, was the name of the man he sought, but the screen was an enormous doorway and across its threshold the boy could not advance.

What will there be?
What will I find if I click now?
Ahmed Sharif. What if Ahmed Sharif is ...
What?
What are you afraid of?
The boy sat perfectly still. He knew the answer:
Yourself.

And ten minutes passed. If in the chapel Bridget was praying for him there was no evidence of assistance or guidance. He felt as alone then as he had on the road on the first night. He felt his loneliness like a suffocating cloak thrown about his shoulders; it was something he could not cast off and while

174

within it none could reach him. It was his burden. He sat and began to twist slightly in the seat, then more so, avoiding something sharp inside him, as though he had swallowed the broken pieces of the mirror of himself.

You have to.

You have to.

Do it.

At last he turned back to the screen. Many of the entries were in French and he had to work at understanding what they might be. He moved his hand to the mouse and scrolled slowly, then clicked one in English. The seconds it took to arrive on the screen were a kind of hyper e-chase, a flickering pursuit through unlit zillions of bytes, vast info-domains where none could hide from the searing brilliance of the search. From the numberless legions of the world's known people the engine of detection tracked down its prey, it corralled a million like-named, and then in nano-instants portioned these and these again until there, into the light was thrown the exact one.

'THE BEGINNING OF THE END' was the title, an article by Ahmed Sharif, dated three months earlier. Beneath the headline in brackets it read: 'This article was turned down for publication by *The Times* of London, who commissioned it, and subsequently by various other newspapers. It was posted on the WorldWideWeb by the author; the views expressed are his alone.'

In time to come, when histories are written, I believe it will be clear that the Third World War began in the first years of the twenty-first century. It began, the historians will say, in small cramped apartments on the outskirts of the great cities of the world. In London, in Paris, in Berlin and Rome, as well as in New York and Chicago, in Washington, in Sydney and Singapore. In the city nearest you as you read these words there are some already engaged in this war. The army of the aggressor wears no uniforms, has no national flag, and does not covet any foreign land. It is an army that is all but invisible; its various battalions do not gather on hillsides and face the enemy. No generals sit on white horses, or in armoured cars with maps and co-ordinates. It is an army whose various divisions do not even know each other, whose soldiers may pass each other in the street, roll trolleys through the same supermarket aisles, without the slightest inkling of their allegiance. For it is an army of belief, of believers.

To witness first-hand what is happening in the world, to understand, I have lived for long periods of time with people who believe their god wants them to destroy the West. I will not reveal their names or where they live. Some of them have already gone to what they believe is an everlasting afterlife of bliss. Some of them have been my friends.

For the journalist there is only the responsibility to tell what is, to say, this I have seen. Below are accounts of life with various groups I have lived with over the last three years. All of them were difficult to infiltrate and required months, and in some cases years, of pretence. I did so because I wanted to know why. Why did some people hate others so much? Why would they kill themselves and men and women and children on buses, in trains, and in bars and restaurants?

Perhaps I have the beginnings of answers. I have found too an understanding. But I fear I have also found something else, the beginning of the end of a way of life, an end to freedoms taken for granted. There is coming a time when armed police will ride on buses, when you will be stopped on the street and searched, when cameras will be installed at every corner and we will live in a prison world.

Almost certainly, within a short time, there will commence a wave of bombings across Europe. And this will be followed by or simultaneous with similar explosions in America, and elsewhere in the world. I believe this is inevitable, for we have entered a time now when a war has begun, not for the territory of another man, not for his physical freedom, but for what – even as an unbeliever – I would call the soul of the world.

There were footsteps. The boy heard them too late. They were just beyond the door. He had no time to disconnect but threw himself to one side so he was below the desk as the door to the library opened. The footsteps approached. He did not breathe. He heard the soft swish of a nun's habit, the rubber-soled shoes. She stood before the computer and read the screen and then the boy heard the click of disconnection.

But she did not leave. The nun went to one of the rows of shelves and after some moments took down a book. Then she sat with it at a small table nearby.

The boy did not dare to move. He feared that if he was found they might be asked to leave the shelter of the convent. He was a boy who had grown up fearing to do anything that was wrong. He had from his first day in school worked so carefully with his pencil that there was never the possibility of a mistake, never was anything crossed out, and the pages of his copies became a series of endless correct ticks like so many one-winged birds flying to the right. Now, since the evening he had run away, he was learning a different way of living. What was right and wrong was not so easy to know any more. And if, in the deeps of his identity, he could sense that the reason he had wanted always to be right was for fear the Master would think less of him if he was wrong, that he would lose a little love, then now no such response was possible. The Master was dead. Love was gone.

But still he did not move. He breathed thinly and clung to his knees. Through his head fizzed the words he had read. They offered a version of the world the boy had not considered. They were like the opening of a science-fiction story, a telling that seemed both real and far-fetched at the same time.

Do people really gather in secret meetings all over the world?

Is there really this splintered army that cannot be stopped?

And what have I and everyone else done that was so wrong that all these people want us dead?

And are those the words of my father?

Beneath the desk the boy lay curled about the thorns of these questions.

An hour passed.

At one stage he heard another set of footsteps enter the library and Sister Bridget's voice say '*Excusez-moi*' in Irish-accented French, but he didn't dare reveal himself and she went away again.

It was not until the bells rang for noon that the nun put up her book and left. The boy uncoiled himself. He wanted to read more, but knew that now was not the time, and instead made his way stealthily back along the corridors to his cell.

'Where were you? I was going frantic.' Bridget's face was a pink bloom of anxiety. 'Thank God I am not a mother, that's all I can say, because my heart couldn't take it.' She sighed and sat on the bed and the boy felt sorry for her. 'I knew that at least you hadn't gone away,' she said, 'because you left your flute and your bag, but . . .'

'I'm sorry,' he said. 'I was trapped in the library. There was a nun. I heard you come in.'

He stood beside her.

'Well?' Bridget asked. 'Did my prayers work?'

'That depends.'

'Tell me.'

And so the boy did. He told her almost word for word what he had read and watched the pink fade out of her face.

He told her of the many entries under the name 'Ahmed Sharif' and how from what he understood he spent long periods of time living with people who planned to set off bombs.

'But he doesn't stop them? He doesn't do anything about it?' Bridget said angrily. 'He does nothing but write about it? Make money off it!' She couldn't stop herself. The frustration of everything suddenly sparked into flame in her eyes. 'I think that's dreadful. I'm not surprised the newspapers wouldn't publish it. What is he doing, he's spreading terror. Spreading their message. That's as bad as anything else. They must be delighted with him.'

The boy's face flushed brightly. 'That's not fair!'

'Why is it not fair, it's exactly what he's doing!'

'He's telling what he thinks. That's all. He's a journalist. He's telling the truth.'

'It's not as simple as that. Some truths you don't tell.'

'That's stupid.'

Bridget had got up from the bed and was pacing, her hands making fists of annoyance. 'It's not stupid, there's responsibility. Responsibility for what you say and how it affects others. And especially in a time like this when everything is so sensitive, when everything can be set off by someone preaching terror and . . .'

'He's not preaching. He's not a liar, he's telling the truth, and I believe him! He's my father!' The boy shouted and Bridget stopped at once and saw the blaze of indignation and hurt in his face. She shut her eyes tightly and shook her head.

'I'm so sorry,' she said, 'so much for Christian example.'

There was an injured moment, the boy's eyes dark with pride and puzzlement.

'I'm going to go back there tonight and read more,' he said.

Bridget swallowed a sudden reply. Then very gently she answered, 'I'm not sure you should.'

'I have to.'

She sighed, aware that she was to press on a bruise. 'Maybe,' she softened her tone further still, 'maybe you shouldn't even try and find this man any more. I mean, what chance have you got? He could be anywhere in the world.'

'I know.'

'I am sorry,' Bridget said, 'but, well, how could you possibly find him?'

There was a silence between them. It was as if a great rock had fallen into the room and opened an enormous hole. If you looked down you risked falling for ever.

The boy took some time. He felt the nun's eyes upon him searching, then he said, 'The same way you believe the camel goes through the eye of the needle, or something like that. I believe it because it seems impossible.'

TWENTY-THREE

When the convent was asleep, and in the cool dark of the corridors there moved only dreams, the boy slipped from his cell and returned to the library. Against her own judgement, Sister Bridget accompanied him and stood guard at the doorway.

Dear God help me. What am I doing? Shouldn't I be showing guidance here? Should I be protecting him from this? Dear God, You have to make Your messages more clear to me. I am not that good at reading them at present. Think of me as a religious slow-learner. You have to spell it out. What should I be doing?

Sister Bridget shut her eyes tightly, as if this might make the prayer go faster, or the answer more clear.

I am standing here letting him read the most appalling articles on the evil in the world. Is that right? Shouldn't I be stopping him? Shouldn't I be telling him it's all a lie, that everything will be all right? That this is just a few bad weeks and soon it will all be forgotten? Every other child comes to Paris and sees the sights, sees the beautiful city, goes to EuroDisney, and buys souvenirs.

She felt a sudden wave of nostalgia for a more innocent time. She glanced over at the boy at the computer, his head leaning forward towards the screen, the page scrolling slowly, and who knew what entering his head.

You could make the electricity blow out as a sign. I could read that. You could make the mouse lock and the computer break down. That would do. Then I'd know.

The boy read on, and the nun found no relief from the briary tangle of emotions inside her. She felt she was betraying the world. She felt the sick feeling all feel when they know that, however small, they are destroying a portion of innocence.

But this boy is not innocent. This boy was never innocent. There is something about him. When you look in his eyes you think the world is bound to hurt him. You think: what can I do to protect him? But there is nothing.

At the door she stood. Spirits and dreams travelled past her but nothing that made a sound. Across from her a narrow window gave on to the rooftops of Paris. There were small lights burning. It looked no different, she imagined, to how it had looked two days ago. But she knew it was. Fear and sorrow were everywhere out there now, and huddled in their homes Parisians were watching over again images of smoke and police-tape, firefighters and ambulances.

As she watched over the rooftops of the city Bridget felt little beyond grief and hopelessness.

I am lost. Dear my Lord, where are You?

What is happening to the world? I have no idea what I am supposed to do.

Are we all lost? O God, please help.

In her mind there was darkness.

Then the boy touched her shoulder. 'Come on,' he whispered, 'let's go back.'

'Are you finished?'

'For tonight,' he said, 'the computer kept getting stuck and I had to keep shutting it down and restarting it.'

* * *

182

The next day neither boy nor nun left the convent. During ten o'clock Mass he again made his way to the library. He read more of the articles by Ahmed Sharif. He read of terror cells around the world, and accounts of men now dead. He read voraciously, and in the click and scroll of the screens there was no obstacle or censor. Everything could be found out. From the boy's eyes nothing was hidden, and he was hindered only by the shortness of the time.

He returned to his cell just as the Sisters were leaving the chapel. Bridget came and said the city was too dangerous for them.

'Besides,' she said, 'we have no plan, have we? We may as well stay quietly here.'

The boy nodded. He could tell there was another reason; he knew she was afraid of his seeing the bombed places and of the trauma he might feel, and was considering how she would convince him to return to Ireland.

'So, will you be all right here? I'll bring you some food later.'

Again he nodded. His mind was like the site of a multiple car crash. In it everything was broken.

Bridget left him. In his journal the boy wrote, but his sentences seemed garbled and in fragments. For the first time in a very long while he did not know what to write; he did not know what he thought. He put the pen and journal aside. He lay on the bed for half an hour, then sat up and took up the flute and played a portion of a slow air poorly, then stopped that as well.

He sat on the edge of the thin bed. About him the convent was utterly still.

He thought of the Master and the thought was like an ache in his side.

I want to see you.

I want you to be here.

I want you to tell me what to do.

183

Time moved slowly onward, and the Master made no appearance, and the boy mocked himself for thinking like a child and went and stood and stared out of the small window at nothing.

'Everything is destroyed,' he said.

When in the early afternoon Bridget brought him his tray he was sitting again on the edge of the bed and looking intently down in front of him, like a player in the middle of a chess game.

'Chicken, I think,' she said, taking a sniff.

But the boy did not respond.

'Chicken,' she tried again, 'all right?'

'I will be going back into the library tonight.'

'What? Well, I don't think that's such a good idea is it? I mean what can you find out there only, you know . . . things that are . . . well, you see, I'm not sure a boy your age should be . . .' Her words trailed off as she approached the difficulty she had.

'I read this morning there were riots in England against Muslims because of the bombing,' said the boy quietly.

'Well, that's exactly the kind of thing I mean.'

'You cannot hide the world from me.'

'No, but you don't need to know everything either. Do you? I mean what good did that piece of knowledge do you? None I'd say.'

'I want to know.'

'Yes, but . . .' Bridget's expression twisted, it was a complex case. 'Knowledge doesn't always lead to understanding.'

'What do you think I don't understand?' the boy asked irritably.

'No, I'm not saying . . . I know you are a very clever boy . . .'

'I hate that phrase, very clever boy.'

'I'm sorry.'

'I have to go to the library. If I can't go here I will leave and find some other place to get on the Internet.' The boy paused. He knew he was being more forceful and direct with an adult than he ever had been before. 'It's my only hope,' he said, 'my only clue.'

And in a moment Sister Bridget left him to the boiled chicken and went away.

Silence fell over the cell again. The boy ate what he didn't like because he was seized by hunger. Afterwards he thought to pass some of the long wait until evening by reading the one book he had brought with him. He took out the copy of *David Copperfield* and opened it at the passage where David brings his school friend Steerforth to visit the warm Peggotty family in their houseboat down by the sea. He read:

> Mr Peggotty, his face lighted up with uncommon satisfaction, and laughing with all his might, held his rough arms wide open, as if for little Em'ly to run into them; Ham, with a mixed expression in his face of admiration, exultation, and a lumbering sort of bashfulness that sat upon him very well, held little Em'ly by the hand, as if he were presenting her to Mr Peggotty; little Em'ly herself, blushing and shy, but delighted with Mr Peggotty's delight, as her joyous eyes expressed, was stopped by our entrance (for she saw us first) in the very act of springing from Ham to nestle in Mr Peggotty's embrace.

But for the first time since he had started reading the books of Charles Dickens, the words seemed somehow silly, and the story too contrived and unreal. He could not keep his attention on it. Who were these people and what did it matter what happened? Why should he spend his time reading about them now? The boy fought against an inner voice and tried to read on, to blot out the world and escape inside a good chapter of one of the greatest books ever written.

But it was no use. He read a sentence and then another

and another and realized he had no idea what any of it meant.

Then he did what he would never have done before. He took the book and fired it through the air so it crashed against the far wall and fell like a shot bird to the floor.

It was not yet three o'clock in the afternoon. The boy had nine hours to wait. He sat on the edge of the bed. He put his hands on his knees and leaned forward and stared at the invisible chess game.

'If it gets stuck tonight, you're to stop, all right? We'll say it's a sign, agreed?' Bridget's voice was an urgent whisper as they entered the library.

'It's a sign it's an old machine,' the boy said.

'Yes but, agreed, all right? For my sake?'

The boy nodded reluctantly and left her to go and sit by the computer.

Now You've no excuse. Dear God make it get stuck if You think You should. Thank You. Yours sincerely, Your friend, Bridget.

She stood by the door and listened for footsteps. Behind her she heard only the soft clicking of the computer as the boy went further and further into the Web.

An hour passed.

'Well?' she whispered over to him. 'Is it not getting stuck?'

'No.'

Bridget took a stool from one of the tables and placed it just inside the open doorway. *Whenever You are ready, Lord,* she thought. And another hour passed.

That afternoon while the boy was in his room she had slipped out into the city and found an English newspaper. In the aftermath of the London bombing all manner of experts had offered opinions why such a thing had happened. Most said they had predicted it. Many referred to policies on immigration, and some

186

of the more extreme called for a ban on Asians entering the country. There were reports of crude late-night attacks on members of Muslim communities in various cities. There were photographs of small shops with windows smashed and slogans daubed upon them. The more Bridget had read the lower her spirits had sunk. In only a few days the world she knew seemed changed utterly. And yet, there was an eerie familiarity. She remembered from her own first days in England some of the nuns telling her how it was to be Irish there when the IRA were conducting a bombing campaign. How an Irish voice overheard was enough to bring insult or beery challenge. And now here it was again, a time of hatred, only much worse. In the small hours of the night she sat on the stool and did what she considered best when faced with the mystery of how things were. She prayed. She prayed old prayers, for herself and for the boy and for there to come some sign, some fragment of hope.

The boy tapped her shoulder.

'Are you asleep?'

She jumped. 'I'm not asleep.'

'Shsh.'

'I am shsh. Well, is it stuck?'

'I can't read any more. In all the articles, in every piece there is not a single photograph of him.'

'No?'

'No. Nor is there any mention of Ireland.'

'Maybe he was never there.'

'Maybe.'

She could see the defeat in the boy's eyes. He hung his head. Silently they made their way back to the cells.

'You should sleep now,' Bridget said, 'you are very tired.'

He looked at her. 'I can't sleep. I have bad dreams.'

She held his shoulder and felt how thin it was. 'Well, what would the Master want you to do now?'

'The Master believed things worked out.'

'Well there you are.'

'He also called himself a fool. Very often. And he also died in a car crash.'

Bridget let her arm fall. The air was full of bruises.

'He mentions a place.'

'What?'

'In one of the articles he mentions a place just outside Paris. It's the mosque. He hints at meetings there.' The boy paused. 'I want to go tomorrow.'

'No!' Bridget said sharply. 'No. I don't think so. Really, it's dangerous. It's bound to be dangerous. And why? He's not going to be there. There's no need for you to . . .'

'You don't understand.'

'I do. I do understand, but . . .'

'I have to go there. Then maybe to Germany, to Berlin.'

Bridget's jaw dropped. 'Berlin?'

'In an article he writes about an apartment building there. He uses a code to hide its name but I think I have it figured out.' He looked at her with defiance and triumph.

'But no. No no no. There may be more bombings.'

'Yes, I know. There will be,' said the boy, 'maybe many, and then in Rome. And Madrid. Where the bombs are, that's where he has been.'

'But he will be gone. Don't you see? Even if he was there he won't be still.'

'That doesn't matter.' The boy looked at her, his dark eyes filled with exasperation. 'It doesn't have to make sense,' he said. 'Nothing makes sense. Have you never done something that didn't make sense, that was just . . . because you had to do something, because it's . . . I can't explain. Just . . . It's what I have to do. Don't you see?'

He paused. Then he said, 'For me there is nothing else.' And it was as if on the floor between them he had dropped an unliftable stone.

TWENTY-FOUR

Ben Dack came running. With his newspaper rolled he came breathlessly along the corridor, his face red and his eyes popped forward with news. At the door to the darkened ward he paused and let the hammering ease in his heart. Then he could delay no longer and pushed forward the heavy door and stepped inside. Cool air and the soft sounds of the machines met him. He drew the chair close to the bed. He patted the lifeless hand of the Master.

'Well I have never been accused of being clever,' he began. 'Not a chance. If it wasn't for Josie, we'd still be none the wiser. That's the thing. That's the thing saved Ben Dack from life in permanent foolishness, Josie Mary Plunkett. She's the one says to me, "Ben, is that the boy? The boy you told me about. Because he's the one missing from that man the Master. He's the one they can't find. Do you see?" And clap,' Ben Dack clapped his right hand on his small round forehead, 'the brain kicked in, just like that, and I said give me a look there. And she passed me the paper and though the photo wasn't the best, I'll grant myself that, I'll grant myself I might have seen it and had I not been thinking – which Josie says is a fair bit of the time – I might not have twigged it. But no, fair is fair, it was him.'

189

Ben paused as though to catch up with himself. He nodded at what he had told so far. No inch of the Master moved. Through the gap in the bandages his eyes remained lifelessly staring, his breath hissed and paused and sucked with the machines.

'And of course everybody knew. Everybody knew that day you were dead – not that you were as it happened – but well, when the crash happened, everybody was looking for him, the boy, to tell him. And he couldn't be found. And then the newspapers had the story of his running off on the morning of his Confirmation, that something had got into him. And that he hadn't been seen since. They had the police over watching the house in case he . . . but no, he didn't. And he was just The Missing Boy in all the papers, and still I didn't twig it. I didn't because you see as Josie says Ben Dack doesn't put two and two together. Ben Dack has his own sums, Ben Dack can add two and two and get four hundred and four. And to that I says fair enough, but. But Josie,' he raised a fat finger in his defence. 'Sometimes I can have four hundred and four and see where the two and two came from. Do you see?'

The Master was not impressed by this pupil. All stayed perfectly still. But Ben Dack was not put off.

'So, anyway,' he said. 'Where was I? Yes, I saw the photograph and twigged it was the boy. "You're right," I says. "By Jingo you're right. That is the boy I gave the lift to. That is the one I brought to Dublin in the lorry," I says. And Josie is up before me and holding out the keys. "Come on," says she, "we've got to tell the police." And quick as a flash we're down in the station and I'm waiting in a line of sad-looking people – you never think what the world's troubles are, do you? – you never think when you're home in your sitting-room watching the telly that right then someone is waiting in a queue at a police station with the world of troubles. Well there they were. One woman crying her eyes out and Josie went over

190

and held her hand. Just that. Held her hand, and soon enough the crying became sobs and that became shudders kind of, and by stages like, like there was a ladder or something, back to courage, back to being able to carry on, the woman stopped altogether. Josie, boy she's a saint. Did I tell you?

'Well, where was I? Oh yes, the station, and eventually there's this big guard calls us forward. Big slow wave of the hand like that. And then he's flattening down a fresh page of his ledger and picking up the pen to write whatever it is we're going to tell him. "Name?" says he. "Address?" says he. "You'll want to hear this," says Josie. "Address?" says he, not lifting his big head. The kind of fellow he was. And Josie patience of a, well, you know, she holds her whist and tells him the address.

'"Nature of problem?" he asks.

'"Nature of problem?" says I. "Boy."

'"Missing boy," says Josie.

'And what does he do but write that down. Big slow writing. Nice and cool he was. No excitement at all.

'"Missing since?" The fellow's head didn't raise an inch. Didn't so much as show the slightest interest. No, he wasn't connecting the dots, do you see? Though there was this countrywide search for this one missing boy since you di – since your crash – and still this fellow when he heard "missing boy" didn't. Well, the world is full of Liquorice Allsorts, as Josie says. And as he's paused to write the answer to "missing since?" doesn't Josie see a poster of the same boy in Confirmation jacket and tie right behind him and on it the date. So she asks the policeman to stand a little to one side and he kind of looks at her and then around at the poster she is pointing to.

'You see Josie can make her point all the same. Indeed she can.

'"That's the boy?" says he.

'"That's the boy."

'"You're sure?"

'"Certain."

'"Wait here, don't go away."

'"Why would we go away when we just came here?"Josie whispered to me. And I gave a bit of a chuckle. I did. She can have an edge, do you see, a little edge. I like that in Josie.

'Anyway back comes this fellow and a sergeant with him, and we're brought in this bright room and that's where I tell them I gave a lift to this boy and dropped him in Dublin by the docks. And they take down a full description and of course the sergeant asks me why I didn't come forward sooner and Josie explains that I'm sometimes a few bends on the road behind and the big slow fellow smiles like he's happy to have company back there. Then the sergeant asks me will I be at my home over the next while. I say I will. There, and on the road, like. "I have the address," says Big Slow, and makes a little-mouth smile at Josie, little tiny mouth in a big fat face, just to show he knew all along the address was important.

'And anyway, that was last night. And so today, I says to Josie, "I won't make that run to Tipp. I'll go in direct and tell the Master. I'll tell him I carried the boy to Dublin and that he was all right. And is probably all right still, and that he shouldn't worry." You shouldn't. They have all kinds of means nowadays. There's nobody they can't find nowadays,' Ben said. 'Especially in London.'

He paused then. He didn't want to tell the Master that the boy had said he was going to London to see his father, and that the police had not been able to find any such person. He didn't want to indicate that maybe the boy had been lying and had run away for other reasons. He looked down at the old man immobile on the bed.

Hiss.

And pause.

And suck.

192

'Now,' said Ben, 'you see, there's hope. There's always hope.'
He sat a moment and tapped the palms of his hands on his
knees. Then he picked up the paper. 'I'll read you what's
happening,' he said, 'keep you abreast, as the fella says.' He
opened the newspaper, but the first pages were filled with
images of the Paris bombings, and he turned past these in the
hope of finding something more positive.

'Terrible business, in Paris now too,' he muttered. Page after
page he turned, the images flickering past the old man's face.
'How do you like sports?' Ben asked at last, and in his best
school-day voice began to read aloud a report on the recent
decline of Manchester United.

Hiss.

And pause.

And suck.

Outside a timid sun rose. Through the horizontal slats of
the blind bars of light fell into the room. Caught in one of
them the pale blue of the Master's eyes seemed a bottomless
pool in which his spirit swam and searched.

TWENTY-FIVE

'*Qui êtes-vous?*'

The boy and the nun stood beneath the thin shade of a poplar tree. The man before them was dressed in white. He had seen them standing some time ago, and because they had not moved, because they were there when he entered the mosque and were there still when he came out, and because the time was now full of suspicion, he crossed directly to them.

It was still early morning. Another innocent blue sky was spread over Paris. At first light the boy had knocked on Bridget's door and with her left the convent for the first time. He had told her she didn't need to come, but she had grasped his arm and said if he was going she was and there was to be no argument. The boy had given her none. They came outside the railings and the boy felt the strange atmosphere that pervaded the city. It was not something you could name, but it was as if you were visiting the home of a family who had recently buried a child. There was a damaged quality still. The first people that emerged in the half-light on their way to work moved with a kind of deference, soft-stepping, hastening through the streets as if they did not wish to be there, going as silently as possible, as though any noise could cause alarm. In this atmosphere the boy saw some of the great sights of the city for the first time, the places he only knew from the school library books. He saw Notre Dame, and across the river the grey and strangely unreal Eiffel Tower; the magnificence of the Louvre; the Tuileries gardens; the Place de la Concorde where the boy was struck by the image of a wheel, harmony, of roads meeting, and even more so, by the Arc de Triomphe. They had agreed not to take the Métro, and so walked some distance before they could find a bus that would take them out into the further suburbs. In that time, they had spoken hardly at all. The boy had a small map he had taken from the convent, and directed them where he wanted to go. At last they had arrived at a quiet street no different from dozens of others; but at one end of it, across from a small dusty park where pigeons ruffled their feathers, was a white mosque.

'Well, what do we do now?' Bridget had asked him.

'I don't know.'

They had stood there. Men had passed and entered, many giving them a quizzical look.

'Well?'

'I don't know,' said the boy again. He didn't want to tell her he was waiting for a sign, for something to happen.

But nothing did. They stood so long the sun rose and was too warm on their faces and they moved back a little into the shade of the tree.

'How long will we wait?'

'I don't know. If you want to go back you can. I am staying here.'

Bridget had not replied. She had heard the stubbornness in the boy's voice.

They waited.

Then at last the doors of the mosque had opened and the men filed out. When one of them noticed the nun and the boy still waiting he approached them.

Neither of them understood his question. But the tone in

which he asked it demanded response. He was standing squarely in front of them, a short strong-shouldered man with tightly cut black hair turning silver and a full beard.

'No thank you,' Bridget said politely, and turned her head to look very intently at something in the distance.

'*Qu'est-ce que vous faites ici?*'

'Really a very pleasant day, yes, thank you very much. Come on now.' She took the boy's arm, but he did not move with her. He was staring directly at the man. 'Come on, now,' she tried again, then whispered urgently, 'it's rude to stare.'

But already the man had understood the boy did not want to leave.

'English?' he said to the boy.

'Irish actually,' Bridget replied over her shoulder.

'What do you want here? You are waiting here a long time.'

'Yes,' said the boy. He pressed his lips together, he gathered himself, then he asked, 'Do you know a man called Ahmed Sharif?'

The man in white stared at him. The sun beat down upon the question. The answer seemed a long time coming. Then the man shook his head.

'That is why you are here? To ask this question?'

'I think he is my father.'

The sun grew hotter by the moment. The man's eyes studied the boy. 'You are Muslim?' he asked.

'I am nothing,' the boy told him.

'He's an Irish Catholic,' Bridget cut in.

But the man was not listening to her. He did not let his gaze leave the boy for an instant, and said to him: 'Everyone is something.'

'Not me,' said the boy.

The man pressed his lips together in a thin line. 'You have been in a mosque?' he asked.

'No.'

'And we have to be going now,' said Bridget, pulling his arm again and finding the boy a solid immovable weight.

'You want to come?' The man's voice was perfectly calm. There was nothing threatening about his tone or manner. But still Sister Bridget pulled at the boy to leave.

'Yes. All right.' The boy raised his arm free of the nun and stepped forward, following the man as he turned towards the mosque. Bridget followed closely, but at the entrance the man in white paused, raised a hand, and shook his head softly.

'You can't come in,' the boy told her.

'I'm not leaving you.'

'You have to. I'll be all right.'

'You have no idea if you will be all right or not,' she whispered.

'You're right,' said the boy, 'I haven't.' He looked directly into her eyes, and then he shrugged. 'I guess you just have to have faith,' he said.

'Oh that's not fair, you just . . .'

The boy placed his hand on her shoulder. 'You worry too much,' he said.

Then he turned and followed the man inside the mosque.

The air was cool. Out of the dazzle of the sun the curved space the boy entered seemed at once a place in another world. Inside there was no sound from the traffic, no noise of any kind. There were narrow windows that caught only the sky; the walls were white, with here and there scriptures he could not read. His washed bare feet felt cool on the tiled floor. All there was serene and composed and timeless.

And holy.

By the man the boy stood, and then whether from politeness or fear followed his movements as the man lowered himself to his knees and then bent forward to the floor.

What do I pray here?
What, for what?
And to who?

In response there was a profound white silence. At length the man rose stiffly from the floor, pressed his hands briefly on the soreness of his knees, and then gestured for the boy to follow him. They entered a small clean room where there were many books, some it seemed of considerable age, bound in leather with ornate gilt spines.

'So,' said the man. 'What did you feel?'

'I don't know. Something.'

The man smiled. 'My name is Imam Ali.'

The boy did not know if he should offer his hand. 'I am called J,' he said.

'Sit; tell me about this Ahmed Sharif.'

'I think he is my father. I want to find him. He is a writer. He thinks the world is going to be destroyed.'

'I see.' Imam Ali pressed his hands flatly together and tapped them just below his beard. 'Many have thought this down the centuries. I believe he is wrong.'

'He said there would be bombs and he was right.'

'Indeed.'

'He says there will be more too.'

'And he may not be wrong.'

'So?'

'You are young to be thinking of these things.'

'That's not an answer.'

'What is the question? Why will the world not be destroyed? You see these books here. These are the books I read. In books is the whole history of man, of many battles over religion, many terrible times, conflicts of rulers and believers, bloody wars over small pieces of nothing but desert, sand that covered the footprints of the soldiers before the battles ended. Here I read the endless struggles of man, and what I think is, despite

199

this, man goes on. Muslims and Christians and Jews go on. They go on believing.'

'I don't.'

'Your life is still short. There are many experiences ahead of you.'

'My mother is dead. My grandfather is dead. And I don't know my father.'

'I am sorry.'

There was a pause for grief to be felt or ghosts to pass.

'What do you know of Islam?'

'I know the terrorists are Muslims.'

A pained expression crossed the man's face. 'You are part Irish,' he said. 'You should know better. Some terrorists were Irish, but not all Irish were terrorists. So too, with Muslims. So too with Christians. A youth fires a gun at pupils in his school in America, kills many. The news does not say, "A Christian opened fire today." You are an intelligent boy, you cannot ignore the world. You should look deeply into things before you make choices.'

Because the boy did not speak, Imam Ali continued. 'Muslims believe there is one God whose name is Allah and that we must submit ourselves to his will. For the Muslim, to submit is important. Our holy book is –'

'The Koran, I know.'

'Qur'an, yes. You know what this means? It means to recite. What else do you know?'

'I know there was a prophet Muhammad born in Mecca.'

'Who was orphaned and brought up by his grandfather, and who later became married and had six children. At that time there was belief in many gods, and there were many shrines, idols to pagan beliefs. There was much corruption and fighting among the tribes of Arabia. Muhammad witnessed this and saw the rich merchants abuse the poor. You have heard of Mount Hira?'

'No.'

'There, near Mecca, Muhammad went to meditate. And alone in a cave on the mount, on the twenty-seventh day of the month of Ramadan, he had a vision. An angel came with a piece of paper upon which were words written that Muhammad could not read. But the angel said read, and then Muhammad found that he could and he heard a voice tell him, "Muhammad, you are the messenger of Allah and I am Gabriel."'

'The Angel Gabriel?'

'Yes. The same name you know.' The old man nodded to the boy. He could see his understanding. 'This we call the Night of Power. In Arabic there is a word, *hijra*, it means departure. Muhammad decided he had to leave the pagan city of Mecca with his followers, about seventy families, no more, and move to Medina. There, he began what are the practices of Islam. Prayer, fasting, and the giving of alms. In the Qur'an are 114 *suras*, chapters, and each one begins "In the name of God, the Merciful, the Compassionate." Think of this. Also, there are what we call the Five Pillars of Islam. These are *Shahadah,* Faith; *Salat*, Prayer; *Zakat*, Almsgiving; *Saum*, Fasting; and The *Hajj,* Pilgrimage.'

The man continued speaking for a long time, telling the boy of the principles and practice of Islam. He spoke in a manner calm and deliberate, as though reading from a long scroll without any intent of influence or persuasion. But at no time did he take his eyes from those of the boy. At last he paused.

'Well,' he said, 'you will see I have not spoken of terror or bombs.'

'No,' said the boy, who had listened intently all the time, with some words echoing in his head, the Night of Power, the Pilgrimage.

'There is more I could tell. Much more. Religion is a deep pool. But now I fear your guardian will batter down these walls if I do not release you to her soon.'

201

He stood up, and again squeezed his two knees. He led the boy to a side door. Before he opened it to the daylight, Imam Ali said, 'Thank you for your visit. I hope you find Ahmed. When you do, tell him the world will not be destroyed as long as there are some like you. Tell him that. You and all like you are the hope, though you do not know it.' The old man was about to say something more, but seemed to stop himself, then change his mind again. 'If this Ahmed Sharif was here, I would say he is not here now. He is more likely to be gone to some other country.'

'To Germany.'

'If I were to guess I would say Frankfurt. *Hoffen*, is this "hope" in German language? Hoffenstrasse maybe?'

'Why do you say that?'

The old man did not reply, but made a slight bow then, and opened the door, and the boy stepped out into the blinding sunshine where Sister Bridget was just then ending her prayers for him.

'Well?'

'You knew I'd be all right, didn't you?'

Bridget bit her lip. 'What did he say?'

'He told me about Islam.'

O God.

'And?'

'And it's interesting.'

'Well, yes, of course it is. But so is Christianity. So is Judaism.'

The boy looked at her as though she was telling him the thing above them was the sky. 'I know that,' he said.

'Yes, well, just, you know, he wasn't trying to convince you that you should . . . because if you wanted I could tell you things about, I mean I am a Catholic nun and maybe I should be giving you a better example but . . .'

O God, shut up Bridget. Just shut up.

'He wasn't trying to convince me,' said the boy crossly.

'Oh. OK. Fine. I mean, just I was worried and –'

'You think I am so innocent I could join up to a religion just after that?'

'No,' Bridget said, 'no, no of course not.' She bit her lip again and felt it was sore. 'Besides,' she added, 'I know you don't believe in any god.'

'That's right,' said the boy.

They walked away from the mosque through the small dusty park where pigeons foraged.

'So I was thinking, listen, maybe we should go back now. To England at least. I can't stay away from the convent much longer, and if we went back there I could work with social services, get you some place nearby, and . . .'

'I'm not going back, I told you. I am going on.'

'But . . .'

'I am going on. I am going to a place in Frankfurt where he might be.'

'How do you know? Did he tell you?'

'Sort of.'

'What do you mean sort of?'

'He didn't exactly. But I think he knew.'

'It makes no sense,' Bridget said, louder than she meant. 'You'll never find him! He doesn't want to be found.'

They had stopped on the edge of the park, the pigeons moving from their feet.

'Nothing in my life makes sense,' said the boy. 'If there is a God or an Allah or Whoever, then let Him or Her make sense of it. I am going on. Thank you for helping me. But I am going back to the convent to get my things and leave. Maybe he will be there, maybe something will happen, maybe I will be blown up, I don't know. Maybe that's the sense that's to be made of it. Goodbye.'

He walked out of the gate away from her.

Oh brilliant. Now look.

Bridget hurried after him, but let him remain five or six yards ahead of her while they both cooled down. They were progressing in this way, singly, down the shadowed side of the Rue d'Arnac when suddenly, without apparent signal, doorways opened and from all sides people stepped outside on to the pavements. Cars in the road stopped. The few pedestrians ahead of the boy and the nun slowed and then they too came to a halt.

They all stood perfectly silent and still.

In the streets ahead the same thing had happened, and was in fact happening all over France. At that moment all came to a pause. In field and factory, in office and shop, men, women and children fell quiet. Traffic lights turned green and red and green again without response. It was as if in a fairytale an antique spell had been cast in a single, wide, forearmed stroke, and there had descended on the heads of all this moment of stillness and reflection. In weird quiet that seemed unnatural everyone stood, amidst them the boy and the nun. Bridget had not heard the announcement on the television, three minutes of silence for the dead. And now, as though each were a statue, or a figure frozen in grief, she and the boy stopped some yards from each other and waited.

It was an extraordinary thing. For although none spoke, none said aloud a prayer, no music played, no flag flew overhead, the three minutes bound everyone more forcibly than at any other time in their lives. They paused for sorrow, and it came and met each one of them, and some wept softly and others were bowed and blanched with sadness, and more – aged women leaning on windowsills for support, men who had survived wars long ago – were stone-faced in solidarity. There was not a whisper of wind. The sun halved the street. A ball rolled along the kerbside, unfollowed. A fat dog by the wall dreaming shuddered and dreamt on.

Bridget watched the boy paused in front of her. She wanted to say something to him. She wanted to be better than she was, to be of greater use, to be a guide to him. In the sunlit side of the street she stood with a vision of her own true vocation, to be a help to others, and fractionally she raised her head higher. She was suffused with a great wave of warm belief, and her sense of inadequacy fell away. She would be able to help him, she could be his guide. It was what she was meant to do.

She stood and silently she prayed.

In all of France there were perhaps no moments more prayerful than in those three minutes. The supplications rose like a great invisible cloud into the blue above.

But in response nothing at all appeared to happen.

Then, suddenly, bells in churches rang out, and it was over. The people went back inside their houses, or walked on, and the cars drove away slowly as though bearing heavy burdens.

The boy did not look behind him, but hurried on, and Bridget followed.

TWENTY-SIX

When they returned to the convent the nuns were at lunch and the boy went directly to the library.

'Why? There's nothing more you need to read.'

'Two things,' he said.

This time she stood at his shoulder and watched the ease with which he used the computer. He did not need to run a search, but knew exactly the site he wanted. To Bridget it seemed some kind of noticeboard.

'It's a chatroom,' said the boy. The screen asked his password. BOY1 he typed, and then he waited.

'A chatroom?'

'Yes. It's on terrorism. Sort of. Do you know what blogging is?'

'Blogging?' Bridget's eyebrows lifted. 'It doesn't sound pleasant.'

'Well, all right forget that. In the chatroom last night I sent this question. "Does anyone know the whereabouts of Ahmed Sharif?"'

'Who did you send it to?'

'The world.'

'What do you mean?'

'I sent it to whoever is on this. Whoever. Wherever. Out there.'

'But . . .' Bridget stopped as the screen delivered to the boy fifteen responses and he clicked on them. Her mouth dropped as she saw the nature of some of the e-mails to BOY1.

'This isn't right,' she said abruptly, reaching in to try and take control of the mouse. 'I can't let you . . .'

The boy pulled her hand away. 'Stop! I need to read them. I am not a child. I know what they are. But they are the best way.' His eyes glared at her.

'I am going to stand right over you and watch.'

'Fine,' he said. Then he finished clicking through the coarse correspondence the world had sent to him, and deleted them all.

In the message box he typed: NEED TO FIND AHMED SHARIF. PLEASE HELP. ANYONE WHO HAS SEEN OR HEARD OF HIM PLEASE WRITE HERE. BOY1.

He clicked 'Send' and watched for a second as though the posting of the e-mail was a physical thing and he was seeing it being dropped into a thousand postboxes.

'Now,' he said, when they were back in his cell.

'Now what?'

'Are you going back to England?'

'You have no idea where you are going, or where he might be, or how you will find him.'

'I have an address in Frankfurt. Maybe.'

'Maybe?'

The boy shrugged. 'I am going there.'

They were back at the same wall, the same blockage to which their conversations returned, but this time Bridget did not crash into it.

'I'm coming with you,' she said. 'And I'll tell you why. Because it's what I am supposed to do.'

'How do you know?' The boy was unable to keep away a smile.

'I'm getting better at reading the signals. Besides I still have to have a talk with you about Christianity. Now how much have you got? I have less than two hundred pounds. We won't get too far on that.'

An hour later, they were back inside the high-roofed cavern of a Paris train station buying one-way tickets to Germany. The cheapest route was to go into Belgium, via Brussels, and then cross into Germany at Aachen, and from there to Frankfurt. The station had not yet fully reopened after the bombing, and the passengers waited outside where they were taken in a fleet of buses out of the city to a smaller suburban platform where the train was waiting. Once aboard the carriage, the boy felt unburdened of some weight on his spirit. Though he did not name it to himself yet, he had developed a need to be constantly moving. He felt better once the train made its first shudders away from the platform. When the countryside of north-eastern France unrolled past the window he had an immediate sense of ease. It was as if now, only when he was in motion could his spirit feel still.

While the boy sat with his forehead resting against the window, Sister Bridget took out some papers from her bag. 'I said your thanks to the Mother Superior,' she said, 'and she said to give you her blessing. So, here, God bless.' She made a quick invisible cross with her right hand. Passengers across the aisle looked at her, whether in alarm or puzzlement she couldn't be sure. The train was less than half-full. Since the bombings there had been a sharp decrease in people travelling in general. They preferred to stay at home, in the imagined safety of their apartment buildings, gathered around the twenty-four-hour news on the television to see what was happening outside.

After an hour or so, policemen who looked like soldiers

walked the length of the carriages. They asked no questions, stopped at no one, simply looked and passed on.

'I have the addresses of convents all over Europe,' Bridget said. 'We can probably stay a night or two in one in Brussels if you like.'

The boy did not appear to be listening. He was staring into the sunlit pastures of France, looking at them as if they were a fantasy. Cattle stood in poses; in a great flat meadow a mowing machine began to make fall the grass. Blackbirds rose and hung at a small distance, then landed on the stubble and hunted for worms.

At Brussels they changed trains. Before long they were at the German border where the train stopped, and there was a passport control. One bearded man became agitated and was shouting something in a language the officers did not understand. At once, as though they had dropped from the sky, there were four armed men in uniform about him, and he was being taken away from the front of the queue, shouting and waving his arms.

'Maybe he was only complaining about the train being late,' said the boy to Bridget. 'Did they understand him?'

'I'm not sure.'

'He didn't seem dangerous.'

'No. Not really.'

The queuing took for ever. While they waited, other officers with dogs moved through the train.

'Things are so different now,' Bridget said.

Later, when they were moving across Germany and the silence of the boy became too unsettling, the nun said to him: 'There is something I think I should say.'

He turned from the window to her.

'Well, that makes it sound dramatic, and it's not. It's just, what is my role in all this? I mean I am a Catholic nun and I think I should be doing something here other than just, well, doing a very mediocre job of protecting you.'

'This is because I went in the mosque?'

'No. No. Well . . . no. Just because . . .' Sister Bridget fished for the words.

'I'm not a battleground to be fought over.'

'No, no of course. That's not . . . It's not that I want you to be a, I don't know, priest or whatever. It's just, it's about me. What I realized is this. Well, imagine that I'm here with you because I have some little tiny piece of knowledge that I am supposed to give you. You know? Like it's a small gift that will help you on your . . .'

'Pilgrimage.'

'Well, in your life. All right?'

'All right. So?'

'So?'

'So, what is it?'

Bridget's face collapsed around a scowl. 'That's the thing. It's not as simple as that. There's not just one thing. At least not that I have figured out yet. But I will. It's something. And it has to be to do with this, what's happening now, and why I am in a train in Germany with you.'

The boy shrugged. 'Maybe it's a mistake,' he said. 'Maybe you're not supposed to be here.'

'It's not a mistake,' Bridget said. 'I have decided that I don't believe there are such things as mistakes.'

'That's handy.'

They looked at each other a moment, then the boy turned back to the window. Forests flew past.

'You know, when you say that you don't believe . . .' Bridget continued.

'In God?'

'That.' He was facing her again, something in his face wide open like a door. 'Well, whenever you say that, I think, "Go on Bridget, tell him, show him, be Sister Super-Bridget," you know, whatever it is I should do. Because it pains me a little.'

'I don't mean it to. It's the truth.'

'I know. I know. But well, then I thought I should tell you something. And well, maybe you know this already. You know nearly everything. But when Mother Clare told me I didn't. It was a time I was having a, well, crisis in faith, and I really didn't know what I thought or believed any more and I went to her and – you know – not the best thing for a nun to be saying, "Mother, I'm not sure I believe in God any more" – and what she said to me was the most surprising thing.'

'What did she say?'

'She said sometimes she wasn't sure that she did either. But that she was following Pascal's advice. Do you know about him?'

The boy shook his head.

'Blaise Pascal was a French mathematician and theologian, he wrote a book called *Pensées*.'

'Thinks. Thoughts.'

'Yes. And in it there was this. It's called Pascal's Gamble, or Wager. And it goes like this. If you don't know whether God exists or not, you can look at the best bet. If you live your life believing he exists and you are wrong, you have lost nothing, but have lived a life of goodness. If you live your life believing he doesn't exist and you are wrong, then in the end you will have to face him and the possibility of his displeasure at the life you have led. So,' Bridget paused for breath. The forests were thick on both sides of them. 'So, the best bet is to believe he does. Because it is logically the best thing to do. You have the least to lose.'

The boy did not speak. Bridget saw his brain turning the argument over.

'Sounds very scientific,' he said.

'Exactly.'

'It's not very religious.'

'No.'

'I never heard gambling used as a good thing before. But it's logical. I like logic. I like it when things make sense.'

'I know you do. We all do.'

'And in a way it's what I'm doing, gambling, and waiting to find out.'

'Well, yes,' Bridget said, 'but . . .'

'So is that what you're doing too? Helping me because it's a good bet that God exists and is watching? Shouldn't people just do good anyway? Shouldn't it not matter whether there is anything after? Shouldn't it be just, I don't know, *human*?'

The look in the boy's eyes was absolute and disarming. Beyond the window ran the trees, a green-feathered fur.

There was a long pause, the train bearing them onward.

'So,' said the boy at last, 'is that it?'

'What?'

'Is that the thing you were supposed to tell me?'

Bridget did not answer. She was still thinking of the boy's earlier question and what it meant to be human. She reached across and briefly squeezed his hand.

TWENTY-SEVEN

It had happened overnight, Gertie the nurse told Ben Dack. It was as if the old man's healing powers had just turned themselves on.

'When the doctor in charge, Doctor Prendergast, came in to check on him – routine, just a glance he usually gives, nothing more, he wasn't expecting anything more – he noticed something. He did. And he called me then and I thought Oh dear the poor old man's taken a turn for the worse, because you do, because in that stage, well anyway, it wasn't. Doctor Prendergast says to me, "We need to cut away these bandages now, nurse." And he was bent right down over the old man's face, so close you'd think he was about to kiss him. You would. And I started with the shears, and you remember after the crash how bad his wounds were, oh, and all that jagged scarring from the glass along his neck and . . . Well, I'm cutting away and there's no sign. No sign at all. Everything's not only without scars, it's, well, how would you say, fresh. Like new. Like a baby. Skin just that soft and smooth and not dried out or chafed or anything. And I keep on cutting and we take off all the bandages and Doctor Prendergast is standing there and he just says, "Amazing, amazing." Over and over like that.

And so then we had to take him down for new X-rays because of the broken legs and the various fractures and that.

'And bingo, same story. Healed. Fastest ever. And Doctor Prendergast is there with the two copies, the old ones and the new ones side by side and he is just shaking his head slowly like he believes there is some kind of mistake and that I must be the one made it. Must be the nurse's fault – you know doctors. And there's no mistake, those are the X-rays, I tell him. And well, there's a look on his face. It's like unscientific, you know. And he leans down again to the poor old man's face and I think the doctor whispers something to him. He does. And I swear it's like he thinks he might get an answer, the old man in a coma and all, the machines still beeping and all connected. But there's no answer, and so we wheel him back here to his room and I get the pyjamas for him, my father's actually, and there he is. Fresh and clean and all healed. And still as far away as ever.'

Ben Dack pressed open the heavy door. The room smelled and sounded just the same, there were just the same noises from the machines, the same suck and pause and hiss from the ventilator, the same dim half-light in which life seemed to balance on a ledge, but at once he felt the difference. He felt a sense not only of the man refusing to fade away but also of his beginning to come back from a great distance away.

'Well now, Master,' he said, grinning broadly and drawing up his chair by the bedside. 'You're some character, aren't you? Are you on your way back to us? Maybe to say Ben Dack would you ever shut up, you're driving me nuts with all your old talk. That'd be it, eh? That'd bring anyone back, wouldn't it? And you know, now that I can get a good gander at you, now that the bandages are gone, you know, I'd have to say you look like a very, I don't know, and you'll excuse me if I'm embarrassing – Josie says I could embarrass for Ireland – but you look a bit like my own father. In his younger days, of course. He's with the dearly departed now. But now, you do. I'd have to say you look like a man I'd enjoy having a chat with.'

Upon the Master's face was an immobile expression, placid and pale. His right eyebrow seemed raised just slightly. His gaze was far away. In his steady unblinking scrutiny was the frontier of another world where his wife and daughter had gone before him. But which he was not to cross now. The deep blues of his eyes were the colour of loss and longing, and in them at times without warning or apparent cause water pooled and spilled, tears running from some secret source down the soft damp flesh of his cheeks where Ben Dack dabbed with a tissue. The Master's eyes wept, and then did not. There was a stop to the flow; as if – Ben told Josie – something had been decided. Though in the Master's expression no doctor or nurse would notice a difference, to Ben Dack the sorrowing seemed replaced by resolve. And sitting by the bedside for long empty hours, he would come to think it was as if the old man had turned back from the very gates of heaven, like someone who has forgotten a key, and was now, moment by moment, across a vast country, returning.

TWENTY-EIGHT

Where are you now?
  Tell me. Is Bridget right? Is there a heaven?
  Is there an afterlife place?
  If there is, is there just one, or is there one for every religion?
  Is there Catholic heaven and Jewish heaven and Muslim heaven and Buddhist heaven and heavens for all the other religions too?
  And are they all separate places?
  Are there boundaries between them?
  Are there guards on the walls?

Down through the west of Germany the train raced. The boy watched the names pass, and sounded each one to himself, as if reading a chapter deeper into a book in a foreign language, and hoping that soon he would understand what it was all about. He thought on what Bridget had told him of Pascal and for a time he tried to imagine placing his life like a stack of coins on a table and gambling. He tried to see things in a way that made sense, to believe there was a pattern, a logic that was being followed. But no matter how he turned things about in his mind, nothing became clear. If there is a God, the boy told himself, He has gone away to some other world and left this one for now. Once maybe there was life on Mars too, and then God looked the other way. Maybe now He is considering starting again somewhere.

At stations along the way the train did not stop. Platforms flew past, sometimes with passengers standing like flat cutouts with pasted expressions. The boy looked away from them. He preferred when they were out in the open landscape. The German countryside was green and pleasant in the glow of summer. Fields were flat and straight, and in them tractors and other machines moved purposefully. Sometimes there were great high-roofed barns and funnels and storage tanks and such buildings as suggested the farmers had room enough to store supplies for several winters. Sometimes there was simply a man walking out into a waist-high sea of green, bending to examine the coming crop, turning to watch the faces at the windows passing.

The train made them drowse. Beside the boy the nun was praying or sleeping, he could not tell. Her eyes were closed.

The boy looked at her and thought again how strange it was that she was with him. She was kind. She was the way he imagined his mother might have been. But the moment he thought this, something inside him rejected it as childish and he scolded himself for even allowing the thought to cross his mind. She was helping him, that was all. She wanted to do it, just out of kindness. It wasn't her wager. She wasn't trying to win anything. Sometimes there could be just an act of kindness. It didn't have to mean anything more. She was trying to show him what it was to be human, that was it. That was what she said.

This understanding settled in him for a hundred miles. But then, somewhere as the train crossed the Rhineland to Frankfurt, a darker voice made itself heard in the boy's head. He looked at the nun and he suddenly thought:

220

She'll die.

Just that. It came to him from nowhere. It came with a bitter taste like late-season berries soured with their dying. It rose in his throat, this vinegar foreknowledge and he tried to swallow it back, but still it was there.

She'll die.

Those who are near me die. My mother, my grandmother, the Master.

She has come with me because she wants to protect me.

She wants to help me.

But I shouldn't let her. It's selfish of me. No one can help me.

She nearly died already by coming on the train to Paris.

I am risking her life as well as mine.

She feels bound to stay with me. She has made a promise she can't break even if she wants to. She is going to come with me no matter what.

But she shouldn't. Those who get close to me die.

She'll die.

I shouldn't have let her come.

The boy had his arms folded tightly, his chin lowered, and eyebrows furrowed. He was staring at the invisible chessboard in front of him trying to understand what he must do.

Then the train slowed, and stopped.

They were not at a station.

Like a small creature released from its cage, a murmuring in several languages ran through the carriage. Sister Bridget did not move from sleep or prayer. Out of the windows on either side was a landscape of trees.

It was as if in mid-sentence a speaker paused, unsure if the speech was for the right occasion.

Nothing happened, and continued to happen.

The boy opened his journal and softly tore out a page. He wrote four sentences and placed the page on his seat. Then he stood up quietly and slipped past the nun. Taking his bag he walked down the corridor, opened the door between carriages, and released the emergency door lock. It beeped for a moment, and stopped as the door closed again when he jumped down on to the tracks. He stumbled forward, his hands in gravel. Then he got up and ran as fast as he could towards the trees.

TWENTY-NINE

In dreams Bridget was returned to herself. She was carried back to the moment when she was a teenage girl coming home from school in the rain. Her bag was on her back; her hair was smooth wet streaks painted on both sides of her face. She had done well that day in a Geography test and was looking forward to telling her parents. She got down from the bus at the cross and began to walk along the narrow road home. It was the month of March. The rain was cold and carried on a chill wind. The hedgerows were leafless briary tangles beaded with silvery drops. She remembered that. She remembered looking at them in their crazy puzzle, the twists and turns of the wood, blackthorn, whitethorn, one interlocking with the next, its own branch vanishing in the midst of others.

As she walked home along the road in her gabardine coat the rain thickened. It splashed back up off the road. Puddles were a thousand-eyed blinking. In the bare ash trees the branches resisted swaying. Above her the sky was a firm lid of grey. Now the rain hardened further still. In her dreams of that day she could still feel the sting on her cheeks, the sense that each drop *pinched*, that there was in the falling something insistent, urging her to pay attention. She was soaked through. On the road no cars came or went, and for no reason at all then, she stopped. And she began to laugh. She laughed at how wet she was, at how fierce the rain was, at how her shoes were standing in water now and the whole place was filling up about her with the flood, and she laughed out loud and could not stop herself. She blinked back the rain that fell in her eyes. She opened her mouth and put out her tongue and the rain needled it numb.

Then somewhere inside her, at that very moment, her life was changed. She couldn't tell anyone exactly how, only her brother, Peter, seemed to understand. The following week she tried to explain to the Sister asking her. It wasn't a case of her connecting the Geography test, the question on famine in Africa, and the rain, or the tangles of the hedgerow and the need she felt to entwine her life with others. She couldn't break it down into any clear moment when things were revealed. But by the time she was so washed through with rain that she herself was dripping a puddle that leaked to the others all about her, she knew she was going to become a nun.

In her dream she was brought there. The rain that fell in her mind refreshed her and she had her face lifted towards it, and kept it there a long time, the water splashing upon her.

Two particular drops struck hard on her shoulder.

She turned her head slightly away from them.

Two more again. Then they were not drops but the hand of a uniformed officer tapping to wake her up.

'Oh dear, I'm sorry,' she pressed a hand to the stiffness in her neck.

The man said something in German she didn't understand.

'Where are we?' Out of the window she saw a sprawl of concrete apartment buildings closely clustered together.

'*Ausfahrt*,' the officer was saying, and pointing down the carriage.

'Where are we?' Bridget asked again. 'This isn't Frankfurt

is it? And where is . . .' She looked for the boy and saw the note. It read: *I am going on. You must go back. If I stay with you you'll die. Thank you for everything.*

'What? Where is the boy that was here, that was sitting here? Just a few minutes ago? Where is he?' She had stood up and the officer had stepped back to allow her to leave. All of the other passengers were already on buses outside, but Bridget turned about in panic, looking wildly around her for the boy. 'Is he already outside? Are there buses? Are you listening to me? Tell me. What's happening? Why has the train stopped here? Where is he?'

To none of her questions did the officer reply. He kept holding one arm out in front of them pointing the direction he wanted her to follow. When Bridget came off the train she saw the fleet of buses filled with the train passengers.

'He must be in one of these,' she said. 'I need to look for him.'

But the officer wanted her to board one that was not yet full.

'*Nein, nein,*' he shook his head at her and pointed.

'A boy, a boy, I am with *mit* boy, *herr* small, young.' She held her hand at the head-height of an invisible boy, and hurried up the steps of a crowded bus. From the ground the officer spoke up to her, but she paid him no attention. She descended from the bus and hurried across into the next, and the one after that, and after that too, until she had looked in all of them.

'Where is he? Where is he gone?'

'Who?' It was a thin silver-haired man in an overcoat.

'A boy. I was travelling with a boy. He's disappeared.'

'This boy is yours?' The man stood close to her, his eyes steady, his accent only slightly German.

'Yes, no. Yes. He is. Mine.'

'Where is he?'

'That's what I'm . . .' Bridget stopped herself and took breath. 'He's missing,' she said.

'Please get in the bus,' said the man. 'We will look.'

'I have to find him.'

'Yes. Please. In the bus.' Into a small receiver in his hand the man spoke in German.

'Why is the train stopped? Why is it not going on?' Bridget asked him.

The man did not reply. He seemed to consider the truth and its variants.

'Has there been a bomb?'

'Why do you ask that?'

'Has there?'

'When did you notice the boy was missing?'

'Just now. I was dreaming. He . . . he left me a note. He's run away.'

'The train was stopped some miles back for ten minutes. The emergency door lock was opened and then closed. Could this be him? Could he have left the train?'

Bridget felt a rush of heat to her face betraying the boy. But she answered, 'He could.'

'You come in my car, please.' The man in the overcoat held out his arm.

For Bridget there was nowhere else to go.

She was sitting in a white room lit by neon, waiting. It was in a police station on the outskirts of Frankfurt. There was a bare table, a clock on the wall. She had been given a glass of luke-warm water and told to wait. Nothing happened. The waiting went on and on. Twice she got up and opened the door and a man in his shirtsleeves said something commanding in German and indicated that she had to wait inside, that there would be someone with her soon. The glimpse she had of the police station gave her a sense of tremendous urgency and focus. At every desk people were speaking on phones, and to Bridget's ear the German language seemed to make their conversations brusque and authoritative, as though they were speaking under extreme duress. In the white room the wait continued. Hours passed, and Bridget's patience had run out as her mind went after the boy.

Where is he?

What happened?

'If I stay with you, you will die.'

O God.

As if from an endless ball of wool, she pulled the questions to the needles in her mind, knitting back and forth row after row, making nothing but a long one-sided garment without purpose that she then unravelled and began anew.

At last the inspector came in. He carried a brown file.

'Have you found him?'

'No. We have not.' He took off his coat, dropped it on another chair, sat down. He drew one hand along his temple, pressing flat his silver hair.

'Miss Bridget,' he began.

'Sister Bridget.'

'Sister Bridget, can you tell me why the boy was with you?'

'We were going to find his father.'

'Is he your relative, this boy?'

'No, he's my friend.'

'Your friend. This boy of twelve years?'

'Yes. I am his guardian, well, sort of.'

There was a pause. The inspector tapped his fingertips. 'I see. And where was his father?'

'He didn't know. We were looking for him.'

The man's grey eyes held her steadily. 'In Germany? In all of Germany?'

'Yes. Maybe. The boy believed he would find him. He believed it was what he had to do. Faith is a strange thing,' she said.

'Indeed. Do you know why this boy got off the train?'

'No. Well . . .'

'Yes?'

'Because maybe he thought it was dangerous for me to be with him.'

The inspector leaned forward. 'Why would he think that?'

'It's hard to explain.'

'Please. It's important, tell me.'

And Bridget did. She told him of the boy believing that those close to him died. She told him of how near he had come to death in the bombing in London, and again in Paris, and how these things may have led him to believe in some way that it was only a matter of time before he would be killed.

'It is the strangest puzzle, Inspector, if you can imagine it. The boy says that he does not believe in God, but that it is up to God to prove to him that He exists by finding the boy's father. Then the boy comes so near to death, twice, that he begins to think there is certainly no God. He finds out the person he cares most about is killed in a car crash. He gets no nearer to finding this man, and everything is suddenly ruined, and he thinks, well, that he brought all this on somehow, he thinks that not only has he made a mistake, but that, well, he is a mistake, himself.'

The inspector's eyes did not leave her. 'What is the boy's father's name?'

'Ahmed Sharif, he thinks.'

'Ahmed Sharif?'

'Yes.'

'A moment, please.'

The inspector rose and took the folder and left the room. Bridget took a sip of the water and scowled. She looked at the clock. Hours had passed since she had been brought there. *Where is he? Where is he right now? What kind of useless guardian am I? Just when I thought I had understood.* Pictures

228

of Jay ran in her head, images of him in trouble, fallen down and lying in a ditch bleeding. *Did someone take him away? What if he was . . .*

The inspector returned with another man, short and middle-aged with thick eyebrows shadowing his eyes. His face was glistening with sweat.

'Miss,' he began.

'Sister,' corrected the inspector.

'Sister, is this boy a Muslim?' asked the man.

'What?' Bridget could not believe what he had asked her. 'Well, that's not anyone's business whether he is or not. I can't believe you can even ask that question. That's discrimination. You can't –'

'I can. And I do ask it.' The man's mouth was small, his eyes narrow and hard. 'Again, is this boy a Muslim? Has he had contact with any Islamic clerics?'

'I will not answer that.'

'I take that for yes.'

'You will not take that for anything. This is outrageous. I am not staying here.' Bridget stood up, and at once the inspector was on his feet and held up both of his hands.

'No, please,' he said, 'sit down, Sister.'

Bridget didn't move. She felt the firmness of his voice.

'There is a boy missing,' she said. 'With every minute he is further away. This is wasting time. I have to go after him. If you can't help . . .'

'Please.' The inspector gestured towards the chair. 'There is something you do not know.'

The tone of his voice made her sit down.

'You see,' he said, 'in the last hour there has been an attack in Germany, three bombs in stations, Berlin, Bonn and Munich. There are many people dead. Many injured.'

Bridget's face was white. Her lower lip trembled and she bit on it.

229

'There was another bomb. In the train station in Frankfurt where your train was due,' the inspector continued. 'But its timer stopped. Maybe chance, or maybe controlled by mobile phone. We don't know yet. It stopped at just about the same time the train driver reported the emergency door lock opening.'

O God.

'He has nothing to do with this. He has nothing to do with anything. He's looking for his father. He is just a boy.'

'One other thing,' said the inspector, and he leaned forward on the table so his face was close to the nun's and his eyes kept her trapped. 'This man, you say, Ahmed Sharif.'

'Yes.'

'Police in Germany have been looking for him for two years. We believe he is very close to terrorist cells here. In fact, there is considerable opinion that Ahmed Sharif is himself one of them.'

'One of them?'

'A terrorist, *Fräulein.*'

THIRTY

Into the trees the boy ran. He did not look behind him. He did not see those few passengers on the nearside of the train who turned from their books or cards or travel-games or sleep and briefly saw the running figure they would describe to the police later. He ran across uneven grassy ground, his bag jumping on his back, his mind thinking only that the further he distanced himself from Bridget the safer she would be. He ducked in among the pine trees and hurried on over the million fallen needles of the forest floor. The light there was dim, the air cooler than the day. The trees were so closely grown that between them where he entered there was no path so he crouched and leaned and stood upright by turns, all the time going deeper. He moved as if pursued. He had a sense inexplicable to himself that it was what he had to do, and this he followed.

He dipped and ducked from lower branches, and some caught him by the arms and shoulders and dragged or whisked and sprang back and some scratched at the sides of his face as if to detain him there. He pressed on. Deeper and deeper he went into a forest of whose size he had no concept. He hurried on in a green and brown world where sunlight didn't fall. What light there was fell thin and frail from unseen heights until diminished to faint pallor. In the denseness of the trees no birds sounded. It seemed a lifeless wooden sea, an unfooted place of pine, forgotten.

The boy hurried to nowhere. He made a path Z-shaped and C-shaped and jumbled, then an alphabet of routes. A branch whipped at the top of his head and he turned from it and another stung his eye. But he ran on.

He did not know for how long. He was deep in trees moments after he began. Now he was deeper.

And then, as suddenly as he had begun, he stopped. There was a small clearing where some tall trees had toppled. He stood absolutely still and listened. He heard only his breath heaving, and had to hold and release it slowly to steady himself and bring all to silence.

Then there was nothing.

He took the bag from his back and put it on the ground.

As if some part of him was struck then, and buckled violently, suddenly he vomited.

'Well now, there you are.'

The boy was sitting on the forest floor; the Master stood opposite him.

''Tisn't easy always to find you,' the Master said. 'But you've a fine spot here.' He was wearing his old jacket and corduroy trousers, the hair upright on his forehead. He kicked the base of one of the great trees as if testing it was real. Then with some effort he lowered himself to sit against it. 'The back isn't great for travelling,' he explained, pressing a hand firmly against his lower spine.

He sat opposite the boy who watched him but did not speak. It was late now. High above them the last light was fast fading out of the day and thick green syrup of darkness dropping. The boy had his arms clutched about his knees. Before the

Master found him, he had lowered his head and begun to rock softly for comfort. As the evening had come on quickly, he had realized that he might not be able to find his way out of the trees. Then he knew he couldn't, there wouldn't be time. He was there for the night at least. A cold fear had paralysed him. He had sunk to the ground as his spirit faltered, and then felt how profoundly alone he was. He missed the world as it was before. He missed the smallest things, a pair of black trainers he had left beneath his bed, the bowl in which he poured his breakfast, the loose handle on the fridge, the uneven table, the smell of his own pillow. Such things. Longing rose in him like a fierce hunger. It devoured everything inside him. He could not think of his unknown father or the bombings or the state of the world or the big questions now. Instead he had only this growing emptiness inside him, this ache that was like a creature of sharp teeth invisibly gnawing away on his heart. He had clutched his knees so that he could feel there was someone. Lost in the trees, he had held tightly to himself, making of his body a circle, a smaller world in which things might be simpler. Then the Master had come.

Once he had sat down the old man said nothing for a long time. The night fell.

The boy did not let go of his knees. He was afraid. He heard sounds high in the roof of the trees, then others, scurryings, scratchings, something that made the air move softly above them, and then was no more.

'Don't be afraid,' said the Master at last. 'Nothing here means you any harm.' He looked straight up where the arms of the trees crossed the darkness. 'It's fairly mysterious, isn't it. A place like this. Darkness. Makes you wonder. What I think is of all the places in the world where there are no people tonight, just the night falling into them, and how sort of . . . lovely they are. You know? You know what Albert Einstein said? You know he was – of course you do – well, here in

Germany, he said, "A sense of the mysterious is one of the most beautiful and deepest experiences a man can have." And do you know, that, from a man of science. Einstein. I thought it very good. You know, the sense of the mysterious. That things can be mysterious, and that's all right. That not everything has to be solved. Some things, love, belief, the kind eyes of a dog, these, you know, can't be explained.'

There was almost complete darkness now.

The boy moved closer.

'I read a lot of books. But a lot of them, well, I read them all right, and then finished them, and put them down by the side of the couch and, well, forgot about them. But a strange thing, now, now is when a lot of them are coming back to me. It's like when your body stops, or is stopped,' the Master chuckled, 'then the mind or maybe the spirit, takes over. Something like that. So, it's now that books by great writers – books that I read – are coming back. Whole sections of them. Characters. The storylines, all of it.'

In the black-on-black the boy made out the figure of the Master leaning forward to untie the laces of his shoes. His socks were toe-holed. His hands reached to hold his feet and gently rubbed.

'Sometimes I can't quite feel my toes,' he said. 'Terrible. You feel you're not walking on the ground at all.'

'That's because you're dead,' said the boy.

The Master laughed out loud, and his laugh echoed out through the trees and was perhaps the first laughter in that place in all of time. 'Good,' he chuckled, 'very good. Do you remember times in my class you'd give me an answer blunt and direct like that? You did, so often. You have such a precise mind. Marvellous, marvellous.' He clapped his hands together twice in appreciation. 'I used to think you thought I knew nothing. You had more and more correct answers, and then soon enough, you did know more History and more Geography and the rest, because you forgot nothing – not like me. And well, that's part of your journey, to find out what is over the edge of the border of the things you know. A man said once that the beginning of wisdom is to know that you know nothing.'

'That's stupid. Everybody knows something.'

'No, no, well, yes, but, maybe I'm not putting it right. It's the mystery thing again, you know? To acknowledge the immensity of things. Infinity. That's a thing, isn't it? That's a thing to try and get your mind around.'

There fell a silence between them while they thought of infinity. And in the silence of their thinking the darkness seemed to grow darker still and the trees about them endless. Then, suddenly the Master spoke.

'"*I carried about me a cut and bleeding soul, that could not bear to be carried by me, and where I could put it, I could not discover. Not in pleasant groves, not in games and singing, nor in the fragrant corners of a garden. Not in the company of a dinner table, not in the delights of the bed: not even in my books and poetry. It floundered in a void and fell back on me. I remained a haunted spot, which gave me no rest, from which I could not escape. For where could my heart flee from my heart? Where could I escape myself?*" That's the kind of thing I'm talking about. Suddenly coming back to me. I must have read that thirty-five years ago. It's from Saint Augustine, a book called *Confessions*. And now, so clear in my old head.'

'Do you remember more?'

'I do. I remember whole chunks of it.'

'Will you say it?'

'Now?'

'Yes.'

The boy heard the Master swallow some hesitation, and then the man angled himself more comfortably against the tree.

235

'I will if you sleep,' he said.

'I don't know if I can.'

'You can. You will. There is nothing to harm you here. For all its troubles, the world is still beautiful and good.'

The boy curled on the bed of pine needles, the forest floor fragrant and cool and undisturbed since forever. The dark was deeper than any he had known, and it was a relief to him to close his eyes. No sooner was he lain down than the Master began. His voice was soft and firm both, like a road loosely gravelled. Once it began it did not stop, but wound on and on as he coaxed the sentences out of his memory.

'Here's the beginning of it,' he said, 'it begins like a prayer that's afraid it's not a good enough prayer; "*Can any praise be worthy of the Lord's majesty? How magnificent His strength! How inscrutable His wisdom!*"'

And soon the boy was on the edge of sleep, and dreaming of this Lord and His majesty and His strength and His wisdom, and dreaming too that the Master was continuing to read to him as he had so many nights before when the boy was young and could not sleep.

All around him the sentences continued. The words had been written hundreds of years before, and read in a million places on the planet since, but sounded now for the boy like a spell or a prayer or a summons for help: that he might not feel so alone. And in the way of such things, in his dreaming mind, hearing the words that were prayer and praise and longing for God, the boy felt an immense peace, as though cradled in kindness with someone watching over him. This, though all the time he lay lost in the starless dark of that forest in Germany.

THIRTY-ONE

Ben Dack drew up his chair. It was evening. A few hours earlier he had returned from a lorry journey into Connemara. On the radio he had heard the news of the bombings in Germany and when he got home he told Josie the world was breaking his heart. He couldn't go and read the newspaper to the Master as had become his habit. 'It would depress a saint,' he had told Josie, 'how is the man going to want to come back to us when all he hears is that?' He had waved the newspaper once and thrown it to the side of the sofa. Josie had smiled the blue china of her eyes and brought him tea in a large mug and half-wedge buttered and jammed scones and told Ben Dack he was the kindest man. 'Read him something else,' she had said.

'And so,' Ben told the Master, drawing the chair closer still to the hospital bed until he was inches from the old man's face and could see how serene and peaceful it seemed, the eyes gazing into the far-away, the skin pale and almost translucent. 'It's really Josie's doing. But I thought to myself, what will I read him if I'm not reading the newspaper? And of course then it hit me, slap, like that. "The man was a Master," I said

237

to Josie. "In his house there must be his books." "Must be," says she. And one thing and another, a word on the phone to the station and I had the key and just paid a short visit to your house – and everything is fine there, everything just perfect – anyway, I came away with these, a fistful from your shelves.'

Ben held up his clutch of books like trophies.

One he opened randomly and read: '"*I carried about me a cut and bleeding soul, that could not bear to be carried by me, and where I could put it, I could not discover. Not in pleasant groves, not in games and singing, nor in the fragrant corners of a garden. Not in the company of a dinner table, not in the delights of the bed: not even in my books and poetry. It floundered in a void and fell back on me. I remained a haunted spot, which gave me no rest, from which I could not escape. For where could my heart flee from my heart? Where could I escape myself?*"'

He paused then and scratched his head. 'Gee whizz. That's something isn't it? Maybe you don't want that one? Maybe there's something a bit lighter?' Ben began to lean down to the other books on the floor, but as he did there occurred the very slightest change.

It was nothing.

It was infinitely small.

It was perhaps only some minor adjustment in the ventilator. In suck and pause and wheeze an extra something, a very slight, fractional, what?

A suck of breath.

Ben Dack raised his head. The Master's face was unchanged.

But something had happened. Ben was certain. 'Did you . . . I think you . . . All right then,' he said, 'you think we should give it a shot? Fair enough.' He let the other books drop back on to the hospital floor. He brought the *Confessions* of Saint Augustine back up and opened the first page. He licked his lips and made serious his expression, as though here at last

238

was the chance he had never been given, to read from the altar on a Sunday, to participate in what he knew would be a miracle.

Softly into his fist he coughed, and then he began. "*Can any praise be worthy . . .*"

THIRTY-TWO

There were birds in the boy's dream. There were white birds that may have been doves and when his eyes followed their flight higher and higher into the air they lost their shapes and became instead his mother and his grandmother. He gasped in his dream to see them. His mother was a figment in his memory, a blur of photographs and stories of which the boy had made a concentration, an essence of loving. His grandmother was the more real, her small eyes smiling, her short figure in a blue and yellow apron with brown tights and fur-lined ankle boots; if she reached to hold his head her hands would smell of warm brown bread, her cheeks of rosewater. And that he yearned for now, and tried to rise up from the forest floor towards the vision, but swiftly the figures dissolved into fragments of light. Still more pale than the sky, their movement seemed out of time or timeless, and their crossing of great distance without effort, as though they were blown slivers of light. In his dream the boy screwed tight his eyes to follow them. He peered upwards into brightness that was all but blind. And he lost them. His eyes blinked. He heard the wing-beat of a small bird, and then another. Then there were three notes, not musical but repetitious, and when they sounded

241

again they seemed like things tapping on his mind annoyingly and he turned slightly to the side so his face brushed the needled ground and made rise a strong scent of pine. He turned back, eyes still shut, still clinging to the flimsiest thread of dream, still wanting to see fly those white wings. Then there was a flickering against his eyelids, and a further flicker, and the three notes repeating, and he opened his eyes to realize that the slight movement in the treetops above had, like a movement of birds of light, patterned his face with sunlight.

He sat up. The Master was not there. The boy had known he would not be, but felt the loss nonetheless. It was as if he pulled away a bandage and discovered the wound still there and bleeding.

The forest in the dawn light was cool and green and filled with small birds. They moved constantly from branch to branch. Their song was not tuneful, but rather a series of broken chains, notes short and staccato sung with urgent announcement. They seemed oblivious of the boy sitting on the ground below. Perhaps they had never flown from the forest. Perhaps they had never learned fear of man. The boy sat in the strange beauty of that place and was drawn to the dream of staying there, of going no further. He imagined what it would be like if humans could know perfect stillness. If they could simply stop and not fade away. He heard all about him now the secret life of those woods, movement of minor creatures, of leaf and stem and branch. Flies and other insects buzzed and cross-hatched patches of air. Light played down from above. The loveliness of the natural world seemed here restored, and to the boy as he sat, it was as though he had never quite realized it before. It seemed he had not in a very long time sat still.

Into his mind came a memory of years before when the Master had one afternoon told him to put up his books because he was going to teach him fishing. They had gone off in the yellow car to a small river not far away, and set up on the bank. The Master had brought all manner of jumbled tackle in a small canvas bag. He assembled two rods and attached the first flies he could manage to untangle. Then he led the boy down to the water's edge and showed him how to cast. Soon they were both fishing the fast brown river. But whether because the flies were unsuitable, the site on the bank poorly chosen, or the fish too clever, they caught none at all. And then the boy realized that he had actually never known the Master to bring home any fish he had caught. When he asked about this, the Master told him that in fact, he had never in his life caught a fish. Fishing is not the same as catching fish, he had said. They had stood there, their lines running into the water, all afternoon. And at some stage – after how long exactly the boy couldn't say – there had occurred the most peculiar experience. The boy *forgot* that he was fishing. He was simply sitting by the bank, connected to the river. He could feel its pulse in his hand. He could feel the *life* of things in the natural world. The river that moved with his line in it had been moving so since time began, and the boy had looked to the Master and seen the soft creases of contentment in his face and realized something then of the mystery and beauty in the world.

He remembered. In the forest now he had the same feeling of *connection*. He hugged his knees and sat still and silent while the life of the woods, winged and crawling, marvellous and many-voiced, woke about him.

If I could stay here.

He watched light grow and turn and change on tree trunks and in branches overhead. He followed the flight of a small brown bird until it left, swooping away upward where the growth seemed too dense for flight and where the bird soon became part of it.

If I could stay here for ever.

*   *   *

He might never have moved away, but for the hunger. His body reminded him he was not only a spirit. The hunger was keen as a knife. It worked its way into his stomach and twisted its blade. He had no idea which direction to go. There was no trail, nothing which indicated how he had got there.

Perhaps this was a forest of thousands of acres, he thought. He would never find his way out. Then he remembered once, when he was lost in a sum, the Master telling him we are only ever lost because we don't recognize where we are.

'All right, so I recognize this place,' said the boy to no one. 'I am not lost. I am here. I came this way.' He took some steps to the right, stopped, looked back. 'Yes. That's right. Not lost. Not lost at all.'

He went on through the trees another few yards, stopped again, again looked back so the way behind at least was familiar. Then on again. All the time the hunger worked its way up under his ribs. His throat was dry; he had no water.

'If I don't find my way out I can come back here,' he said out loud, and stooped down beneath a branch he seemed to remember had caught his shoulder the day before.

'If I don't find my way out I will die here. Is that what You want?' he asked, and only paused a moment, as though to emphasize his point.

He walked for an hour without the slightest sense that he was reaching the forest edge. The trees were as thick as ever. In green shade and dappled light he was a small figure walking in the hope that his footsteps were guided.

He arrived at a place where two thin branches were bent half-broken at his shoulder-height, but he could not be sure if this had happened today or yesterday. Was he going in circles?

'You're not doing a very good job,' he said to the air above him. 'What kind of guide are You? Just because I don't believe in You doesn't mean You can't help me.'

The hunger was intense now. He had to clutch at his stomach sometimes and wait for it to lessen, then move on.

He had been walking about two hours, he thought, when the trees closed before him so tightly that there was no way forward. Some tall pines had fallen in a storm, toppling sideways only to be held half-upright, balanced against their brothers. Their great roots had lifted on one side. Here the boy was forced to stop. He sank down to his knees. He could go no further. Across his mind passed the words of the Imam that he was the hope for the world. If he was, the world would have to turn hopelessly from now on. He gave up.

Then he heard the chainsaw.

He thought he heard it first inside himself. He thought it was the sound of his hunger. Then he got up and moved off to one side through the trees towards it.

The man in the visor was startled when he appeared. He stopped the blade and pushed up his visor and over the sound of the engine running shouted some question in German.

'Road?' the boy shouted back and pointed.

Again the man shouted something. He seemed to be asking where the boy had come from, but the boy only repeated his question and pointed more urgently.

The man shook his head. '*Autobahn*,' he said, '*Autobahn*,' and pointed the saw in the direction. Then again he asked a question.

But the boy was already hurrying past him, and the man was left staring after him as if he had been a deer or a ghost discovered in the vastness of that forest. Then he revved up the saw again and turned down his visor and did not see the white butterfly above him.

The boy followed a track into a clearing, and passed the man's truck until he was out on a narrow gravelled service

245

road. Already he could hear the hum of cars on the motorway. A hundred yards further on he could see it, silver cars flashing in the sunshine. Relief hid his hunger for a time.

By the side of the autobahn he stood and put out his thumb. But the cars moved too fast, were past him before they saw him, and the drivers were not expecting to stop.

Stop one.

Stop one.

If You are there You will guide me.

Then I will know.

There was a noise. An exasperated pop of sound as a tyre blew out and a small blue Volkswagen pulled over twenty yards down the road. The boy ran down to it as a young man with long hair got out.

'Can I get a lift? I can help if you like,' said the boy.

The man looked at him as if he had just dropped from the sky. He had not even seen him on the side of the road. 'English?' he asked, his accent eastern European.

'Irish. I'm from Ireland.'

'You don't look Irish.'

'I am Irish,' the boy said forcefully.

'Ah, good,' said the man and smiled. He kicked the flat tyre and vigorously scratched his woolly hair. 'Gus,' he said, 'Gus, from Poland.' He offered his hand.

Twenty minutes later, they were on the road. To sit down the boy had to lift a sprawl of opened biscuit and cake packages from the seat.

'Can I . . .'

'Eat. Eat,' Gus told him. There was soft rock music playing on the car stereo. Gus sang along out of key in Polish English. 'Knock, knock, knocking on hea-van's door, feel like I'm knocking on hea-van's doooooooooor.'

They were a further few miles down the autobahn when the boy asked: 'This goes to Frankfurt?'

'Frankfurt? No, other way. This goes south, to Stuttgart. You want Frankfurt?'

The boy didn't know what to answer.

'Frankfurt is not good now,' Gus told him. 'Police everywhere.'

'What?'

'Bombs. You heard?'

'No.'

'No? Whole world is mentally sick. Bombs even in Germany. They thought, never in Germany, but yes. Here too.'

'Were people killed?'

'Yes. Many.'

'Who, I mean where?'

Gus told him.

'But in Frankfurt the bomb failed, or it would have blown up the train station. So, some fortune. You never know, eh?'

'No,' said the boy.

'But police now everywhere. You have no bomb, I hope?' Gus gestured with his head to the boy's bag. 'You're not suicide bomber?' he smiled. 'So, you need Frankfurt?'

He had asked for a car to stop, he had asked for guidance. A car had stopped. But it was taking him to Stuttgart. If he believed the car had been stopped for him, did he have to believe he was *supposed* to go to Stuttgart? Was this a sign? Was he never meant to go to Frankfurt? Then this: had his getting off the train in some way saved it? How connected was everything, or was it all just chance? The questions bubbled; his face burned.

And what about Bridget?

There was no time to find clear answers.

'So, yes, Stuttgart?' asked Gus.

Slowly the boy nodded. Everything was a puzzle once more.

THIRTY-THREE

On the autobahn below Mannheim the traffic caterpillared and stopped. There was a roadblock.

Gus let out a sigh. 'This all over Germany now,' he said. 'Said on the radio. Maybe all over Europe.' He turned off the engine, opened the door and stood out to look up the line ahead of them. 'End of freedom, eh?' He shook his head at the sight of the armed policemen moving from car to car, then leaned back in and opened the glove compartment. 'Identity papers,' he said mockingly, 'means nothing. I am who? Oh yes, Gustave Maski.' Then he saw the boy looked fearful. 'You have something?'

'I have a passport.'

'Good. That's good. No problem. Here,' he offered the boy a cigarette from a crumpled box in his shirt pocket.

The policemen were at the cars in front of them.

'Relax,' said Gus.

For no reason he could explain the boy took a cigarette. When Gus had lit his own and blown the first smoke at a sharp angle upwards, he leaned over with the match. The boy's eyes followed the flame. He could smell the phosphorus burning and saw the white endpaper curl back with swift collapse and the slightest noise of ignition. Then the tip glowed, and, while Gus was shaking out the match and tossing it outside, the boy did as he thought smokers did and sucked hard.

The smoke filled his mouth and caught like fine mesh on the soft membrane of his tonsils. Immediately he coughed. It was as if he had tried to drink netting. His head pressed forward and his eyes watered. And he was like this, small-coughing and gasping, as a young German policeman tapped on his window.

The policeman said something and Gus answered him shortly, and looked away, and in protest began singing the off-key 'Knock knock knocking on hea-van's door.'

The boy gave up his passport and held the cigarette out in his left hand where he watched with strange fascination the smoke rising in a straight plume. It was as if some part of him was quietly burning away.

The young policeman's face was empty of expression. He wore a black gun snapped into a leather holsterbelt. To this was attached a black unit from which sprang the coiled wiring of his radio. This was at the boy's eye-level while the officer studied his passport on the car roof.

The cigarette burned.

Pausing in his song, Gus took a long deep pull, narrowing his cheeks and then exhaling while shaking his head so the smoke fanned wide. 'Mama take dis bahdge offa meee,' he sang again, and to the boy pointed with his thumb to indicate what he thought of the officer.

Still the officer was not returning their papers. Still he had them resting on the car roof. Then, at the boy's eye-level he saw the great pink hand of the policeman come down and unhook his radio and say something loud in that language that the boy thought harsh and intimidating.

The policeman's body was blocking the door. On the other side Gus was tapping the tune and singing. The boy felt afraid.

He felt guilty and trapped and he wished he could hide. He wished he could be invisible. He lowered his face and then he brought the cigarette to his mouth again. Again he sucked the smoke hard into his mouth and again it rushed into him and his mind took the shock of this not-air arriving and made him gag and he sputtered smoke-spit and leaned forward and Gus stopped singing and looked at him and laughed. He slapped the boy hard on the back.

'Polish cigarettes,' he laughed. 'Strong. Yes.'

The policeman had bent down now, and without speaking studied the two faces. He handed Gus back his folded identity card. To the boy he said in English: 'Irish?'

'Yes.'

'Irish?' he asked again looking at the boy with disbelief.

'Yes, Irish.'

'Where are you going?'

'He doesn't have to answer that. You don't have to answer that!' Gus cut in, poking his finger. 'You forget? There is still a thing called freedom.'

The cigarette was burning in the boy's hand. He had the strange idea that if he brought it to his mouth he could hide behind the smoke.

The officer replied in fierce German. Through thin lips he spat words full of threat and violence until Gus grew quiet and looked away.

'Stuttgart,' said the boy, and brought the cigarette to his mouth. This time he did not suck hard. He held the tip against his lips and saw his right hand was shaking.

The officer stared at him. Then one of the other policemen who had moved three cars ahead now called back to him because there were cars waiting to move on.

'Stuttgart?' he asked. It was as though he was pulling at a thread waiting for a hole to open.

'Yes.'

The cars behind them had their engines running. The smoke had passed inside the boy's mouth and he held it there, a cloud waiting release.

'Holiday?'

The boy nodded. In the officer's forehead three lines glistened. His eyes were shallow grey medals without depth. He should have followed procedure then and called in the two names to check against descriptions of those wanted. But his mind was excited and when he saw something in the back of the car he barked, 'What is in that bag?'

The driver in the car behind them pressed on his accelerator and the engine roared and the policeman shouted something and waved his arm angrily. The boy gasped the smoke from him. He leaned forward coughing. Then the policeman opened the car door.

'Please. The bag.'

In the moment he had placed it on the ground outside and spoken into his radio two other officers had arrived. None of them knew what to do.

The boy put the cigarette again to his mouth. Still his hand was shaking.

Gus leaned across him and said something in German to the policemen in which the only words the boy understood were *Nein* and *Bombe*. The young officer bent down and patted the bag gingerly. Now the cars behind them began to reverse, and angle on to the hard shoulder and spin across into the free lane, racing away, drivers and passengers momentarily staring.

The officer felt something. He told the others. One of them who had his hand on the butt of his gun now commanded '*Aus! Aus! Aus!*'

Another drew his gun and aimed it.

Gus and the boy stood from the car and raised their hands. The officer who had shouted pushed his hand roughly on Gus's back and turned him around so he stood facing the Volkswagen. The boy copied him. In his raised hand the cigarette still smoked.

Among the officers there was excited discussion.

Gus half-turned his head to the boy, whispered, 'There's no bomb, right?'

The officer with the gun aimed at them shouted. There was another flurry of excited phrases and half-phrases in German, and the thin mechanized crackle of instructions on the radio, then the sound of the young officer pulling gently at the bag's zip.

In the light breeze the cigarette burned to its end. The boy felt the heat, and then the pain as it scorched his skin. He didn't move. He held his hands in the air. His eyes pooled.

The sound of the zip quickened as the officer saw there was no bomb. The thing he had felt was the flute.

The other Germans teased the officer, and hearing the change in their tone, Gus slowly lowered his hands. The boy dropped the cigarette and clutched his hand.

The officer had his journal opened, puzzling over the writing. Then he snapped it shut and handed it and the bag back. Laughing, his colleagues moved away.

Moments later, Gus drove them back on to the autobahn. The boy was pressing his thumb against the burn.

'For one minute, I was worried,' Gus said. 'For one minute, I thought, maybe a bomb. Maybe I am knocking on hea-van's door!' He laughed and his long hair shook. 'Here,' while the car pressed forward at full speed he reached down beneath the seat and took out a bottle of beer and then another. 'We cele-brate life. In there, look.' He pointed to the glove compartment where the boy found a bottle opener. Gus held out his bottle to clink it. 'Life,' he said and tilted the beer into his mouth.

The boy had not drunk beer before. He was thirsty and shaken and full of worms of guilt. He was speeding in a car towards a place he did not want to go because he asked for a car to stop, because he had asked for help, because Frankfurt was full of police. He was thinking of Bridget and where she was and how upset she would be. He was thinking of the train and of the bomb that had not gone off. *If I had stayed on the train would we both be dead now?*

And if I was spared, what was I spared for?

He drank a mouthful of the beer and found it bitter. He tried to hide his scowl.

'Polish beer, cheap, strong, good,' Gus said, drinking again. He had his bottle finished before the boy was even a third through. He pulled another one from beneath the seat and though the boy thought to ask him not to drink it while they were driving, he did not. He pulled off the top and handed the bottle over. Gus pressed a cassette into the machine and began to sing along.

The boy drank the beer. It was strong. Gus gave him another one, 'Last one, Irish,' he said. The boy drank from the bottle. He wasn't sure if he was imagining it made him a bit dizzy. He had a sense of cloud. There was a cloud some-where, maybe it was inside him, or it was in his head, or his head was in it. Some kind of cloud floating a bit, and he was floating just a little and sort of sick, especially when he watched the line marked on the edge of the motorway lane. He looked at the burn mark near his knuckle; it stung. To the tape Gus was singing: 'How does it feeeeeel? To be on your owen, jus like a rollin stoooone.' He nodded to the beat, smiled over at the boy, his eyes lit, as if burning from the inside.

The old car sped onward, various parts rattling and loose, bottles rolling on the floor, music blaring. Dizzy, in cloud, lost, the boy pressed his head back against the seat as though to stop the motion of things racing relentlessly forward into the unknown.

In a café in Frankfurt, Bridget sat, staring out over a cup of cold weak tea. She had already been there two hours. Twice already a waiter had come down to her and broken the surface of her deep contemplation to ask if there was something else she wished to order. Twice she had shaken her head. She stared out through the large window at the street. Cars and pedestrians passed in perfect mimicry of ordinary life. But things were not ordinary. Beneath the blaze of the summer sun the city moved in fear. Radios and televisions were left on. At every hour it seemed other bombing plots were rumoured and news reports filed on new fears in other cities across Europe. Above the café-bar the twenty-four-hour channel kept news-flashing.

But Bridget couldn't even begin to think about it all. She couldn't even start to imagine how she might make sense of it all. All she could think of was:

I lost him.

I lost the boy.

The acid of blame kept rising in her gorge. No matter how she considered it, she was at fault.

He was in my care. I was supposed to be minding him. I was supposed to be his guardian.

Where is he, now?

How can I help him now?

And his father, if it is his father, what will the boy think when he finds out? And that's when he'll need me most, and I won't be there.

She stared out of the window. This truth pierced her. The waiter, watching, waiting for fresh coffee to percolate, might have seen the spear where it angled into her. Upon its point she remained, motionless, a long time.

He'll be all right. They won't find him. But he will be all right? Won't he? Won't he?

And I was some help to him, wasn't I?

There was no comfort, only questions and grief.

Sorrow poured from her, the wounds of her life opened. Here revisited was the moment when she learned that her brother Peter had leukaemia, here the slow agony of her mother's death, the swift blow of her father's. The cold wet graveyard home to the three of them. So much loss. With a sharp twist Bridget realized that in some manner she must have thought of the boy as her brother. Now he was lost too. It was too much. She did not think she could bear it. What life was for her now? To return to Birmingham and the convent, sitting back at her desk and peeling off that day's 'Thought for the Day'?

I cannot go back now.

I cannot.

I cannot take another step.

Elbows pressed on the table, hands holding her head, Bridget stared out at nothing.

She was still so, an hour later, when a black African woman, moving wearily along the footpath opposite, suddenly stopped, and, as if she was a puppet or a kite whose strings were just then snapped, slid softly down onto the ground. No one seemed to notice.

THIRTY-FOUR

Write-thoughts. Right-thoughts.

What am I doing? Is this where I am supposed to be?

Is anyone supposed to be anywhere?

Do I go to Frankfurt to find him? Or do You bring him to me? Is that it?

Do You bring everyone together?

I don't trust You.

He had been ill. When they had arrived in the city, Gus had asked the boy where he was going, and when he saw the sickness in the boy's eyes he told him he had plenty of room. This was an old dance studio in a dilapidated building in a part of Stuttgart that was awaiting demolition. It consisted of a large single space with mirrors along the walls and long windows at one end. On the floor were a dozen or more scattered blankets and sleeping bags, some with figures curled in them in mid-afternoon. It resembled a refugee shelter. The sprawl of clothes and covers, coats rolled for pillows, towels, plastic bags of food, boots, gave an impression of people paused in flight and desperation, of those whose worlds were fractured. There was a blue man of indefinite age with tattooed face and neck and arms rolling a cigarette; another with shaven head and eyebrows, a face polished smooth and eyes almost colourless staring into nothing; there was a tousle-headed woman who looked a thousand years old; she smiled at the boy and showed the broken tombstones of her teeth; a pair of girls who could not have been older than twelve but whose eyes and lips were painted and startling. The boy had felt the gaze of all turning wearily on him. He had tried not to look at the sights before him. He had felt ill and dizzy and things were in danger of toppling. Gus had put the boy's arm over his shoulder and was leading him. In the mirrors the boy saw another of himself who looked so slightly face-twisted. He could barely recognize this other. In the back of his throat he tasted slimed coating, like an oily egg not fully fried. He tried to swallow, and swallowed nothing and tried again because he knew the vomit was coming. Across the dance studio and the mute gaze of the bemused spectators Gus led him to a corner. He said it was that morning vacated. 'For you,' he told the boy, and lowered him to the floor where there was a litter of cigarette ends and burnt matches. The boy curled and groaned. Gus left him his bag. 'Polish beer,' he said, and shook his head, leaving. Ten minutes later the boy had vomited on himself. The two girls who were nearest shouted at him loudly in a language he couldn't understand.

In the lavatory he held on to the sink. He was startled by the dirt of him. He splashed cold water on his face and took off his shirt and washed it. There were three sinks in a row and two cubicles with no doors. In one of them the woman with the ravaged thousand-year-old face was sitting peeing. She said something to him in what he thought was French. Then she laughed. Along the walls and tiles in the room many things were written in pen and pencil and marker. There were even words cut with a penknife. Words in many languages. In

258

English: 'Tommy O Sulli' and in one place 'Irene' and 'Screw you God' and 'Banger + Digger' and in deep green felt pen 'All You Need is Love Love Love'.

The boy dipped his head into the running tapwater. In the mirror his face was barely recognizable. It seemed so many years older than the one that had looked out at him on the morning of the Confirmation. He looked at himself, and then in swift spasm he gagged and vomited once more. When he raised his head a second time, the woman was standing behind him. Her hair was fine red wool matted and knotted, her skin blotched like an old map left in sun and rain.

'Qu'est-ce que tu as? Hein?'

She put a thin hand on his back, bony fingers like a small creature clinging.

The boy turned. In pale pools thinly wormed with red, her eyes swam. They were green as glass. From the ravaged gape of her mouth came a breath of blackness – soot, stale smoke, charred meat, the boy thought and angled back against the sink. The hand came to his face.

'Qu'est-ce que tu as? Hein?' she said again, the long yellow-brown-nailed fingers scuttling up his cheek and then sliding down in awful caress.

A shiver passed down the length of the boy's spine. The woman's mouth smiled, cracking small scabs in her lips so they glistened blood. She moved closer to him, the thousand lines in her face like the wandering route of the lost. Her fingers were on his face, her black breath close. In near air she kissed her bleeding lips together and made a small thin chortling sound. Her second hand she closed over the boy's and she brought it up to her, placing it over her heart where a smooth flat place told that her breast had been removed.

In dream-like sequences, the boy became a puppet in the old woman's thin hands. The fingers were at his face, and then the boy was pushing her back.

259

'Go away, go away, stop,' he was saying, and trying to shove her back. But she clung on to him and his head was spinning and he was afraid he was going to be sick again. 'Go away!' he shouted, and pushed her hard in the chest and her hand came out of where it had burrowed into his pocket and she slipped and fell backwards. Against the partition of a cubicle she crashed and her head popped forward with contact and across her eyes flashed the strange astonishment of this and she blinked and then laughed where she was on all fours. The boy could see the wound in her scalp bleed. He stepped forward to help her, but she let out a fierce cry and shook a fist at him. And then, still kneeling on the floor, blood travelling in a crazy trickle sideways across her face, she opened the fist to show her cleverness and victory: she had stolen what few notes he had. She shut the fist and made the cry again. The boy stood back from her. On hands and knees she moved along a few paces on the ground. She laughed a loop of drool out of her, then a hand came up to find the support of the sink and she righted herself. She held out the fist to the boy, opened and closed it quickly, cackled, spat a strand of wild hair and bloodied scab, then opened and closed the fist again, as though showing the greatest triumph.

'Your head is bleeding,' said the boy, pointing.

But the woman did not listen or care. As though a joke was being told over and over on a continuous reel in her head, she cackled a strangulated birdsound, and then did a skip-step, and another, and in this way went out of the room past him.

When the boy returned to his place on the floor, his bag had been emptied.

'My things! Where are my things?'

There came no answer. No heads were turned in his direction. In the mirrored gloom of the studio figures shifted like shadows. Deep in a bedroll an old man snored. The boy got up to look. His head pulsed with pain. Carefully he stepped through

260

the scattered blankets and clothes and rubbish. By the two young girls with made-up faces he found his journal discarded.

'This is mine,' he said. 'You shouldn't have taken it. Where's my other things?'

'We don't 'ave them,' answered one of the girls in an accent of middle Europe. Her hair was bright orange. She was painting the other's toes blue. 'Piss away.'

The boy stared at her. She turned to her friend and said something and they both laughed.

At the doorway to the studio, he found Gus. He was sitting with his back propped against the wall, smoking.

'Gus, my things, they're gone. Did somebody go out of the door with them? I was only away for a minute, did you see them?'

Gus's eyes as he turned them to the boy were far away. He spoke very slowly, as though he had to go and bring each word back from a great distance.

'Things . . . are . . . good,' he said. 'Nice things, Irish. Things . . . elephants and . . . caravan and my mother . . . in Poland, yeah? Yeah.' He sucked on his cigarette.

'Gus? Gus?'

It was futile. The pungent scent of drugsmoke filled the air, and within it, the boy realized, Gus was lost. He watched him. For a moment he felt like crying, and the enormity of his own sense of loss came like a great tide racing towards him. It turned over and broke everything in its wake. It whooshed aside reason and logic and belief, and inside the boy smashed to pieces any thought that what he was doing was right. The pain in his head beat like an iron bar. He went back through the studio searching.

'You have my things! You stole them,' he said to the orange-head.

'I don't 'ave them! We don't 'ave them, go away you fool.' Her head shook with anger. 'You mind your own things here, no mammy here.'

261

'Shut up!' he shouted. 'You have my things.'

Quickly the orange-head shot to her feet and raised her hands. At the far wall behind her the old-faced woman began laughing again. 'I said I don't 'ave them, I am not a liar, go away.'

'How did you get my journal then? How did it just happen to be here, right beside you?'

'It was a miracle.'

'Give me back my things!'

'Idiot.'

'Give them back!'

The girl went to hit him on the face. Her hand flew and the boy caught it. Her wrist was thin and twisted in his grasp.

'Let me go! Let me go!'

'Where are my things?'

'Let go! Katrina?' she appealed to her friend, but she, with black lipstick and eyes, did not move. 'Agh! You are hurting me!'

'Tell me!'

'They are gone!'

'Where?'

'To be sold.'

The boy let go her arm. She stood back from him rubbing the place where he had held her. 'Where do you think you are?' she sneered. 'We have no things here. Only what we hold.'

'Who took them?'

'Nuno took flute. He is gone. It is already sold. Your book is . . .' she nodded towards the far side of the studio where the boy made out the silhouette of a man.

THIRTY-FIVE

'Excellent,' said the tattooed man as the boy approached. 'Fighting for your things, excellent.' In his large hands he held the boy's copy of *David Copperfield*. 'That's excellent.'

'That's my book.'

'Indeed it is.'

'I want it back.'

'Yes, you do,' said the man, but he made no motion to return it. The tattoos covered every inch of him the boy could see. His eyes peered out from swirls and curls of blue ink that made it seem he was deeply hidden in tropical undergrowth. The boy was staring.

'You like tattoos?'

He didn't know what to answer. 'I want my book,' he said.

'You want to fight me for it? No you don't. I am Maori warrior. I break bones like sticks.'

The man sat, cross-legged, watching him.

'My name is Whatarangi,' he said and offered the boy his hand. His grasp was powerful. 'Sit.' He indicated a small heap of clothing beside him.

The boy sat. 'Can I have my book back?'

'Passion. This is good.'

'It's my book.'

'Nothing belongs to anyone.'

'That's mine.'

'Well, true. It is not mine, I will agree to that.'

'You stole it.'

'Oh! Painful. I see you are one who believes there are such things as right and wrong.' He shook his head. 'How old do you think I am, boy? Go on, guess.'

'Thirty-five?'

'I am sixty years.' He held his arms out wide to show the strength of him. 'Do you know, boy, I have learned some things in that time. I have travelled around the world. Around the world from my own home in New Zealand for nearly forty of those years, and I have learned a bunch. I have. But not this one thing. One thing I had no time for. I was too busy on seas, or in forests or on the sides of mountains. Too busy trying to live and not let my enemies kill me. These hands have killed two men,' he said, and raised his great paws and looked at them with faint puzzlement as if they were part-bear.

The boy hesitated. Then he said: 'I want my book.'

'Yes, yes. I am coming to that. Patience, boy.'

'I also want my flute back.'

'The flute is gone. Nuno will have sold it already. This can't be helped. This is the nature of the place you find yourself. Now. This is important, a little patience. So now, here you arrive. And here I am thinking I should learn this last thing. It seems now is maybe a good time.' Whatarangi paused and snuffled hard and closed his eyes so the boy saw that even his eyelids were blued. He smiled with remarkable white teeth. 'I have a proposal for you.'

'About my book?'

'About your book. I will return your book to you when you help with this last thing.'

'What is it?'

'Do you accept?'

'I don't know what it is yet.'

'You will not get your book back. That is clear. I will eat it.' In the man's eyes was a startling wildness.

'I accept,' said the boy.

'Good.'

'What is the last thing?'

'Careful, boy, you respond wrong the hands may have to kill you.' The paws rose again and held trapped a parcel of air. Out of the blue the eyes studied the boy intently. Then Whatarangi said: 'I have never learned to read. '

Promising that he would begin later that night, and Whatarangi promising that he would get his book back when his pupil could read the first page, the boy went out into the city. He stepped across the body of Gus lying by the front door. The pain in the boy's head had numbed now. It was early evening. He had no idea of the layout of the street system or where exactly he was. He was hungry and tired. He had no money. He walked with his hands deep in his pockets and his shoulders curved.

It took him some time to find his way out of the derelict district. He crossed great open spaces where the ground was broken and vast cranes towered, places where heaps of sand and gravel were piled, ring-fenced rectangles of nothing where dogs came bounding and slavered against the chain-link fencing. He moved by instinct, hoping he could find his way, making note of landmarks for his return. In the sky above him the last light was retreating. A few figures hurried homeward. Cars followed their headlights into the falling dark.

At last he found a broad street of shops, shut now, and in a side street a half-dozen restaurants. Smells of cooking caught in his stomach like hooks. Onions were frying sweetly, tomatoes blistering their skins in a baking oven. He stood against a wall and imagined eating.

So hungry I could . . .

Of his right hand he made a fist and banged the knuckles on the wall. Then he had to get away from there. He hurried like one on a mission, overtaking strollers, hopping down off the pavement into the street and running. He ran without knowing where he was going. He ran following the direction that came to his feet while above his head streetlights fizzed and lit.

When his chest hurt and his throat was tight and the air burned and he thought he would fall down, he slowed and stopped. Hands on his knees, he bent over, gasping. He thought he had run away from the hunger and the sadness, but it was beside him. He sat on the kerb and looked into the starless dark.

'There is no one,' he said, 'is there? There is just nothing.'

He lowered his head so it fell almost between his knees. He wanted then to see the Master. He wanted to close his eyes and open them and see him there in his old tweed jacket. The boy wanted the Master to put a hand out on to his shoulder and squeeze it gently and say: 'Time for home, now.' He wanted the loneliness and puzzlement to go away. He wanted to have no quest, to have nothing to be searching for, for there to be no yearning inside him. Why was his life this difficult? Why did it not fit together the way others seemed to? What was he doing? There was no point in any of it. Sadness rained down on him. He screwed tight his eyes and rocked himself softly back and forth. Then he did something he did not expect. Without forethought or even intent, he began to say very quietly the 'Our Father'. He said it not out of hope or even real belief, but like a desperate gambler sliding his chips to the number seven square. He said it with head low and eyes closed, moving the words through his mind like beads beneath fingers. When he finished there was a fragment of peace, and he stopped rocking. He opened his eyes, but the Master was not there.

As the night deepened police cars patrolled as if they were nocturnal creatures, weird flat-topped beetles with firefly attachments flickering, they crawled softly in the streets. Four-eyed, they watched everything. The boy turned down alley-ways away from them. In one such place he came upon a small café with a cardboard sign saying 'Internet'. Inside, before a narrow counter, two bearded Arab men stood talking by tiny cups of coffee. They looked at him as if he was some other, alien, kind. From inside a curtain of beads, another man appeared. He was older, with a beard long and silvered. He gestured with a ringed hand towards an old computer.

'Internet, ya?' he asked.

'Ya.'

The owner came to the machine and moved the mouse and the screen showed a desert scene studded with icons. The mouse was sluggish. He shook it and said something in Arabic, then clicked to connect.

It took a moment. The boy heard the old machine dial out.

'*Deutsch?*' asked the man.

'English.'

'English.' He set it, then pointed to the cardboard sign saying the rate was two euros an hour.

The boy nodded. The man waved his hand for him to proceed and he bowed slightly and moved back to his customers.

The boy went directly to the chatroom. He waited while the hour-glass turned. He glanced back at the men at the counter whose talk quietened. He had no money to pay, but he couldn't think of that now. The window opened. He had a dozen replies. Quickly he clicked on them in turn. But in none was there anything he sought. There were predictions of further

267

bombings. Next one would be in Rome. Then Madrid. There were wild forecasts – buy petrol cans now. Fill all petrol you can. Buy and store water. Canned goods. Weapons. There were offers of special deals on protective clothing for chemical warfare, masks and gloves and whole suits for biological agents. Don't open any large envelopes. Avoid all fruit. Those who have entered this chatroom know that only some will be able to survive what is coming. Only those who are prepared. Go to: www.beprepared.com. Of warnings and forecasts there was an avalanche; cyberspace filling by the instant with messages of doom. The boy deleted one after the other, blanking the warnings into space. There was nothing about Ahmed Sharif.

He typed the question: 'Where are you, Ahmed Sharif?' and sent it.

At the bottom of the page he clicked on a link for 'German bombings latest'.

When it came he read feverishly. He felt a kind of ghoulish fascination, for the horror reached out and grabbed him and though what he read was terrible and filled with accounts of pain and suffering, he could not look away. He read for an hour. He clicked and waited for pictures to download. They downloaded on to his spirit and took up all the space. The burden of wanting to know was so great in him that he could not stop himself. The old Arab came after an hour and put a small cup of coffee and a biscuit beside him. He raised a finger to indicate one hour had passed and then held out an open palm for the boy to continue, before he withdrew again. At the counter he told the two men something, perhaps of what he had seen on the screen, and both looked back at the boy briefly.

He read. And it was as if through the screen he had entered into the secret core of the world. As if here everything was made bare and you could see just what had happened and stare at the words that told it thinking 'this is not a story, this is real.'

The boy wolfed the biscuit and drank the bitter coffee in a single gulp. While he was paused so for an instant, across the screen in a single line of teleprint came: `Frankfurt explosion tonight during police raid. More click here.`

Again the hour-glass turned.

Up came a photograph of a building with black smoke pluming out of it. The address was 5 Hoffenstrasse.

There, where Imam Ali had said. The caption read:

This evening German police had followed intelligence suggesting that a terrorist cell had been working from this location. During the raid a large explosion had detonated instantly, killing the officers as they entered. The following are the names of the terrorists believed to have been in the building at the time: Omar Hussain, Ramzi Hussain, Yasin Fawa, Said Anwar, and Ahmed Sharif.

The boy could not move.

He just kept staring at the name on the screen. *AhmedSharif AhmedSharif*. His eyes pooled and he tilted up his head and stiffened his chin and looked again. The name was still there.

Couldn't be.

It couldn't be.

It made no sense.

It couldn't be that he was dead. It couldn't be that after coming all this way.

It. He wasn't. It was another. It was someone else.

It made no sense.

He stared at the name on the screen.

Ahmed Sharif.

Ahmed Sharif.

Ahmed Sharif.

No.

No no no no no.

He sat a long time, trying to breathe. Then he got up from the seat and approached the old man at the counter. The two customers stood back and looked at him. The boy reached his hand into his pocket as if to find money he knew was not there. Then he spun about and ran out through the door. He tore down the street and heard the voices of the three men calling out after him, and then one of them was chasing him and waving something and the boy thought *is that a gun?*. Involuntarily his head stooped down and he was running crouched expecting that at any moment the man would realize the boy was too fast for him and decide it was time just to shoot him. In those moments he ran with eyes screwed and mouth open almost feeling the bullet coming through the air after him, expanding the instant of its journey to a long slow-motion piercing, so that in his mind's eye he could see it the way it sometimes was in films, and see too the moment of its impact as it burst through his skin and flowered a huge pain. He ran. The man's heavy feet beat some way behind. Then they stopped, and the boy was still running but ready to be shot. He felt the aim was on him, and he fled to the right and into a car park where he dropped to his knees and crawled into the dark.

It was after midnight when he found his way back to the dance studio. The entire area was in utter darkness. He came like the blind with hands out to find his way up the stairs. In the great mirrored room there were many shapes sleeping. He crossed to the far corner, but his place was taken now by a man with a long beard. He found a narrow space near the lavatory door and collapsed.

He had no blanket or pillow. He lay on the ground. He wept, and bit hard on his sleeve to keep from making noise but his heart cried out.

Suddenly there was a flick of sound. Standing beside him, Whatarangi held a cigarette lighter aloft, in his blue face fierce eyes.

'You don't forget your promise,' he said. 'I have been waiting.'

He held the book up to show.

'Not now, I can't.'

'You cannot break your promise.'

'Go away. I can't.'

Whatarangi opened the book to its last page. 'Now?' he asked.

The boy turned away. Then Whatarangi tore out the final page of *David Copperfield*, balled it in one hand and popped it in his mouth. From the corner of his eye the boy watched in disbelief. But because he did not move, the great tattooed man tore out another page and ate it too.

'Now?' he asked again.

'You're destroying my book!'

'Good paper,' he said, 'this way the book will not be wasted.' He tore out a third page. His blue cheeks filled, the whites of his eyes gleamed in the flamelight.

'Stop! Stop it!'

Sleeping figures stirred on the floor.

Whatarangi raised his finger to his lips. 'Come,' he said. 'Over here, I have candle, we begin.'

THIRTY-SIX

They killed him thinking he was a terrorist.
He is dead too.
Everyone in my life is dead.
I am death. Come near me and you will die.
Nothing is meant.
Everything is just chance. There is nothing else.
Just chance.
And being alone.
He is dead.
I am alone.

Days passed. The boy could make no effort to leave the dance studio. His will was gone. He could go no further. There was nowhere left to search for anything now. Now that the man who might have been his father was dead, the man they were calling a terrorist, it was all for nothing. Hot tides of anger washed up in him. It was a mistake. It was a miserable mistake: Ahmed Sharif had been wrongly identified for a terrorist. He couldn't have been one. He wasn't one. His mother wouldn't have loved him if he was. No, it was the way the world was, it was the stupid way things were now, when everyone was afraid of anyone who was different. It was fear that killed him. A rage to break things burned the boy's insides, to kick at doors, put his fist through windows, to seize on something and wrestle it apart. It was someone's fault. It was wrong. Everything that had happened was wrong. And everything he had done was wrong and had brought nothing but pain. He should have stayed at the altar rails and been confirmed the same as everyone else. When he thought back on that morning it seemed a part of another history not his own. He was no longer that boy.

I am lost.

Is that what You want? Do You want me to be lost?

Are You punishing me? Is that it? You hate me.

Neither could he truly mourn for the dead journalist, because he could not feel for sure that he had in fact been his father. He could not say now, 'My father is dead,' when for the greater part of his life he had already imagined that to be so. Nonetheless he felt guilty, guilty for lacking in grief, and guilty that he was more disturbed about the pointlessness of his search than the death of Ahmed Sharif.

He lay in his place on the floor. He imagined by this time Bridget would have returned to England. She would be wasting time praying for him and hoping he would find his father. She would be watching the news; maybe she would have realized that he had left her to save her, that if he had stayed on the train they would both be dead.

Because I am death.

His spirit collapsed in the way a bird tumbles out of the sky when a pellet embeds in its breast. He lay on the ground, sleepless, dreamless, stunned. He relived the worst moments of his own younger life, recalling days he spent in school when not a single other child spoke to him, winter afternoons he came home and went to his room and cried into the pillow.

The familiar feeling that there was something wrong with him, that he was a mistake, came back to him now. He didn't fit in. Nothing did. He had thought he had found a purpose, to find his father, only for it to come to nothing. It was like travelling a road that went off a cliff. Nor could he now find his way back into childhood. Those days when he was happiest – when he lay on his bed in a summer evening with a book, reading to the clicking of the push-mower outside; walking up the hill fields with the Master to fly their kites, pheasants startling up out of the long grass; doing an autumn dance with him, kicking high the sycamore leaves; baking doughy breads fit only for birds; taking off together in the yellow car to see a place the boy had found on the map – these were like dreams. Now there was nothing in front of him, and nothing behind. All had been erased. He lay on the floor and hugged himself, and, as if beneath him a hole opened, he fell headlong. He fell into utter black, into a blind and absolute emptiness, his spirit turning over and over in free-fall as he descended from the world he had known into nothingness. He did not have the strength to cry out or to reach to save himself. He fell into desolation, beyond sorrow or pity or the possibility of comfort. All was a cold black nothing. He was lying on the floor but at every moment he was falling further, falling from the will to carry on, from the struggle to find a purpose, from the desire to do anything. In that dark deep and wretched place the boy fell to where he thought for the first time of ending his own life. Who was there who would miss him now?

'Boy?' Whatarangi stood over him.

'Go away.'

Whatarangi tore a page from the back of the book and ate it.

'I don't care. Go away.'

The blue man's jaws moved slowly as the balled page pulped.

'You care,' he said.

The boy's pale face flew up at him, his voice fierce. 'I don't care. I don't care about anything now. My father's dead, my mother's dead, my grandfather's dead! Now! Go away!'

But Whatarangi did not move. 'You are not dead,' he said. 'You made a promise.'

'I don't care about it. I am going to kill myself.' The boy lay back on the ground and curled himself small. Then the big man's hand was on his shoulder and grasping painfully. The boy cried out. 'Let me go!'

'I will not.'

'Let me go!'

'I will break your bones off and eat them.'

'Stop that, you're hurting!'

'You made a promise. Come.'

His fingers locked on the boy, Whatarangi led him across the studio to the weak light of the window. 'Here, sit. Now read. Keep your promise. Do some good. If you want, you kill yourself when the book is done.'

The boy rubbed the pain in his shoulder. The giant figure squatted before him and held out the book. 'Read,' he commanded.

And so the boy did. At first he read only out of fear of being hurt. Then gradually the rhythm of the sentences lulled him, and he read as if he were the one being read to.

At different times of day and night Whatarangi came for him and told him it was time to read. He studied the boy's moods and judged the reading like a medicine prescribed. If the boy showed any hesitation Whatarangi threatened to tear out and eat a page, and, surrendering easily, the boy rose wearily and sat on the far side of the mirrored room in the dirty sunlight and continued his lesson.

The tattooed man made slow progress. His big blue finger touched the letters, as though they were scratched on the wall of a cave. The even swirls of his forehead buckled with frowns of concentration and he pushed his purplish lips forward waiting for the sound to be right. The boy could not quite understand how a man who had spoken English all his life, who knew a broad vocabulary, could struggle so to pick the words off the page. But between the message and its reception in the big man's brain there fell a shadow. The sense was obscured. The boy worked on the first page of the novel until he knew it by heart, and thought Whatarangi must also. At some stage during the lesson – which could last any length of time, and one time endured the entire day – Whatarangi gave the boy food in exchange for teaching. With a sharp knife he peeled off slices of pineapple, cubes of cheese, hunks of bread.

'Where do you get the food?' the boy asked him.

'Out about,' came the answer, 'at night I steal. Read, read!'

Like all before him, Whatarangi too soon fell under the spell of the story, and was not happy for the boy to read him over and over the same page. He wanted to know what happened next. So though the boy had no energy of his own and came and went from a pool of disillusion on the far side of the studio, he read on. The blue man watched him. He did not enquire of the boy's troubles. Sometimes he made gruff comments about others who sheltered there. 'Those girls? Romanian,' he said, 'lived in an orphanage all their lives. Arms thin as sticks, snap 'em like that.' He cracked a chicken bone in his gleaming teeth, crunched away then swallowed it. 'Ran away age twelve. Now, needles.' He jabbed a finger at his arm. 'Bald man, know him? Shaven head, Valerie, a Finn, very careful there, not good upstairs, sees rats everywhere. Helene you know.'

'Who?'

Whatarangi indicated where the red-haired woman with the aged face lay sleeping. 'Beautiful one time. One time in magazines. Indeed yes. Beauty queen of Lyon. Then her heart broke and she went into a bottle. That's what came out, boy. Think she may have killed her child. Raves about it sometimes.' With his smallest finger he picked at a fragment of bone caught in his teeth.

'What about Gus?'

'The priest?'

'Gus, he's a priest?'

'Near enough. Three years in Poland, had a vision, went walkabout.'

'How long ago?'

'Don't know, boy. He'll go back though.'

'But he does nothing but smoke dr –'

'That's right. I reckon God will be happy to have him back, all the same. We're all here because Gus brought us,' said Whatarangi. 'Now, read!'

And so, while yellow summer light caught in the grimed panes of the high studio windows, and all those who found refuge there slept and dreamt fitful dreams of other lives, the boy read to the tattooed man. All became accustomed to it. Some waking to the steady tone of the sentences lay and blinked and listened though the language was not theirs. They folded their arms behind their head and stared into what memory they had of childhood, and the brief moment perhaps when their mother or father had once read to them. And in that, though they may not have understood what the boy read, though the excitements of the plot or the nature of the characters were lost to them, still, there was comfort.

'What about the one who stole my flute?'

'Oh, that was Nuno.'

'Will he come back?'

'He hasn't been here since. But he'll be back. He always comes back.'

'I'll kill him.'

'No, I don't think you will.'

'I will. He stole my flute.'

'That he did. Still, you won't kill him. Now, this is good Parma ham, two slices, two chapters? Read.'

'Hey Irish.'

During the night the studio was unlit and through it moved a hushed traffic of souls. Those who slept during the day stirred now and went to the streets. Others the boy did not recognize appeared in the paler shadow of the doorway and lumbered in to find floor space like travellers from a great distance, Russians, Latvians, thin suspicious youths who, it seemed, had walked from Albania. They arrived with Gus or Gus's friends and for a day or two or sometimes longer joined the crowded population of the shelter. Solitary men, women, young and old, loomed briefly above the bedded, then, as though in a crowded graveyard finding a narrow space, they dropped down and lay still. They brought with them the smells of their country and their travelling, stories of terror, of road-blocks and night searches, of a ruined world. They exuded sunburn and dust and tar and from their fallen shapes in sleep the boy imagined their stories floating. The breath of a bearded man next to him whistled through toothlessness. It smelled of fuel. The boy turned to the other side where the two Romanian girls had left their place for the night. Then Gus tapped him on the shoulder.

'Hey Irish, can you help me?'

The boy rose and followed Gus to the doorway and down the stairs where in the poor light a small figure lay slumped.

'Help me carry, yeah?'

'What's the matter with him?'

'He's bad, he's beaten very bad. Here.'

Gus crouched down and slid his arm around the uncon-scious figure and the boy took the legs.

'He's just a child,' the boy whispered.

'Eight years of age,' Gus said. 'Up, go.'

They bore this child up the chairs, his head rolling on Gus's chest, strange guttural noises escaping his mouth. On the legs he held the boy felt the slippery ooze of blood. They brought him inside the studio and on Gus's bed laid him down gently.

'Oh Jesus. Oh Jesus help him.' Gus lit a match and a small stub of candle. The sight of the injuries took their breath away. The child had been beaten and whipped; his face, dark-skinned, was covered in lumpish black bruises. There were lacerations on his right cheek that gleamed where flaps of flesh opened. His right arm hung loosely from his shoulder. His legs too were whip-scarred and bleeding. But it was his eyes, his eyes that made Gus bring his hand to his mouth and cry out.

'Oh Jesus.'

For it appeared that a bat had been swung at the child's head and landed full on his face above the bridge of his nose, shattering bone and destroying both eyes. They were bloodied purses, puffed, jellied with ooze, half-shut. Neither Gus nor the boy could move.

They didn't know what to do next, where to begin. They were frozen in horror and anger that lasted only moments but felt like for ever. The boy said, 'I will get water.' And Gus placed his hand on the child's forehead and may have said a prayer or made the sign of the cross, the boy could not be sure. He ran to the sink and filled two plastic water bottles and took a cloth from the bed of the two girls. Gus was still standing where the boy had left him.

'Quick, Gus, we need to start. Have you anything?'

'I have pills.'

'Something for pain?'

'Yes.'

The boy tore the cloth in two. He dribbled water over one part and then placed it very gently across the wounded eyes. With the other he began to clean blood. Gus came with a small bottle of tablets, and a long black cloak he began to tear into bandages. It was a priest's cassock. With spoon and knife they ground the tablets to powder then tilted the child's head and the boy had to put his finger on the lips to open them slightly before the drops of water would carry the chemicals down. The child's breathing laboured. It came and went shallowly, and sometimes in spasms of pain. They tried to soothe the eyes, changing the compress every few minutes. Still the child lingered in an unconscious state, blanked from knowledge of what had happened to him, or his mind arrested on the very instant of horror. For an hour, more, they bathed and bound him in black bandages.

Up the stairs in the small hours Whatarangi's giant figure appeared. The moment he saw what had happened, he let out a loud curse, startling those sleeping and he waved his arms in the air over the bed as though driving back winged figures of Death now gathering. Then he leaned down, took the loose arm and with a swift jolt and press returned it to its socket. There was a sickening crack, but the arm seemed restored. Then Whatarangi grabbed the boy by the sleeve roughly.

'Come.'

'I want to stay. I want to help.'

'You will help with me. Come!'

They hurried down into the deserted street, and across the baked mud of empty spaces, until they arrived at a street of shops.

'This way.' The tattooed man led the boy around the back of a pharmacy, and with his elbow broke the door glass. At once an alarm sounded.

'Quick. Quick now.' He opened the door.

'What? What do I get?'

'Medicines. You read what ones. Get many.'

'I don't read German!'

'Get them, quickly.'

'But . . .'

'Quickly!'

The shrill alarm shredding the air, the blue-inked man standing in the doorway, the boy shot over to the shelves and began searching frantically. Penicillin, he thought.

Micin. Something Micin is it. And for eyes opti or opto something. God I don't know.

His hands shook taking the bottles. When he had a half-dozen, Whatarangi took them from him into his coat pockets and they ran out across the crunching glass into the night.

Just so were the medicines inexactly prescribed, no doctor was consulted. They were a selection wildly made, and the boy and the tattooed man and the walkabout Polish priest administered them through that night and the next day and the night that followed. They dropped clear unction into the battered eyes. They dabbed and applied cool compresses so the eyelids calmed and eventually the eyes opened for a single instant when consciousness returned. For one moment the battered child opened his eyes but whether he had vision was unknown as he quickly succumbed to another world.

Through all, the boy sat beside him. In the outrageous woundedness of this other, he forgot his own pains. In the stillness of one evening, squatting there, waiting, changing the dressing, he asked the invisible that if Bridget were praying prayers for him, let them now be exchanged like foreign currency and spent instead on this child.

In the dark of the third night when Whatarangi appeared and sat in vigil next to the boy, he said to him, 'So, boy, I miss our book. Read to us both.'

'I don't think he would –'

'Oh yes. I think so.' From inside his greatcoat Whatarangi took out the novel.

The boy opened it to read.

'I was correct, yes?' Whatarangi asked.

'About what?'

'That you would not kill him.'

'Who?'

'Nuno,' he said and pointed, 'this is Nuno that stole your flute.'

THIRTY-SEVEN

This is what Whatarangi told the boy.

Nuno Serafim was eight years old. He came from Lagos in the south of Portugal. His father was a fisherman who on the feast day of Saint Peter caught a great white fish in which there was discovered a pearl. It was of great value. Nuno's mother and father held a party for three days. For three days all of the fishermen and their families drank and danced in the streets outside the Serafim house. A sickle moon lay on its back among the stars. In and out of the house paraded dancers. Chains of laughter and singing coiled around everything until at last exhaustion overcame them and every chair and bed filled with bodies fallen into dreams of their own good fortune. In the morning, the pearl was missing. It was not where Nuno's father had left it hidden inside a jug on the kitchen shelf. When he discovered this, the fisher-father roared awake all of those who were just then dreaming themselves on the point of reaching out and picking up gleaming pearls of their own. Each one was told about the theft and questioned closely; each shook their head in disbelief that Philippe Serafim could imagine it was they.

The pearl was not found. In the house it was as if a child had died. The fisher-father took to the boat alone. Following his accusations, none wished for his company, nor did he wish theirs. On a sour swollen sea of mistrust he bobbed, sucking on the last as yet unpaid-for three bottles of wine that had survived the celebration. Under the arrival of a grim armada of grey cloud, in the midst of roiling waters, the father fell or leapt overboard, and drowned.

That evening, when the body of Philippe Serafim was laid on the kitchen table and the parade of dancers had become a file of mourners, Nuno gave his mother the pearl. He told her he didn't know why he had stolen it.

'Maybe he was afraid the father and mother loved it more than him,' Whatarangi said. 'He was the only child. Maybe he was afraid of the many guests in the house. Maybe he knew that it would ruin the family, that maybe his father would drink the pearl away. Maybe, boy, he was trying to save them from doom.' He shrugged. 'Either way, doom was coming.' And considering the sad inevitability of that, Whatarangi shook his blue head and rose and told the boy no more.

When Nuno woke he was blind.

He reached up and pulled away the poultice from his eyes and then shouted and sat up and tried to move and stumbled instead into the boy sitting next to him.

'Stop, shsh, you're all right. You're all right,' said the boy, though he knew Nuno was not. 'You're here, you're back, Gus found you.'

Nuno had brought his hands to his eyes, touching them gingerly. 'No. Cannot see,' he said. 'Can see nothing.'

'Here, here,' the boy stood and offered his hand and then realized of course that Nuno couldn't find it, so he reached and grabbed on to the other's fingers and held tight. Nuno grimaced with pain.

'I'm sorry. I'm sorry.' He let go of the hand.

286

Nuno patted the air about him for something solid. The boy put out his arm so the blind fingers would fall on it. He let them travel up to his face.

'You?' said Nuno. 'You came with . . .'

'Yes.'

'My eyes, my eyes. Can see nothing!'

'Sit down. Please sit down. Here.'

The boy returned him to the bed on the floor. He put a bottle of water in his hand.

'Nothing to steal,' Nuno said.

'I am not going to steal anything from you.'

Nuno drank the water, and again touched his eyes. 'Will I see?' he asked.

'I don't know,' said the boy, although he could surmise from the shattered bridge and the ruined, blown-out look of the eyes that something had been severed and Nuno would not see again.

'Here,' said Ben Dack, pulling up his chair by the hospital bed. 'I brought a new one. It's a big one this time, looks well enough read, indeed it does, and Josie says to me that I should pick ones that look well read because it stands to reason she says that any that's well read are favourites and favourites are what a man needs when he's in hospital, because there's comfort there isn't there, Josie says. There's comfort and what more can you look for. So, this one, I thought looks like it's been through a number of times.'

He held the cover up so the Master could see it. But as ever his eyes did not move nor in part of him was there the slightest recognition. After a moment, Ben lowered it and opened the first page.

'It's by Charles Dickens,' he said. 'It's called *David Copperfield*.'

THIRTY-EIGHT

Why is everything so sad?
Why do things not work out?
Why is there no goodness?

In the days and weeks that followed, the injuries to Nuno's
body slowly healed. The boy attended him. He couldn't say
exactly why. One evening the tattooed man laid out a great
thick blanket next to Nuno's bed and told the boy to sleep
there. He did so. And gradually he dared to ask Nuno for the
rest of his story, and what had happened after he confessed
to stealing the pearl.

'You have been told?' asked Nuno, raising his eyebrows. In
his blind face it was impossible to say whether he was pleased
or saddened.

'Whatarangi told me something. He said after you confessed
doom was coming.'

'It was.'

'Why?'

'I deserved it.'

'But what happened?'

Nuno's lips smiled thinly, as if he sipped something sour.

'You don't have to tell me.'

'I do,' he said. 'My mother grab me by the throat and begin to choke me. She lift me clear of the floor and screams out so she does not hear that pearl fall to the ground and roll. Old Tomas and Constanca and even Maria-Concepta, the neighbours run in and they try to keep my mother from killing her son. Our kitchen, small room, was then a big crowd, and dogs and cats and the priest too. Shouting and begging and praying and my mother cursing, so none notice the pearl kicked and making its way, bump bump.'

'Oh God.'

'Yes, down front steps and into street. Just when it was to fall in the sewer a woman, Magdalena, cries "la perla!" and my mother she stops choking me and everyone stops and looks out door as, plop, it drops out of sight.'

'Gone?'

'Gone. Then digging. One whole week, the smell, yuck. No pearl found. My mother not talks to me. She believed Nuno has devil inside. She would not ever spoke to me. At six years of age I became – puff!' Nuno raised his palms and blew them softly away. 'Say . . . not visible.'

'Invisible.'

'Yes.'

The sadness struck Nuno then, and the boy, to stop him telling more, said he had to go out for a time. He moved to the other end of the studio and from there watched over his blind charge.

The following day, as though his story was a weight he had to throw off, Nuno began continuing the narrative right away.

'After that, I learn. To survive I begin steal things, little things, pieces of fruit, bread. I see I am good at it. Nobody sees Nuno. I think: maybe my mother is right, maybe have devil inside me. Some things I stole I didn't want. I gave them away on my way home. Sometimes I stole very badly to see could I get caught. But no. Never.

'Then, one afternoon, hot day in old Lagos, streets like this,' he pressed his two hands together, 'tight with tourists, I steal three wallets, and then this clap, clap clap, like this. On the corner was Englishman standing clapping me. "You're a genius," he says. "What's genius?" I ask. He tells me he has been watching me all day. I think: Nuno run. But the man, Ellis, his name is, says, "I want you to come to Spain with me. In Spain with me you will make a fortune."

'"Enough to buy a pearl?" I ask. "Oh yes, many pearls," Ellis says. I go home to my mother. I open the door. She is kneeling to the wooden cross. I say, "Mama, I want to ask only one question." She gets up, comes and closes the door to my face. I am gone. I am invisible.'

'So you went to Spain?'

'I went to Spain. I start learning English. I am nice boy, I pick many wallets. With Ellis we go from Malaga to Alicante and to Barcelona, then to France. Many different jobs. I learn English. I ask Ellis if I have enough for a pearl. Not yet, he tells me. He will buy one for me when I have enough. He drinks too much. In Nice he has trouble with some other men. He gets a wound here, on his cheek, from a knife. I ask him for my pearl. He says we have no money now. He drinks too much. He shows me he has a gun. One night he comes to the door with it. He thinks I am someone else. He will kill me. He is this close to me. Nuno sticks fingers into his face and then bite hard his ear. Some comes away in my mouth. He howls like this, aghaghaghagh, and I run.'

Nuno paused. He knew the boy's eyes were upon him.

'Nuno Serafim did not go home to Lagos. How could he? He had nothing. He had maybe devil inside. He went to Italy. Learned small Italian. I stole even from churches. I came here when I had to run from there.'

The boy did not know what he should say. He said nothing.

He poured Nuno a drink and held it until his hands took it. He thought that if he had nothing in the world but a single pearl he would give it to Nuno then.

From his treks through the hot summertime city Whatarangi brought Nuno and the boy food and drink. So too, others that came and went day and night from the twilight world of the dance studio stopped and enquired of Nuno how he was.

'You look very lovely,' he said, smiling blindly up at the two Romanian girls, whose painted eyes grew glossy with tears. 'Oh yes, very beautiful. Most beautiful girls in the world.'

Gus too watched over him. In moments when he was not away in the place where the drugs he smoked took him, he joined them, sitting cross-legged and nodding gently as though hearing a soft rock tune in his head or having explained the great mystery of how things were.

'You were going to be a priest?' the boy asked him once.

'Maybe still.'

'Why did you leave?'

When Gus smiled his eyes were the blue of heaven. 'Man said to me one time, he said, you left becoming priest because you could not justify ways of God to man. I said to him: no. I said because I could not justify ways of man to God. I go back when I can.' He nodded again to the inner music, drummed his fingers on the floor.

Once his body had recovered, Nuno quickly returned to his old character. He was impish and funny, and pulled his face clownishly with his fingers to make the boy laugh. Remarkably he showed not a trace of self-pity, but seemed to accept his blindness, as if it were a natural inheritance or the to-be-expected result of his life as a thief. He even made jokes about it, and sometimes mimed a blind man meeting a girl, patting the air and then discovering with a huge grin that his fingers had found round breasts. At first the boy was not sure how to take this. Nuno's face was still bruised, the bridge of his nose bore a purple indent, his empty eyes were puffed and crusted. To look at him you could not but feel sorrow, and yet Nuno seemed to feel none.

How are you so happy?
Why are you not bitter?
You will never see again.

Nuno's greatest problem was the length of the day. Used to being on his feet and slipping through the crowded streets in search of what he could take, now he sat long hours on the studio floor, imprisoned unless he had an audience to entertain. This, the boy became. From early morning when Nuno woke him by throwing what he could find in the direction of the boy's breathing, all through the day and into night, the boy was his companion. He was the one who settled the food on a plate in Nuno's hand. ('Don't tell me what is it. I will imagine. Ice cream! Agh! Carrot!') He was the one who laughed and listened when Nuno told of adventures in robbery that featured in cartoon versions fat wealthy women, goateed scoundrels in embroidered waistcoats, open-shirted playboys with gleaming medallions and blow-dry haircuts, whole casts of the foolish and careless, whose money and jewellery and watches were *asking* to be stolen. In these tales, there was something completely disarming. The boy found that when Nuno told them he almost forgot that what he was hearing was criminal. He laughed out loud when Nuno mimed the high-heeled overweight matron running after him down the Promenade des Anglais in Nice when he had taken her handbag. He clapped when Nuno escaped from the pursuit of two policemen in Munich by sliding underneath a parked car.

For his part, Nuno was delighted to have an attentive

audience. He liked that the boy did not seem to judge him. He liked that he was clever, and understood the stories though sometimes Nuno used Portuguese and fragments of other languages so the whole was a patchwork. He liked that the boy knew things, and sat and listened with half-understanding when at night he read with Whatarangi from *David Copperfield*.

One day in late summer the boy offered to take Nuno outside. He gave him his arm and they came down the stairs awkwardly, and out into the daylight. In the baked mud of the building site all about them, Nuno stopped to feel the sun on his face. For some moments he seemed lost in himself. He held his face tilted to the sky and the boy stood waiting beside him.

'Have you ever seen the lemon trees?' Nuno asked.

'No.'

'I can see them,' he said. 'And a whole field smelling of lemons.'

'In Portugal?'

He nodded. They moved off across the site. Nuno knew the way by heart. He told the boy what they were passing. When they came out in the city streets there was apparent at once the presence of great numbers of police.

'What? What is it? I can feel it in your arm.'

The boy steered them away. He led them into the shade of side streets.

'Tell me, tell me what you see. You must be my eyes.'

With his own inherent exactness, his desire to be accurate and true to everything, the boy recounted in detail buildings, people, colours, and in a shop window German newspapers that he could not understand. Only the words, Madrid, and Rome.

'What does that mean? *Bombe Drohung?*' he asked Nuno. 'Does that mean there have been bombings?'

'*Drohung?* I don't know. Maybe.'

A chill ran at the boy's spine, the world as it was outside the studio returning to him, and with it the thought of Ahmed Sharif, of how he had died and taken with him the truth. The boy thought too of Sister Bridget, and how she must be safe in her convent again now, and he wondered if he should send her a note to say he was all right, and let her know where he was.

By late afternoon, exhausted, they were back in the studio. Whatarangi was sitting, the novel open on his lap. As they appeared he began to read out loud in a very slow and careful manner.

'Whether I . . . shall . . . turn . . . out-to-be the . . . hero-of my own life, or . . . whether that . . . station . . . will be held by . . . any . . . anybody else, these pages must show.' He looked up and in his blue face his teeth appeared in a smile.

'Excellent. Very good.'

'He is though, isn't he, boy?'

'What?'

'The hero of his own life,' Whatarangi said.

Their nightly reading had brought them near the end of the book now, or at least the uneaten end.

'I suppose so.'

'Yes, yes, he is. It is sure,' he insisted, as though the boy had reacted half-heartedly to the tattooed man's great friend.

'Yes. All right. He is. He is.'

'To be a hero is not so easy.'

'No.'

'No. It is not.'

Whatarangi stared at the boy and Nuno, as though through his eyes sending a message, then he clicked his tongue against the roof of his mouth making a sound like horses' hooves drumming. 'I need talk to Gus,' he said abruptly, and got up and went past them outside.

Much later, when the long dirty windows showed a sky of

moonless ink and the mirrors of the studio reflected various twists of low candlelight, the shadowy traffic of night guests having quieted, Whatarangi returned. He was black on black in the doorway. Then he beckoned the boy to leave Nuno sleeping and follow him down the stairs.

'Why . . . what's . . .' began the boy, but Whatarangi's finger was to his lips, and his great hand was already pulling him to his feet.

Where thin streetlight fell inside the doorway, Gus was standing, waiting for them.

'What is it? What's happening?' asked the boy.

'We want to talk here where Nuno will not hear,' Gus said.

'Why not, about what?'

'I go to Italy.'

'Going? You mean . . . ?'

'No, there is something I have been looking for. I have found that it is there, in Milano.'

The boy looked at the two men, puzzled. Then Whatarangi said, 'He goes to Italy, yes. And he wants you go with him, and take Nuno.'

'Why?'

'Nuno must go back to Lagos,' said Gus. 'He must go back to his mother. She will forgive him.'

'And we want you to bring him,' added Whatarangi, his great head bowing down to the boy so his eyes were directly in front of him.

'What?'

'You, boy, you can do this.' Whatarangi's eyes gleamed. 'We have now got the money, you take him on the train from Milano to Portugal.'

'Gus, why don't you bring him? Or you Whatarangi?'

'It is not for us to do,' Gus answered. 'It is for you. You are his friend. You are the two of you for now connected. That is the way.' In the half-light he shrugged, as though the mystery of connection was easily grasped.

The boy was unsure, and not a little afraid.

From inside his coat Whatarangi pulled out a fistful of banknotes. 'This is for you to do,' he said. 'Besides boy, you cannot stay here for ever. This only place for waiting. And what else for you to do?'

The truth hit the boy. There was nothing else. There was nothing to go on or go back for.

'What if he does not want to go?' he asked.

'He will go. With you he will go,' said the tattooed man. 'He will go when you tell him you are going there. You tell him you are on your way to Africa.'

'But I'm not going to Africa.'

'Maybe you are. Maybe you are not. No matter. Who knows where anyone is going? Here,' Whatarangi said, taking the boy's hand and putting the money in it. 'Go now, wake him and tell him.'

'Now?'

'Now. Gus must go tonight. He must be in Milano early morning.'

'I can't. I don't know what I am supposed to do.'

'You are supposed to do this.'

'How do you know? How do you know what's right for me?'

'Sometimes, boy, it is not about you. It is about others. This is right for Nuno. Are you not his friend?' The tattooed man brought his great head close to the boy so his eyes were inches away and in his steady gaze was a look urgent and compelling. In shadows in the blueness of his face the boy perceived the image of a butterfly. Had he not noticed it before? Was it actually . . . ?

There was no time. In a moment, the boy was upstairs. There was a bag of clothes Whatarangi and Gus had got for them. He shook Nuno from sleep.

'Nuno, I want to see the lemon trees,' he said. The boy looked from Gus to the Maori warrior to Nuno.

'What?'

'Take me to see the lemon trees.'

THIRTY-NINE

While Gertie, the nurse, was adjusting the pillows under the Master's head, Mr Hopkins arrived with his students. In grey suit and claret tie he sailed into the room ahead of them on a wave of impatience, and after the briefest consultation of the chart, tilted his head downward to address the students across his glasses. 'Patient 7622 in your notes. Comatose 3a. Quantifiable improvement. Patient demonstrated significant above-average healing in early stages. Began two weeks ago breathing on his own. All ventilators removed.' Mr Hopkins pursed his lips. There was talking. None should be speaking when he was. Beneath his glare it evaporated. 'This, Mr Maloney, monitors what?'

'Brain activity, sir.'

'Surprising you should recognize it.'

There was a brief titter.

'Now, we have all read about Comatose 3a, so-called "Miracle Man", our tabloid Master Lazarus. Despite opinions to the contrary, I myself am not of biblical age and cannot attest to Lazarus's medical history. I leave that aside and point out that for our purposes what is remarkable as evidenced here is how the patient demonstrates an extraordinary level of inner activity while remaining to all purposes comatose. There is no physical responsiveness of any kind. Maloney?'

'Sir?'

'Test for responsiveness?'

'Em . . .'

'A pin, Maloney. A pin. Do you have a pin?'

'Sir.' Maloney was given one by a female student behind him. He held it out.

'You, Mr Maloney, fire ahead. Your first procedure.'

Again there was a titter as Maloney stepped forward and hovered with the pin, looking for correct placement.

'Em . . . not sure where, sir.'

Mr Hopkins snorted and grabbed the pin from him. 'Where? Where, are you a complete idiot? If the patient is comatose and cannot feel then it doesn't matter where, does it?' Forcefully he jabbed the pin into the Master's arm, once, twice, while saying to Maloney, 'See, see!' Then, to further his point, he pressed it into the right cheek. 'See, nothing!'

But there *was* something. On the monitor where a green line graphed in steady waves there was suddenly a furious jag, then another, then a frantic series of acute angles like waves backing against a seawall.

'Sir?' Maloney pointed. The semi-circle of students stared at the monitor then at Mr Hopkins.

His face blanched. He stood with the pin poised. He lowered it quickly and stepped forward to the machine. He tapped it on its side and then leaning behind it jiggled the cable.

The even graph returned.

'Faulty bloody thing.' With his right forefinger he pressed the bridge of his glasses back into place. Disdainfully he shook his head. 'In medicine,' he said, 'there are no miracles.' Then he swept past the students and out of the room.

Nurse Gertie moved from the place by the wall where she had stood the whole time. To the specialists, nurses like her

300

were invisible. She bent down over the Master and touched the place on his cheek where the pin had been jabbed. 'You poor man,' she said. 'I am very sorry about all that. They can be monsters, so they can. You're not to pay him any attention. You're coming back to us, Ben says. And I believe you are, aren't you?' Gently she patted down the hair that rose off his forehead. The skin of his face was pale. His eyes were open, unmoving. In their stillness was not death, but intensity, a serene focus, as if he could see across sea and mountains, as if right then, he was watching another story unfold.

FORTY

Before the boy left with Nuno and Gus, Whatarangi embraced him. He held the boy firmly by his shoulders and squeezed.

'Boy, hero of your own life,' he whispered hotly, and then handed over the copy of *David Copperfield*.

'You keep it,' the boy told him. 'It's for you.'

Whatarangi beamed. 'My first book,' he said.

'After this you can try *Moby Dick*, I think there is a character with tattoos.'

'Moby Dick!' shouted the giant man. 'I like this name!' He stood back, almost shyly, showing only his teeth and the whites of his eyes, and suddenly the boy knew how much he would miss him.

'Lemon trees, Nuno!' Whatarangi shouted.

Nuno stuck out his tongue and then grinned. Gus was sitting in the old Volkswagen, the engine running.

'Can I come back here?' the boy asked, a bat of fear crossing in his mind.

Whatarangi nodded. 'Yes. Yes. But see what happens next. The world is . . .' he opened his hands wide to indicate its size, 'very long book, boy. Go! To the lemon trees. You take him, Nuno.'

The boy held out his arm and Nuno reached and took it.

They drove south out of Stuttgart past Ulm and Memmingen towards the Austrian and Swiss borders, the boy in the front passenger seat, Nuno asleep in the back. The autobahn was not busy with traffic. In the night cars came from nowhere and whooshed past them, red tail-lights studding the distance. With Nuno sleeping, Gus played no music, but drove crouched forward peering at the road as if it were a difficult translation.

He narrowed his eyes at a giant road sign. 'We have to find the right tunnel.'

'Tunnel?'

'There,' he waved his right hand, 'the Alps.'

The boy looked at flecks of light in the foothills of the great mountains, and tried to discern their shapes. But although he knew they were there, *knew* that just over beyond the edge of the motorway, were the greatest mountains of Europe, they were, like toys of God taken away, entirely invisible. In books in the old rack of the school library, slim hardbacked books that were twenty, thirty years old, he had seen photographs of them. In copies of *National Geographic* he had seen the white peaks against dazzling blue sky, photographs from which he could almost breathe the ice-clear air. Now, because he could not see the mountains, he saw only the memory of them. And this returned him to school, and to a time that seemed so long ago when he had sat at a desk in the Master's room.

If I could go back.

If I could just be back before this happened. Just sitting at my desk and turning the pages of a book with pictures of the Alps.

If there had been no letter.

If my mother knew what would happen, would she have written it?

I messed it all up didn't I?

Didn't I?

The Alps, folds of their darkness opening under starlight, loomed above.

Are you out there now, all of you, my mother, the Master, and my father? Are you all out there somewhere?

The car and its passengers were minute, a fleck of light, approaching.

The boy stopped the questions in his head. He imagined his hand chalking a single phrase on the old blackboard in the school. Concentrating deeply he wrote it as straight as he could.

I am bringing Nuno home.

And again: *I am bringing Nuno home.*

He stood back and stared at that phrase on the board. The classroom was empty. In its windows there was no glass, in its doorway there was no door.

He pressed his head back against the seat, and closed his eyes.

The car entered a tunnel cut into the heart of the mountain.

'Are you sleep?'

'No. Nuno is.'

'Good. We stop here for fuel. Rest the car little bit. Very old car.'

Gus opened a packet of biscuits. The night was deep about them, but the place was brightly lit.

'Can I ask you a question?' said the boy.

'Yes.'

'How do you explain things? You said you would go back to being a priest when you could explain things. How? How will you?'

Gus shrugged. He snapped a biscuit in the palm of his right hand and ate it. 'I will choose to see things making sense,' he said.

'But how can you? The world is chaos. What will you say about disasters? About when somebody good gets killed for no reason?'

Gus blew air at the questions as if they were flies. 'I will think there is a reason. I will think this one or that one was needed by God. Maybe had other business upstairs. If God created you, then he can be allowed change his mind about his creation. He can take you, use you some other place. I don't know. Maybe God didn't stop creating after seven days.'

'What do you mean?'

'Well, who stops after seven days? More likely he is very creative, yes? Is a master artist. Every minute creating. Not a moment he is not working out new plans with his creations and for his creations. Only sometimes they go wrong, because he allows that. So then he has to make things work out another way. Maybe this creator, is absolute genius, yes? Maybe better than anyone on earth can imagine. See, made these mountains too, look.'

All about them in thin slivers of sidereal light, like permanent witnesses, stood the Alps.

> If You are there, if You are the creator
> that Gus says, then create here.
> Create happiness for Nuno.
> Forget about me.
> Let his mother be happy to see him.

The journey took them through endless tunnels, the road curving in a hundred bends until they crossed down into the north of Italy. Dawn fringed the horizon, the light drawing in the silhouette of mountains and silvering the surface of lakes. As the sun rose the landscape wore ribbons of low mist. Broad fields lay in perfect tranquillity, farmhouses shouldered into the shelter of hills, tall elegant plumes of cypress trees lined avenues. Lake waters blued with morning.

'Tell me,' Nuno said, leaning forward.

And so the boy did, talking the way, putting words on everything.

'Is all of Italy like this?' he asked Gus.

'Italy is very beautiful.' He squinted through the windscreen as though he himself could not quite believe it, as though they travelled through a mirage.

It was morning when they reached the outskirts of Milan.

'We go into Milano for a short time,' Gus told them. 'I have to see someone. You walk about, wait. Then I will bring you to Genoa.'

He parked the car on the side of a street, told them to meet him in an hour.

'Gus, do you understand German?'

'Yes, a little.'

'What does *Drohung* mean?'

'It means a threat.'

'Do you think it is safe? Do you think . . .' The boy didn't finish.

'Nothing is safe,' Gus said, 'you must put away the fear in a box and live anyway.'

He left them.

'What is Milan like?' Nuno asked. 'I smell pastries, nice pastries.' He inhaled deeply. 'And shoes,' he said. He put his hand on the boy's arm to lead him. About them now moved the ordinary life of the city, commuters and pedestrians, elegantly dressed men and women in summer suits, hurrying to shop or office.

The world goes on.

'There's no smell of pastries here,' Nuno said. He sniffed. 'There's candles.'

'There is a huge church. It's black and white.'

'Take me. I like the smell of candles.'

They stepped out of sunlight into the vast cavern of the Duomo. The boy's eyes peered at obscure figures scattered through the pews. On the far altar a Mass was being celebrated by a small congregation. With intense sincerity the priest half-sang the prayers, his voice hanging the Italian phrases like short-lived banners down the empty length of the great cathedral. There was no audible response. Those kneeling, others standing to watch, others still preparing their cameras for a snapshot, returned to the priest not a sound. Still his voice sang on. In the chanted rhythm of his phrases the boy recognized some words, *absolvo* and *credo* and of course *Jesu Christo*.

'Candles,' Nuno whispered and pointed to where they were.

'Yes.' The boy led him. 'There are metal stands with trays, long thin candles on them,' he whispered.

They stood close enough for Nuno to feel their heat. Before them an old woman in a black shawl dropped a coin into the box. Then she took out a candle and held it out to them to light.

Later, when they were standing by the car waiting for Gus, Nuno asked the boy what he had prayed for.

'I prayed for courage.'

'You have courage.'

'No I haven't. Not really. And I prayed for my grandfather the Master who is not in this life and for my mother.'

'And your father?'

The boy shook his head and said nothing. So Nuno asked again, 'And your father?'

'No. Nuno, what did you pray for?'

'I pray I am sorry for all the time I stole money from churches. I pray my mother will love me.'

When Gus returned he carried a thin package wrapped in brown paper. It was the length of a weapon. He said nothing. They got into the Volkswagen and drove off. They were in the train station in Genoa in little over an hour.

'Here,' Gus said, when they were standing beside the car. 'Here is your flute.'

The boy opened the package. 'How did you . . .'

'Whatarangi found out man who Nuno sold it. He was an Italian. Here in Milano. We explained it was mistake. I bought it back.'

'But how much was it? I can't pay you back.'

Gus said. 'Take Nuno safely and all is returned.'

'To the lemon trees,' he said.

Then he turned away and was gone.

FORTY-ONE

Once the train left Genoa, it ran along the coast of the Ligurian Sea.

'Name everywhere,' Nuno said. 'Tell me.'

And so the boy did. For his blind companion he depicted the country they passed, naming the stations and reading signposts, telling the colours he saw – red clay rooftiles, ochre walls – and describing farmlands, vineyards and olive groves, the graffiti-covered backs of buildings as they approached cities, the white walls of grand villas overlooking the blue Mediterranean.

'San Remo. Nuno, we have to change trains here, we have to change to the faster train. It will go all the way to Spain.'

The boy gave his arm and Nuno took it. They stood in a line for passport control. Nuno had a creased identity card.

'Smells like police,' he said.

'Quiet,' the boy whispered. 'He's just in front of us.'

Nuno made a face. 'Nobody will question a blind boy,' he smiled. 'You are safe with me. Lucky I am blind.'

* * *

'Béziers.'

Like a dream all that blue water. Summer holidays. I can't imagine holidays any more.

'Perpignan. Soon we have to change trains. We're nearly in Spain.'

'Spain is nearly as good as Portugal. But not. Portugal is best!'

As the train moved down the Spanish coast, Nuno slept, and in the heat of the carriage filled with strangers the boy struggled to find his sense of purpose. As always he thought of the Master.

What would you think?

What would you think if you were alive and I phoned you up out of the blue and said, 'Master, guess what, I am in Barcelona.'

Holy God, you'd say. Jeepers. Barcelona. And what are you doing there? You'd say, I thought you were off looking for your father. I thought he was in Germany.

He was. I was.

But he's dead.

If he was my father.

I thought I was meant to find him. I thought that was what my mother would have wanted me to do. But it was all for nothing. And then. I don't know. I don't know.

'Take it easy now. Calm down.'

I never thought I would miss you because I always thought you would be there.

'I am still here.'

But I can't feel you.

At Valencia they changed trains again. The brilliant white light of day thinned and mellowed fast in late afternoon. Across the arid plain clouds of dust followed the train. Parched land of red earth looked to the sky as it had not rained in nine months. Windows in the carriages clouded, finely powdered. Night began to descend.

Make a wish.

I wish Sister Bridget would not be distressed.

I wish she knew that I was sorry for leaving her.

The train clanked to a shuddering stop in the great central station of Madrid. It was past midnight. There was a flurry of movement and Spanish as passengers disembarked. Brakes and engines hissed. Porters and railwaymen in plastic neon jackets walked along the carriages. The ticket collector came down the train and with his fingers indicated a four-hour wait.

There was a vacancy then, a hole in the night. Nuno slept and moaned in his dreams. The boy closed his eyes but could not sleep. He was afraid that if he did something would happen.

You are bringing him home. They trusted you to do this. Maybe they thought you were sixteen. No because.

Because I don't know why.

Because it happened that way. Because there is nothing else for me. Because this is how it happened.

Because of chance.

A squad of uniformed figures appeared on the platform with what looked like a converted ice-cream van. Inside it were a large monitor, lights and cables. The figures carried what appeared to be electric wands and one of them had a long metal pipe with a disc on its end strapped across his shoulder. With these, they went about the train examining it for bombs or chemicals or whatever clever devices had been newly invented to cause destruction. They said not a word. The ice-cream van purred up the train alongside them. The business was conducted with urgent concentration, everything weird and surreal in the way such real scenes were now.

It lasted half an hour. Then they were gone.

Like spirits, soft-footed, bleary-eyed, passengers for the train came in the still dark small hours of morning and found seats in which they yawned away the exit from Madrid. The dark landscape passed without feature.

Aranjuez, Castillejo, Ciudad Real, Puertollano, Cordoba. The boy named these places aloud although Nuno slept. He said them as much for himself now, drawing the schoolroom map into his mind and tracing the route. In this way he began to realize that, since leaving Paris, on the map of Europe he had roughly drawn a great question mark.

The day was burnt white, the Sierra Morena pale and blurred in heat-haze. When the train was in sight of the long slow flowing of the Guadalquivir river, Nuno woke.

'I smell the south,' he said. 'We are nearly there.'

'Not too far now.'

'Portugal is best, you will see. You will see and tell me.'

'I will.'

An hour later, they crossed the border from Spain, and changed trains.

'Well, tell me, tell me!' Nuno tugged excitedly at the boy's sleeve. 'Portugal! Port-u-gal! My home! Your home too now, yes?'

The boy did not answer. The landscape was parched, crisped by the sun as if after fire.

There had been no rain there in a long time.

Now, like an argument running out of words, the train slowed and stopped. It shuddered and moved a little, making gradual progress then pausing as if unclear whether or how to proceed. The white high-rises of the tourist industry hid the blue sea. Burnt brown land under development sloped and curved away to the right where diggers had dismantled a grove.

'Do you see the lemon trees?' Nuno asked.

'Yes,' lied the boy. 'They're wonderful.'

'Beautiful, yes?'

'Yes.'

And after that, Nuno fell silent. They passed the teeming traffic-blocked city of Portimao, then began the last jolting leg of the journey to Lagos.

It was late afternoon. Sea-air salted everything and blunted the fierce edge of the sunlight.

At last they were there. They came out of the station into a street busy with bodies, the smell of fish thick and strong and yet encouraging. The vibrancy of the old city was striking. At once the boy felt a strong sense of a place thriving on this furthest edge of Europe.

But Nuno stopped. 'I don't think I go,' he said.

'Yes, you have to. I am going to bring you,' said the boy. 'It will be all right.'

'How do you know? Maybe not. Maybe she see me and say "Go away". How do you know?'

'I don't,' the boy admitted.

'So?'

'So, we haven't come all this way for that. It can't happen. That's what I believe. I believe it will work out, but I can't explain why.'

Nuno pushed out his lower lip. He stood with his head bowed. Then he put out his hand for the boy to lead him.

'At my house very nice lemon trees, you will see.'

They made their way up the cobbled hill from the market streets, past the old fortress on the port where once slaves had been bought and sold. Nuno gave a few directions but otherwise they walked up beyond the old walls with not a word.

'There is a house here to the right.'

'There is.'

'Number three. It has a blue door.'

'Yes.'

'You see the lemon trees in the garden?'

The boy looked at the sad dried branches without fruit. 'Yes,' he said.

'Beautiful?'

'Very beautiful.'

315

'This is my home,' said Nuno, muscles about his eyes jumping.

Please God if You are passing this way.

Please. If You are in the business of creating still, create here now. Make happiness here.

Now please.

'Come on.'

They walked up a short gravelled path and the boy knocked on the door.

'It will be all right,' he whispered to Nuno and put a hand on his shoulder.

Then the door opened and a woman appeared coming through the darkness within and blinking against the brilliance of the light. When she saw Nuno she cried out. She brought her hands to her mouth to grasp her cry and then to the two sides of Nuno's face. She kissed him and kissed him again and was crying and holding his head and kissing his blinded eyes and thanking God that he had at last forgiven her and answered her prayers.

FORTY-TWO

Ben Dack chuckled. He was just finishing a cross-country delivery, returning from the docks in Dublin with a lorry-load of New Citronic Lemonade when he decided to stop in to see the Master before going home. The truth was he wanted to read him a bit of *David Copperfield*. In Ben Dack the plot hooks of the great novel had sunk deeply, almost without his realizing – he himself had read so few books before – and on the slow congested roads that reached across Ireland, he had found himself thinking of Mr Dick and Aunt Betsey and the constant invasion of donkeys in their garden. In the first fading of evening light he drove into the hospital car park and chuckled. The novel he had left by the Master's bed, for he only read it in his company.

'It makes the visits all the better,' he had told Josie. 'I'd never have found that book if it wasn't for him. Imagine. He's still the Master, eh?'

Now, a smile drawing circles on his cheeks, he winked at Gertie who was on the phone at Reception and walked his short rolling walk down the disinfected corridor to the stairs that took him to Level One.

'Ben?'

317

He didn't see Gertie hold the phone to her chest and lean out across the Reception counter. He didn't hear her call him back. Instead he trotted down the stairs, eager and refreshed by the anticipation of this visit that had become a habit. He pushed open the grey door. But the bed was empty, the Master gone.

'I'm sorry Ben, I tried to catch you.' Gertie's face wore the care-creases of twenty years' work as a nurse. She put her hand on his shoulder. Ben looked as though something had fallen out of the darkness upon him.

'What happened?'

'Oh he's just the same,' Gertie said. 'He's not . . . I'm sorry. No, no. They decided there was nothing more we could do for him.'

'He's the same?'

'Yes.'

'So where is he?'

'He's . . . his insurance wasn't great . . .'

'Gertie, tell me.'

'They took him to Woodley Park.'

'That place! That's . . .' Ben didn't finish. He turned and broke into a run.

'It's too late now, Ben, it's after Visiting, they won't let you in,' Gertie called, but he was already taking the stairs two at a time.

He climbed into the lorry cab and drove to the nursing home whose reputation was for parsimony, strictness and persistent viruses, whose patients arrived only because of lack of funds and left only by hearse. Woodley Park was a three-storey building from the nineteenth century that had been converted and extended with a series of cheap low additions to the rear where the patients' rooms were. There was a tree-lined avenue. There was a tarmac car park. From the front

318

entrance hall and Reception, it seemed a place welcoming and proper. But in these areas no patients were allowed.

Ben Dack rang the doorbell.

There was no answer. He rang it again, this time holding his finger in place and hearing the shrill tone. At last the heavy door opened. A thin matron, sharpened by meanness, glared at him and the lorry behind him.

'Too late for deliveries now. It's too late,' she snapped.

'It's not a delivery. I want to see a patient.' Ben moved to get past her.

'A patient! You can't see a patient now!'

'Madam, do you see that lorry out there? I'll drive that lorry full of lemonade in through the front door here if you don't let me see this patient.'

The matron's lips quivered. Though her eyes were fixed, her mouth betrayed her in meagre trembles. She tugged at invisible torments on the sleeve of her buttoned blouse.

Ben Dack told her the Master's name.

'Him?'

'Yes, him. Room number?'

'Well, excuse me now, but –'

'Room number or the lorry?'

Ben Dack surprised himself by the anger in his voice, by the fury and resolve that were the evidences of love. When the matron told him the room number he hurried ahead of her. With her in pursuit threatening to call the police, he crossed the wheelchair ramp into the patients' quarters, following the stench and room numbers that ran in reverse order until he came to number three. The door was locked.

'Why is it locked? What can he do?' Ben's voice shook with outrage.

'You can see him for one minute, then you can go,' the matron snapped. 'Security for patients in Woodley Park is of top importance,' she added, turning the key.

The room was small and dark and smelled of misery. Outside its window another extension had been built three feet away so the view was of wall. In the narrow bed the Master lay. Whether from carelessness or haste he had been placed awkwardly, his torso twisted as if turning from something feared or beginning on his last journey. One of his legs hung down uncovered.

'Where are his books?'

'I'm sorry?'

'His books, he has books.'

The matron's mouth pursed with indignation. 'He needs no books. All books are put in the Patients' Library.'

It was across the hall.

'Stop, stop, what are you doing? I'm going to call the police!'

The library was not locked. It was not a library in any normal sense, there were some shelves but very few books. The room was a mass of cardboard boxes, vacuum cleaners, broken wheelchairs, and a hodgepodge of general storage. There on top of a giant paper-roll, Ben found the Master's books. He came back into the darkened room.

'He's coming out for a visit,' he said.

'What?'

'He's coming out for a visit with me.'

'You can't take him out now its –'

'I'll sign for him or not,' Ben said. 'Your choice.' Then he came forward, and crouching low used the strength of his years of lifting things on and off his lorry, and took the wasted body of the Master in his arms. He held him there against the lemon smell of his shirt and steadied himself to bear the weight that suddenly seemed like nothing at all.

An hour later, Ben Dack wheeled the Master in out of the night to meet Josie in the kitchen.

320

'Well well well,' she said, rubbing floury hands down her apron to come forward and take the old man's hand in hers. 'You're welcome, you're welcome,' she said. 'Oh your hand is cold, come in to the fire.' The Master did not show any sign of response. But when Ben wheeled him into the sitting-room Josie poked alive the turf and the flames flickered across his eyes.

'Well, Benny Dack,' said Josie, putting her hands on her broad hips and smiling at her husband.

'We have the child's room,' he pointed out.

'We do.'

'We had a room for our son but we never had a son,' Ben told the Master. 'We're thinking maybe you'd stay there?'

While Josie went to ready the room and heat a hot water bottle for the bed, Ben opened the copy of *David Copperfield*.

'This is wonderful,' he said. 'I'll be able to read now in my own house.' He flicked to find the page. 'Here we are. Here we are now. I love this character Mr Dick. How I'd like to meet a fellow like that! You know, the way he flies his kite with the messages on it thinking somebody might read them. I love that. I do, the kite up there flying around in the wind and the messages on it. Here, here it is.

'Chapter Fifteen. I Make Another Beginning.

'*Mr Dick and I soon became the best of friends, and very often, when his day's work was done, went out together to fly the great kite.*'

Ben Dack chuckled softly. He looked over to the Master whose face was fire-lit and serene, and he patted his hand. 'You're warming up nicely now,' he said.

FORTY-THREE

It rained.

Out of the western sky beyond Cape Saint Vincent a great sheet of grey had gathered. All afternoon fishermen in their boats bobbing watched it. They saw the colour of the sea change to iron and the fish swim deeper in the expectation of storm. Some of the fishermen turned their boats around and returned to Lagos with the news of what was coming. But the weather had been for so long the same that some had even forgotten it could change. Others said they did not believe it, when in fact it was only that they were afraid to. The younger sailors, enjoying the sudden sense of peril and learning that Nature, like a lover, was not so predictable, stayed out in the deep. They fished the unfishable tide, their lines running downward to the invisible as if they themselves were the flying kites of another far below. All eyes watched the weather gather. Over the cobbled streets of Lagos a cool curtain of shade fell.

Dogs were first to smell the rain. They rose from the dust and trotted for shelter before a drop fell. Then the sky opened.

The rain sheeted straight down. People went outside to remember what it felt like on their skin. Children laughed, watching how each other's faces looked with hair plastered and their skin glistening, splashing in the first puddles bubbling at street corners where the drains had long ago been blocked. They ran about, played games of reverse rules where it was good to be shot, this time by the rain.

At the small house at the top of the hill, the hammering on the roof grew so insistent that talk was impossible and Nuno and the boy came outside to feel the falling sky. A giant barrel of thunder rolled. Nuno walked into the arid garden and lifted his face so the rain splashed into his blindness. The boy stood alongside him. He could feel the lemon trees drinking greedily as the rain touched all of their surfaces and began too the gradual descent through the dust to their roots. Nuno held his hands out wide. Then the boy did the same. The thunder rolled again. Across the dark sky of late afternoon forked a brilliant lightning. The rain pelted and stung and fell without end, but Nuno and the boy stood, arms out, faces skyward, laughing, as if it were sent for them.

Thank you.

The following days it rained still. The streets ran like rivers, the cobbles shining black. People long unused to the constant whisper of rainfall sat with their doors open listening. Nuno's mother spoke no English, but communicated her gratitude for her son's return in cooking. However long the boys stayed in the house, she fed them. There were plates of smoked fish, fish cakes, bowls of fish stew, fillets of fish, small white C-shaped cuts of moist cheese that turned out to be fish.

The return of Nuno brought all of the neighbours to the house. There were many visitors to see him and the boy who had brought him back. Time and again in the impenetrable rhythms of Portuguese Nuno's mother told the story, and at various points in the telling the neighbours turned as one and looked at the boy.

324

'You are a hero,' Nuno teased him.

'I'm not,' he said. 'You are the one who faced coming back.'

Knowing that Nuno's mother was not well off, the neighbours brought clothes for the boy, as well as figs, plums, lemon cakes, and of course buckets of fish. He was for a time a mysterious celebrity among them. In all of this the boy tried to be gracious. From Nuno he learned some words and phrases in Portuguese and these were always a source of great delight to the people there. In the second week of the rain a white-haired woman called at the house and met with Nuno's mother for a short time, and then with Nuno himself. Later, when she left, Nuno told the boy: 'She will teach me blind language.'

When the rain ended and the thirst of the earth seemed slaked, the season had turned into autumn. The boy grew restive, uncomfortable with charity, and unsure what he was to do next. Was he to stay in Portugal now? Was he to go back to Germany? He belonged in neither place. But nor could he imagine going back to the village in Clare now that the Master was gone. Everywhere there was an absence. The boy's spirits fell into a place low and confined but also familiar. He remembered the first day he went to school, letting go the Master's hand to walk in the yard on his own. Directly the Master went on into the schoolhouse, leaving the boy to meet the other children. The boy had stood on the edge of a circle. For a moment two of the girls looked at him and then one said he had a flat nose and laughed and they ran off. In the open space of the schoolyard the boys seemed charged with manic energy and climbed the walls and leapt down, screaming out and running, crashing into one another. When they paused, momentarily, the boy stood alongside. But really he may have been a thousand miles away. He did not know how to belong; he did not know how to be this way. In time he could learn how to pretend, but always he had sensed that he wore a poor mask and the others knew. So much of his life since was like

325

this. Only at home had he ever been comfortable. In any group the boy had felt a deep sense of his being different. In his journal once, he imagined himself an alien with a coded alien language understood by none.

So, in Lagos, now that he no longer had a sense of purpose, he fell into this familiar loneliness and wondered what his life was for. He had enjoyed the sense of purpose in bringing Nuno home, but what was his purpose now? In the evenings he took his flute and played on the edge of the square collecting some money from the wealthy Germans who dined there. Some of his earnings he gave to Nuno's mother, who one day used them to buy a flute for her son.

Soon Nuno too knew the Irish tunes, and played in duet with the boy, and to some it seemed that they would grow up and live for ever as brothers by the sea.

One afternoon, while Nuno was working with the white-haired woman, the boy wandered in the town. In the emptiness of the time he drifted from street to street until, for no reason he could later remember, he stopped at a narrow café with three computers at a high counter along the front window.

Even as he connected to the Internet he felt a strange sensation in his stomach, as though a butterfly inside him was beating to find a way out. He watched the icon, waiting the instants as he was linked to the Web. Then he typed the address of the chatroom on terrorism he had last visited in Stuttgart. All manner of bulletins were posted, warnings, threats of future attacks, in Washington, Los Angeles, Sydney, Istanbul. The geography of terror was multinational, the flurry of messages constant from Web users all over the world. The boy's eyes flitted down over them. In the pleasant autumnal air of the Algarve it was easy to forget the summer of bombings, to move them further back in your mind so all of that seemed part of the past, not the present.

Then he saw the messages posted in response to his own. He clicked the first.

There was a single line. It read: I AM AHMED SHARIF.

He looked at the date; it was two weeks ago. He clicked the next one from the same sender. I AM AHMED SHARIF, WHY DO YOU WANT TO FIND ME?

Dated a week later, another one: ARE YOU THERE? I AM WAITING FOR YOUR RESPONSE. I AM AHMED SHARIF.

Then the last one, that had been sent that afternoon. I AM AHMED SHARIF. I WANT TO SEE YOU. I KNOW YOU HAVE BEEN LOOKING FOR ME.

The boy clicked 'Reply'. He wrote: YOU ARE DEAD and pressed 'Send'.

He stared at the screen. It was a joke, a trick. Anyone could write that they were anyone else. He waited. No reply came. He paid for the time and went down to the sea.

But the following day he was back. He entered the chatroom and saw there was a message for him.

I AM NOT DEAD. DO YOU WANT TO MEET ME?

He typed: YOU DIED IN GERMANY.

Instantly there was a reply.

HELLO. ARE YOU THERE?

WHO ARE YOU?

I AM AHMED, AND YOU?

I DON'T BELIEVE YOU.

YOU HAVE BEEN LOOKING FOR ME. WILL YOU COME AND SEE ME?

YOU ARE DEAD.

I AM NOT DEAD.

HOW DO I KNOW IT IS YOU?

I KNOW YOU HAVE BEEN LOOKING FOR ME, FIRST IN LONDON, THEN IN PARIS AT THE MOSQUE. I KNOW.

The boy felt his throat tighten, his heart was racing.

Another message came.

WILL YOU COME TO SEE ME, OR WILL YOU GO HOME?
I HAVE NO HOME.
YOU HAVE YOUR COUNTRY. WHERE ARE YOU NOW?
LAGOS, PORTUGAL.
There was a delay. Then: IF I SEND YOU A TICKET WILL
YOU COME TO SEE ME?
HOW CAN I BELIEVE YOU?
YOU WILL COME TO NO HARM, I PROMISE. SEND YOUR
ADDRESS.
The boy did, then wrote: YOU DON'T KNOW MY NAME.
The reply was his name.
WHERE ARE YOU?
This time the answer that came was again two words: IN
EGYPT.
Then the connection ended.

FORTY-FOUR

The boy told no one. But in three days a letter arrived for him at Nuno's house, blooming red roses of excitement in the mother's cheeks at the evidence of her guest's importance. In the envelope there was a return plane ticket in the boy's name to fly from Faro to Cairo in Egypt.

'What is it?' Nuno asked. 'What did you get?'

'I have to go away.'

'Why go away?' Nuno stuck out his lower lip.

'I have to find someone,' said the boy, and he took Nuno's hand and led him outside under the lemon trees.

ARE YOU COMING?

YES.

I WILL BE THERE TO MEET YOU.

HOW WILL YOU KNOW ME?

I WILL KNOW YOU.

When he had read about the death of Ahmed Sharif in the building in Frankfurt, the boy had been angry and confused. But by the time he had accepted the task of bringing Nuno to Lagos, he had let go nearly all thought of Ahmed Sharif.

Whether Ahmed Sharif might have been his lost father ceased to weigh so heavily on his mind. Instead, in the blind boy he saw a way to do something worthwhile. To not look back for what was not there. He had been glad even that it was over.

But now the Internet message had changed everything.

Faced with the fact of a contact, the boy couldn't bring himself to turn away from it although in his heart he wished Ahmed Sharif *were* dead.

On a morning silvered with sun-rain he held both of Nuno's hands in his and told him that he would never forget him.

'You are hero for me,' Nuno said.

'No, you are the hero.'

'You changed my bad luck. Maybe I change yours too?'

'Maybe.'

'You have to go?'

'I don't really want to. But I have to.'

'Why?'

'Just . . . I do.'

'You will come back again sometime?'

'I will.'

'My lemon trees will have lemons,' Nuno grinned, and squeezed small his blind eyes.

The boy took the fierce fish-scented hug of Nuno's mother and the bag of fruit and biscuits she pressed on him. The sun-rain glistened. He sat in a taxi to the airport and waved his hand. He did not see the butterfly leave the lemon tree.

It was impossible to believe that he would go, impossible for him not to.

The plane flew from Faro to Alger where there was a change before the long flight across Tunisia and Libya to Egypt. The boy studied the map. He knew the countries of Africa, but not the inner geography and peered down through cloudless air at brown ground below.

The airport in Cairo was thronged with passengers, voices in many languages, people from all corners of the world. They bustled, the shoed and the sandalled and the barefoot alike, the fair and the tanned and the dark.

In the midst of them was the boy. He presented his passport and stood beneath the scrutiny of the official, his hands trembling slightly. He looked at the opaque sliding glass doors of the exit. He didn't want to move through them. He didn't want to know what happened next.

Then with two sharp thumps the official stamped his passport and returned it to him.

The boy didn't move.

The official waved him to go through. 'Yes, you go. Go.'

Still he stood there.

'Go.'

The boy nodded, as though at the conclusion of an inner argument. He walked forward and the doors slid back. He came out into the Arrivals hall and saw like postage stamps the many faces pressed there. He turned his head downward, his backpack on his shoulder.

Is this where I am from?

Africa?

Is this where I belong?

He went along the barrier to the end. He swallowed hard. There was a trembling in his legs. He was weak and empty. Then he heard his name spoken.

And he turned and Sister Bridget was standing beside him.

'I'm sorry, I'm sorry, I'm sorry, I'm sorry. It was me. I lied. I'm so sorry. It was awful. Will you ever forgive me? I'm really sorry. But I was afraid if I said it was me then you wouldn't come. Will you forgive me?'

The boy stood staring.

'You hate me, don't you? You hate me now. It was a terrible thing to do. I know. I'm sorry, I'm so sorry.

'There was this nun in Germany, she showed me how to work the Internet. And I thought, I'll just say hello. I'll just say: "Bridget here, how are you?" And then I read that your, well that he was killed in that explosion and I thought, how dreadful for you, how really awful. And I said, "now he really thinks everyone who comes into his life dies. And he won't reply to me. He'll be out there somewhere utterly alone." That's why I did it. There was no other way. Please say you'll forgive me, please, I'm so sorry.'

She stood back from him, her hands held together. She looked older than when he had left her on the train. Her clothes were different. She looked less like a nun. In her expression there was more ease and freedom. Her face was freckled and burned, the end of her nose peeled pink.

'It was you?'

Bridget nodded. 'Forgive me?'

The boy said nothing. About them arriving passengers flowed. He stood like a rock in a living stream. How could he forgive her? He felt cheated. Having believed one thing, how could he now simply erase it and believe another? He was puzzled and annoyed. He had been childish, stupid not to have questioned more. She had fooled him and he should have been furious. But the truth was more complex. In his heart he knew that he was glad.

'You know,' Bridget said, 'how you spoke to me about finding what it was you thought you were supposed to do? And how when I asked why you felt you had to go to Frankfurt, you answered that it was because you had to. Well, this is what I had to do. I had to find you again, to show you that not everyone you get close to dies. That's why I did it.' She was looking directly at him. 'You are my unfinished business.'

332

'That doesn't sound good.'

'It *is* good.' Her eyebrows met in consternation then rose again in contrition and appeal. 'I'm *so so* sorry. It was an awful thing to do, even as I was doing it I was praying for forgiveness. Now, there is a café over there. I will go over and sit down and you can think about whether you forgive me or not, and whether you want to hear about what I think happens next.' She smiled thinly, and turned away.

'Bridget.'

She stopped.

'I forgive you.'

She wanted to hug him, but knew not to and instead made small fists and squeezed them. 'Come on so,' she said. They walked out of the airport each with sideways glances one to the other, as if to confirm they were real. Stepping out into the heat and acrid fumes, Bridget said, 'You know of course you nearly killed me going off like that.'

'I am sorry. I thought it was –'

'It's all right,' she cut in, 'I suppose I can forgive *you*.'

They took a taxi into the hot, noisy, traffic-jammed city of Cairo, the crossroads of East and West. The boy watched everything. He saw the forest of minarets pierce the skyline, the mosques that were everywhere, the streets thronged with Arabs and Turks and Jews and black Africans and Europeans alike. They were staying in the old city to the south, a walled enclave of stone houses, crooked streets and ancient bazaars. When the taxi could take them no further, they got out and walked in the colossal heat. Bridget told the boy the convent was not like the one in Paris. 'But they are very welcoming,' she said. 'It's here.'

It was a small stone building in great need of repair. Its steps were crumbled away in the centre.

'How long have you been here?'

'Not very long,' Bridget said, 'shsh, listen.' On the air from

333

one of the mosques travelled chanted prayers. For a moment Bridget did not move and neither did the boy. 'Africa is so extraordinary,' she whispered, and showed him up to a cell, narrow and hot, its window a hole without glass, its bed a wooden bench with a single blanket.

'I thought you would have gone back to England.'

'I couldn't. That life is over for me. And I have you to thank.'

'Me?'

'Oh yes. Through you I realized I should have followed my own instinct. I should never have stayed in England in the first place. Through you I understood I should follow chance.'

'Chance?'

'Yes, chance. I was sitting in a café staring out the window when just across the street a woman stopped. She just stopped, and put down this bundle and plastic bags and sat down on the ground. Just that. She couldn't go any further, and she was sitting there on the path. I am not sure what would have happened to her. But I went outside and well, the bundle was her child. She had no money, she told me, but she wanted to take her son back to Tunisia to see his grandfather who was very old. And the next thing I was telling her I was on my way to Africa myself, and could probably pay for her and her son,' Bridget smiled. 'I was saying it without even thinking. I didn't even have time to say to myself "Oh Bridget here you go again." I just said it, and knew that this was what I was going to do. Because of chance. Because I knew just then that chance is how God shows Himself to us. It's the Holy Spirit.'

The boy did not know what to say. He felt pleased and surprised and faintly guilty.

'Not of course that you believe in Him either,' Bridget added.

'So you are here now? This is where you want to be?'

'Oh no. I am on my way to Ethiopia.'

'Why there?'

'Do you know Ethiopia is one of the oldest centres of Christianity in the world, that legend tells that it goes back to Sheba, the times of Solomon?' The boy was looking at her. 'There was a brochure someone left in the bus station in Tunis,' Bridget said. 'I picked it up.'

'Chance.'

'Exactly. You're so smart. Well, anyway, I think that's the place where I can do the most good.'

The boy nodded. He could tell already that Bridget was changed, that she was more certain of everything. He knew too that the moment was a doorway but he was through it before he could have said for sure what lay beyond it.

'I am going to come with you,' he said.

I am going to Ethiopia.

The journey was epic and arduous and slow and in itself was a thing that could be told the way travellers' tales were told, full of astonishment and wonder at the complex marvel of Africa, with words for a thousand pages. They took a dusty bus from Cairo south along the bank of the Nile, the great sweeps of the eastern desert to their left. Sand blew before them and behind them and was soon ingrained in the folds of their clothes. They sipped on plastic water bottles and sat in sweat, stuck to the red upholstery. The boy told Bridget of his time in Germany, and of Whatarangi and Gus and Nuno. And as he told her he thought of them and missed their strange company and wondered if the tattooed man was reading still. The bus passed places whose names the boy tried to pronounce to himself, El Minya, Asyut, Aswan. Endless hours rolled by. The bus beat along the sand-blown road, its passengers cramped and chattering, opening entire meals out of paper bags or cloth wrappings, scenting the air with dried meats and spices. By the time the journey had concluded its first leg, south of the shores of Lake Nasser, Nile waters slow and moon-silvered, the passengers had fallen into a trance-like state, accustomed to the rattling rhythm of the bus's loose suspension and the endless unrolling of the road.

'We sleep here, I suppose,' Bridget said, pointing to an open-sided bus shelter.

In utter silence the land stretched away on all sides of them, above them hung a vast canopy of stars. It was as though the world had not yet grown old.

In the dawn another bus came. Out of the wilderness, it seemed, passengers arrived, women bearing bundles, old men thin and with weeping eyes, as though the journey ahead of them could only have one destination: Sorrow.

The bus brought them to the border where they changed again, this time – after a delay of five hours – into a vehicle without doors or windows but with a smiling driver who stroked the steering-wheel as though it were the head of his camel. They crossed into Sudan and down the long dry bumpy emptiness of a road that carried them along in deep tracks in the sand.

'That's the Nubian Desert,' said the boy. His face was to the outside, sun and wind burning it more dark. 'Across there is the Red Sea.'

None of the other passengers spoke English. None of them looked at the white-brown expanse of landscape, the tight drum of blue sky. On several occasions, at no particular spot, the driver stopped the bus to let the engine rest, and the passengers were free to get out and stretch. The first time, Sister Bridget and the boy stepped down the way tourists might, walking out onto the arid plain with the easy confidence that Europeans have over their landscape. But the sun was scorching, the temperature over forty degrees. They felt the beams blaze on their skin and hurried back to where the other passengers

336

who had disembarked were huddled in the thin fly-swarmed shade of the bus.

The day's driving brought them to the city of Khartoum, a teeming capital, where the boy knew from maps that the Blue and White Nile rivers met. After sunset the air remained hot, and the small room they found in Omdurman, the old Arab town within the city, was a clay oven in which their sleep was baked and broken like little loaves of no nourishment. Once during the hot dark of the night, Sister Bridget asked: 'Am I mad to have wanted you to come with me?' But the boy was asleep or unable to answer. Long thin insects moved on the wall, and she batted at one with her shoe. They had taken no injections for immunization. 'You are reckless, Bridget,' she said, 'but that's all right. To live a life you have to be a bit reckless. And this is right, I know this is right.' The boy did not move from his dream of the Master sitting by a fire. Bridget said aloud the simple prayer, 'May God guide us,' and then turned over to the wall to watch anew for whichever of God's creatures might require her shoe.

From Khartoum the road went south to Wad Medani where they had to change bus again, and haggle with the driver over the price to Gallabat at the Ethiopian border. There were no other passengers going that far, the route proper ended at Gedaref, over a hundred and fifty kilometres to the north. The price the driver wanted seemed to be the boy's flute. He gestured towards it with his head and said something excitedly that neither the nun nor the boy could understand. Bridget raised and wagged a finger but the wiry figure of the driver skipped three steps of a dance and moved his fingers on an invisible flute while humming high notes until Bridget realized what he wanted was the boy to play. So, through the last leg of the journey to the border, they sat in the front seats of the empty bus rattling through sand and dust with the boy playing an ancient music never heard in that place before.

When they crossed the border, Bridget said to the boy, 'Thank you for coming with me.'

'Yes,' he said, 'chance was the reason.'

The boy held the gaze of Sister Bridget momentarily before confessing with excitement, 'I can't believe we are here.'

'I do. I believe it. Yes, this is where we are.'

They looked into that war-and-famine-ravaged country for the first time. Half a million and more Ethiopians had passed there trekking their way into Sudan to escape. There were clusters of small huts; there were tin and grass constructions and rough tents erected on crooked sticks. There were the mountains ahead of them, a grey dust shadow against the pale sky.

'Here, there is one doctor for eighty thousand people,' the boy said. 'I read that. But how can that be? How can that be *permitted*?'

'At least there is one,' replied Bridget and she smiled.

There was no bus. There was a flat-bottomed truck. They sat at the back in the boiling sun and bumped over the rising road. In the lower hillsides, occasionally they met boys leading one or two thin cattle across great open spaces, looking for grass. There were goat-herders and camel-walkers, there were men working with short wooden-handled hoes in the dry ground. But as they rose into the harsher mountain land, there were no signs of farming. There were scattered members of nomadic tribes. The figures they passed, tall, barefoot, thin, wrapped in a blanket cloak of green or brown, walking slowly but steadily towards that day's destination, did not turn to look at them. They were like apparitions in the dry landscape. There was about these people a sense of the nearness of death. It was as if in their bearing, in the strange nobility of their movement, the serene knowing in their eyes, there was knowledge of what the world could offer in terms of suffering. They were ones who had seen their children starve, seen older men and women fall to the roadside without water, animals become walking skeletons softly collapsing into the dust. They had seen villages burned in civil war, by rebels and government forces alike, they had witnessed disease which took the lives of hundreds of thousands. Now, they wandered, hunting a meagre means to survive another day.

The truck took the nun and the boy about Lake Tana and the highlands of Amhara up into the passes through the Choke Mountains. They said almost nothing to each other. Bridget held her pink cardigan over their two heads as a sunscreen while her knuckles burned. The air grew thinner. They changed into another truck at a place called Fiche that was no more than a scattering of huts without electricity or water, where women sat at the roadside holding the bundles of their babies, brushing away the flies.

The fireball sun descended behind the mountains when they arrived at last in the city of Addis Ababa. Bridget told the boy where they were going. She showed him a paper flyer that she had in her bag.

'I am always looking for a sign,' she said. 'Here is the flyer I found in the bus station. Read it.'

It was in English. It said, 'The House of Angels'. The flyer told of nuns who ran a small hospital in the capital city of Ethiopia where they treated hundreds who arrived at their gates suffering from tuberculosis, malnutrition, and the ravages of AIDS.

The boy handed it back. 'Will they let me help?' he asked.

'Let's find out.' Bridget took his hand and squeezed it, then let it go for fear of embarrassing him. They found their way through the back streets of the city to the small hospital with grey railings.

At the door the face that met them belonged to an elderly nun from Galway. Her name was Sister Eucharia.

'Goodness,' she said. 'Goodness, goodness. From Ireland? All the way from Ireland.' She shook their hands. Hers were thin and frail. She stood, shaking her head at the marvel of their arrival, as though they were messengers unaware of the significance of their message.

To his own reading Ben Dack had nodded off in front of the fire. The Master was in the armchair across from him. Josie had the television on but the sound turned down. There was a short item revealing that the identity of the terrorists killed in Germany may have been mistakenly reported. Some confusion surrounded the details of those involved. But neither Josie nor Ben was listening. Josie was watching the Master from the corner of her eye. His gaze was fixed on the flames moving in the hearth.

'I sometimes think, you know,' Josie said to him, 'that you must be thinking about that boy, about your grandson.'

She said his name. And at that, as if with great effort, having worked his way across a vast and difficult inner landscape where there was none but himself, and as if he had arrived at a final border blocked by boulders, the Master suddenly let out a long low moan.

'Ben! Ben!'

Ben was awake and on his feet before he knew why. Then Josie was beside him and they both moved closer to the Master where he was moaning still with effort, and then his right hand – at first Josie thought he was to bless himself – quivered and Ben grasped on to it.

'He's coming back to us! He is, Josie. He is! Aren't you?'

And Ben Dack looked into the Master's eyes in which there seemed shining a wise and resilient light. He pumped the hand he held up and down, until Josie, fearing the effect of his excitement on the grandfather, stepped forward and held the handshake in her own two hands and steadied it.

'It's the boy,' she said. 'He's coming back for the boy.'

That night the boy and the nun slept on blankets on the floor. In the morning they walked through the wards of the sick. In one there were only small children in cots. The boy offered his finger to a little girl with large brown eyes. She grasped it.

'They are all orphans here,' Sister Eucharia said. 'Many have AIDS.'

That day the boy stayed in the ward. He moved from one child to the next. He tried to make them smile. He made his head appear and disappear over their cots like a dusky moon. While Bridget helped in the kitchen with pans and pots and disinfectant, the boy played however he could with the small children. And sometimes they cried, their crying pitiful because it seemed to come from such a deep place of loss. And sometimes the boy was able to make them stop, to place his hand like the hand of love on their chest or touch the side of their face. Sometimes he played his flute for them and the music soothed them, and other patients along the halls heard too, those lightly dancing melodies from so far away.

The boy moved his blanket into the children's ward. He slept on the floor and woke when a child cried. A week, and then another passed. And then he had already been there a month, then two. The children grew accustomed to him – this slim figure in a white jellaba Bridget brought him. As he grew accustomed to them, it was not that he forgot. It was not that he did not sometimes think of his life before, or in the night seek for the Master in his dreams. For he did. He dreamed of the Master often, waking with the puzzling sense of how real his grandfather had seemed, as if their spirits had travelled out and met in some country of the night. It was not that he forgot how his search for his missing father seemed doomed from the start, or how the summer of bombs in Europe which had one time seemed to signal the end of everything suddenly stopped. It was not that he did not hear of other terrorist outbreaks in America and Australia, the tightening of borders, the religious hatred, and growing waves of racism everywhere. The boy did hear these things. But they came like news from another world now. If things were to end, if a bomb were to explode in the street one morning as he passed, he would, until that moment happened, try to be useful. He would try to love. To him it was a simple mathematics. It was pure as logic, as old as human nature. It was the only apt choice, living in the shadow of death: to love until the last moment. So the boy devoted himself to the children there.

'So many of them, we don't know their names,' Eucharia said. 'They have been left because a family is dying.'

'Well then, that is a job for you,' Bridget asked the boy. 'To find out their names?' She smiled at him. 'Seems fitting somehow.'

She watched him work, patiently, diligently, one by one drawing from the children a response, saying his own name and tapping the top of his head, bringing his face down to theirs and whispering in funny voices until he could make them laugh.

He invented birthdays for each of them, surprising them with a candle and song, finding in that poorest place a pocket of joy. On an afternoon of golden light like ladders in the windows, Bridget bumped into him in the corridor, her arms piled high with bed linen, a stray wisp of hair catching at the corner of her mouth. They paused in the sunlight, Bridget's face flushed with the effort of hurrying about in the heat.

'Hello there,' she said. 'You see, I'm still here. Not dead.' She smiled, and the boy did too, as if they were walking proofs of things improbably true. 'Thank you for coming here with me.'

The boy did not reply. He did not need to. Between them there was a bond now beyond words.

One day in the fly-swarmed market he found rough chalks of different colours, and bargained for them by promising to play his flute at the trader's wedding. He returned to the hospital and asked Eucharia, 'May I have a wall?'

'A wall?'

'Yes, please, Sister.'

'You'll leave it standing, dear?'

'Oh yes, Sister.'

'Any wall in particular?'

'The one in the large children's ward.'

'I see. Well, yes, go ahead. You may have a wall.'

The following morning, the boy took two sisters whose parents had been killed and who would not speak, down to the end of the ward.

'This is not a wall,' he said, 'this is a window. And through it you can see the sky.'

They did not understand him. In the steady gaze of their wide eyes he took a brown chalk and drew a huge rectangle. 'Window,' he said. 'Now, this, watch.' His hand moved in a great arc of blue, and then continued into a second one. It lay against the wall like a sideways number three. The sisters stared impassively.

'I'm not very good at this, but anyway, here goes.' Beneath the first he reversed another three, joining them with slow deliberation. Then he held out chalks of yellow and red to the girls. 'Colour, in here, like this,' he showed them. They took the chalks. Silently they moved to the wall. One sister lifted her long thin arm like a wand and began the magic of the colouring. To her sister watching she said a single word that meant 'begin'. They coloured for an hour that day, two the next. The boy brought other children to the wall. Those who could stand came sometimes only to watch, others had stools brought for them and for the chalks held out hands multicoloured with dust. For periods long and short each day they worked at the wall, covering it until every inch high and low was filled with the flying of extravagant butterflies.

By the year's end the boy was known to all. In the language of one of the tribes the children made a name for him that sounded like *El Hidj-Hadj,* the Mother-Father.

And at last, in the House of Angels, the boy had found a place where he belonged.

He did not think he would ever leave.